# Duets™

**Two brand-new stories in every volume...
twice a month!**

## Duets Vol. #85

Talented Jill Shalvis first launched the
RED-HOT ROYALS miniseries in Temptation
with #861 *A Prince of a Guy*. The romantic regal
romp continues this month with a very special
Double Duets featuring *A Royal Mess* and
*Her Knight To Remember*. Jill is "fast, fanciful
and funny. Get ready for laughs, passion and
toe-curling romance," says *Rendezvous*.

## Duets Vol. #86

Two talented writers make their Duets debut
this month—with a splash. Samantha Connolly,
who hails from Ireland, was an avid reader before
trying her hand at writing, with great results in
*If the Shoe Fits*. Dorien Kelly is still walking on air
after selling her first book, *Designs on Jake,* to Duets.
She's now hard at work on a second novel.
A welcome to this delightful duo!

**Be sure to pick up both Duets volumes today!**

# A Royal Mess

## *With a screech, Natalia whirled around from the counter.*

"Tim! You just took five years off my life." She put a hand on her chest.

"What are you doing?" He pushed away from the wall, a hesitant look on his face.

"Cooking." She took in his expression and narrowed her eyes. "And you know what? Believe it or not, some people think I'm quite good at it."

He tried to remain casual, tried to think of an answer, but at that moment her tongue darted out and licked a spot of chocolate off her lips. His body leapt to attention, and he stared at her, hoping she'd do it again.

She poured the chocolate batter from the bowl into the blender, then put the lid on. She slammed down a button that started the blender whirring, clearly not impressed with him. "I wanted this to be a surprise. Now go away."

"But I—"

Which was all he got out before the top of the blender blew off, spraying the contents across the room. And covering Natalia in rich, thick chocolate.

Looked as if he was getting dessert a little early.

*For more, turn to page 9*

# Her Knight To Remember

## "You're not going to believe this."

Annie burst into the room, hitting Kyle in the butt with the door as he reached for his pants. Righting himself, he caught a flash of pink satin.

She grabbed his arms. "Not in your wildest dreams will you believe this."

"Uh..." He ran his gaze down her pink satin nightmare of a dress. "Your sheep ran away and you need me to herd them for you?"

She grimaced. "See? You think Little Bo Peep, too!"

"Baby, that's the last thing I think of when I look at you."

She went still, hands on his arms, eyes locked on his. "Kyle—" Suddenly she seemed to realize he was more than half-naked. With a hard swallow, she covered her eyes.

"Hey, you've seen it all before," he protested.

"Just...take care of it." She ground out the words.

"Well, okay." Purposely misunderstanding her, he put his hands on the elastic band of his shorts, prepared to take them off. "But you could at least say please."

For more, turn to page 197

HARLEQUIN DUETS

ISBN 0-373-44151-7

Copyright in the collection:
Copyright © 2002 by Harlequin Books S.A.

The publisher acknowledges the copyright holder
of the individual works as follows:

A ROYAL MESS
Copyright © 2002 by Jill Shalvis

HER KNIGHT TO REMEMBER
Copyright © 2002 by Jill Shalvis

This edition published by arrangement with Harlequin Books S.A.

® and TM are trademarks of the publisher. Trademarks indicated with ® are registered in the United States Patent and Trademark Office, the Canadian Trade Marks Office and in other countries.

Visit us at www.eHarlequin.com

**Printed in U.S.A.**

# A Royal Mess

## Jill Shalvis

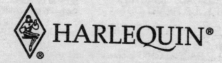

TORONTO • NEW YORK • LONDON
AMSTERDAM • PARIS • SYDNEY • HAMBURG
STOCKHOLM • ATHENS • TOKYO • MILAN • MADRID
PRAGUE • WARSAW • BUDAPEST • AUCKLAND

Dear Reader,

How many of you have dreamed about wearing a tiara? Admit it, we all wanted to be princesses, to marry a prince and never have to clean again.

In *A Royal Mess* and *Her Knight To Remember*, my princesses find out what it's like to live in the real world. Not quite the piece of cake they had imagined. In the real world people don't rush to fulfill their needs. Men don't fall at their feet.

And in the real world, love can blindside. Which is exactly what happens to Natalia and Annie, with two of the most rough-and-tumble, most rugged, most gorgeous men they've ever seen.

I had so much fun torturing my princesses with *real* men. I hope you enjoy their stories.

Happy reading!

*Jill Shalvis*

P.S.—I love to hear from readers! You can reach me at P.O. Box 3945, Truckee, CA 96160-3945.

## Books by Jill Shalvis

### HARLEQUIN DUETS
28—NEW AND...IMPROVED?
42—KISS ME, KATIE!
    HUG ME, HOLLY!
57—BLIND DATE DISASTERS
    EAT YOUR HEART OUT

### HARLEQUIN TEMPTATION
742—WHO'S THE BOSS?
771—THE BACHELOR'S BED
804—OUT OF THE BLUE
822—CHANCE ENCOUNTER
845—AFTERSHOCK
861—A PRINCE OF A GUY
878—HER PERFECT STRANGER
885—FOR THE LOVE OF NICK

### SILHOUETTE INTIMATE MOMENTS
887—HIDING OUT AT THE
    CIRCLE C
905—LONG-LOST MOM
941—THE RANCHER'S
    SURRENDER
1019—THE DETECTIVE'S
    UNDOING

To the real princesses in my life:
Kelsey, Megan and Courtney

# *1*

TIMOTHY BANNING needed a vacation from his New York vacation. That wasn't going to happen, and he could brood all he wanted once he got back to his Texas ranch, but for now he had to at least get there.

The airport was mobbed. A typical Sunday afternoon. He braced himself for an overbooked, underfed flight. At least he'd gotten a boarding pass, which was more than he could say for the angry crowd currently huddled by the check-in counter.

Grateful to be anyone other than the lone, harassed airline employee trying to soothe too many tempers at once, he got in line to board the plane.

He was exhausted, more mentally than anything else, but visiting his so-called retired grandma did that to him. She was unstoppable—shows, shopping, talking. Nothing a good nap wouldn't cure.

Oh, and note to self: next time Grandma says hang gliding over Central Park, she's not kidding. Tim stretched his sore neck and winced. She'd nearly killed him this time.

And still, she'd refused to consider coming back with him to Texas. Refused to even talk about his taking care of her in her golden years.

In front of him was a little girl—maybe five years old—in her mother's arms. She had serious bed head and wore a sundress that said I am Adorable. Wide-eyed, she stared at Tim, loudly sucking and slurping on a bright blue lollipop.

As adorable as she might be, he nonetheless hoped to God she didn't sit near him on the plane.

With an audible *smacking* sound, she pulled the lollipop out of her mouth and smiled, her teeth and tongue a distinctive shade of blue. Drool dripped down her mother's neck. "Tish, careful." Her mother shifted the girl's weight to her other arm. "Keep that in your mouth, now."

*Yeah, Tish, keep that in your mouth.*

Tish finally stuffed the lollipop back into her mouth and eyeballed Tim's hat. "You a cowboy?"

Tipping back the Stetson with a finger, he nodded. "Yep."

"You gots a horse?"

"Yep."

"Does she like sugar?"

"About as much as I'd guess you do."

Tish grinned and sucked on her lollipop some more. The line to get onto the plane hadn't moved. In fact, the crowd pressed in slightly, shifting him closer to Tish and her sticky, blue lollipop.

Chaos continued to reign around him; loud passengers, the crackling of the intercoms, the weary voices of the airline employees and the smell of plane.

Quite different from his usual setting of gently rolling hills and the call of cattle.

"Excuse me." A supremely irritated female voice rung out behind him. "I want on this flight."

Tim glanced over his shoulder and did a double take. The leather-wearing, silver-studded, spiked-hair juvenile delinquent did not match the cultured, demanding voice. Tim spared a moment to feel sorry for the poor attendant facing this newest customer, then gripping his boarding ticket with gratitude, shuffled forward in line with the rest of the lucky ones around him.

"Ma'am," the ticket clerk said. "This flight is overbooked."

"*What?*"

"We've oversold the flight," the ticket clerk said calmly. "Now we can—"

"I don't care if you oversold the entire state of New York!" She sure didn't *sound* like a teenager. "I'm holding a ticket that entitles me to a first-class seat. Now find my boarding pass."

Tim shook his head at the queen-to-peasant tone. His line was moving now, even if only at the pace of a snail. Only three people left ahead of him, and in a moment he'd be on the plane, snoozing.

Then, finally there was just Tish and her lollipop extraordinaire. Soon he'd be prone, eyes closed, lost in dreamland. Tim stepped on board, and smiled at the pretty redheaded flight attendant when she moved in front of him to serve a drink to someone already seated in first class.

"Hi," she said breathlessly, once again squeezing her hot little bod in front of his to get back to her station.

Suddenly catching some Z's took a back seat to his second-favorite hobby.

Women.

But unfortunately for him, it was just a spectator hobby, as most women didn't find his demanding, outdoor lifestyle on the ranch conducive to a long-term relationship. No one wanted to take a back seat to a sick horse or a herd of cattle.

The line wasn't moving again, this time thwarted by the crowd of people in front of him fighting for overhead compartment space.

The pretty flight attendant tipped her head up at him, a sweet smile on her lips. "I'm Fran."

"Hi, Fran."

"We're swamped today." Her eyes were hot as they ate him up.

"I'm just glad to be boarding," he said, enough of a red-blooded male to enjoy her frank appreciation of his body—a body that was so tired he was practically weaving in the aisle. Give him his dawn-to-dusk job of running a ranch over sight-seeing and grandma rustling any day. But finally he could move, and with a last smile for Fran, he found his seat.

He could still hear the furious demands of the passengers not as lucky as he ringing in his ears—the ones who hadn't checked in the requisite hour ahead of time, the ones foiled by both heavy spring storms and an airline that had sold more seats than they had available.

Not his problem. With a wide yawn, he tipped his hat over his eyes, and attempted to stretch his long legs—which resulted in two bruised knees. But he'd long ago learned to sleep anywhere, anytime, and today was no exception. As he drifted off to the tune of a flight attendant's pleas to stow any additional items beneath the seats, he sent out one last, no doubt useless hope that the two seats beside him would remain empty.

It was not going to happen on an overbooked flight, so he adjusted that thought to…may whoever land here please be small and quiet. *Very quiet.*

Slowly he drifted off, only to be jerked awake when someone behind him kicked his seat. Opening his eyes and craning his neck, Tim encountered a set of green eyes and a blue, drooling, grinning mouth.

"Hi, Cowboy!" Tish the lollipop queen grinned and waved, popping her mother in the nose.

With an inward groan, Tim waved and turned back, closing his eyes again, this time dozing off to a rousing rendition of "Old MacDonald's Farm."

THE NEXT TIME Tim was rudely awoken, he expected that it was Tish again, and he feigned sleep in the hope she'd ignore him.

It wasn't Tish.

From beneath his hat he caught a glimpse of long, toned legs sporting black combat boots as the passenger plopped huffily into the seat next to him.

"Unfriggingbelievable," muttered the jailbait juvenile delinquent from the check-in counter. She'd gotten a seat after all, and as luck would have it, right beside him.

"The seats back here are too close together." She wriggled back and forth in an apparent attempt to make him as miserable as she was. It worked.

Her black leather mini hitched a little higher, and Tim wondered how her mother could have let her out of the house dressed like that. Could be worse, he told himself, closing his eyes once again. Could be someone who wanted to gab the entire flight—

"No one's going to believe this." She popped her gum so loud his ears nearly exploded. "Flying *coach.* Ha! I'm packed in here like a sardine."

Ah, hell. She *was* someone who was going to gab the entire flight.

"How is one supposed to stretch— *Ouch!*" She rubbed her leg, and because they were too close together, the backs of her fingers slid against his legs as well. "This should be illegal sitting like this. I should file a complaint."

He wasn't going to look at her. No sirree, not going to even peek. Pressing his hat to his face, he slid farther into his seat, practically jamming his knees to his chin.

"It's astounding, really," she said over his groan of pain. "The luck I've had today."

Who was she talking to in that voice that seemed almost…British? He risked a sideways glance from beneath his hat. Was she talking to him or the rather large woman who sat at the end of their row? Since that woman wasn't responding and he was faking sleep, there was only one conclusion.

She was talking to *herself,* which meant she wasn't just a talker, she was a crazy talker.

"I bet American royalty doesn't have this problem,'' she said. "I mean, really, when was the last time a Kennedy had to sit coach?"

Tim managed to slink a little more in the seat without further mangling his knees. He kept his eyes firmly closed.

"And how could I have gotten bumped from first class? Who do they have up there, Prince William? It's such an insult." She must have tipped to the side, trying to get comfortable again, because Tim felt her hair brush his arm. With it came an exotic, almost irresistible scent. Flowers and woman.

Normally he'd love that—both the sensation and the scent—but he drew the line at far-too-young, crazy women.

The plane started to move. Good. People didn't like to talk during takeoff. At least, he didn't. It was the ultimate sleeping time.

She didn't speak for fifteen whole seconds. His hopes rose.

"Oh, dear." Her voice wobbled, suddenly not sounding confident at all. "You'd think with how many times I've done this, I'd be better at takeoff."

He felt her arm slide against his as she gripped the armrest between them. Soft, smooth skin. Warm to the touch.

*Don't open your eyes, Banning.*

"Did you hear that sputter in the engine?" she

wondered, nudging him. "Excuse me, I'm sorry to disturb you, but was that a sputter, do you think?"

Maybe a different man could have ignored that note of sharp fear in her voice, but he'd never been able to turn from someone who was afraid. Opening his eyes, he craned his neck her way. "Just normal take-off noises," he assured her.

She stopped chewing her gum and bit her lip, hands still clenched on the armrests at her sides, which meant in the small confines they shared, her elbow was plowing into his ribs.

"Really," he added, a little startled at the depth of her dark gold eyes. She had dark gold hair to match, even if it was spiked straight up, showing off ears that were pierced all the way up the outside. "We're going to be fine," he added, wanting to clear that up before his nap in order to avoid another interruption.

She nodded. Her eyes were lined in heavy black, with blue eye shadow, which matched the blue lip gloss she was nibbling off with her nerves.

In front of them, Fran the flight attendant whisked closed the curtain between first class and coach, but not before she sent Tim a saucy little wink.

Next to him, his copassenger sat up straight and pointed. "Did you see that? They were being served lunch up there! That's *my* lunch! Yoo-hoo! *Hello?*"

Fran didn't reappear.

Smart Fran.

"Well." She sat back, looking genuinely surprised at being ignored. "Honestly. I'm starving back here and they're eating." She huffed over that a moment, then raised her voice. "I'm a starving princess, you know!"

Fran poked her head out. "Please. I'm going to have to insist you keep it down."

"But—"

"You can have me beheaded as soon as we land if you'd like, but for now, *I'm* the queen."

The curtain closed with finality.

"I really am starving," Princess-In-Leather said to Tim, somewhat subdued now.

"I'm sorry."

She stared at him. "You have no idea who I am, do you?"

"Let me guess. A starving princess?"

"Yes!" She seemed pleased, until she realized he was humoring her. "Well, this is different, not being recognized." But she laughed and shook her head while putting on a set of headphones.

*Crazy*, thought Tim.

From behind them, Tish popped her head between them. "Hi!"

Princess-In-Leather smiled and removed her earphones. Loud, obnoxious noise pumped out of it. "Hi back," she said to the little girl.

"I'm this many." Tish leaned over the back of the seat, smacking Tim in the head when she held up five sticky fingers.

The princess nodded. "I'm that many times four plus four."

Tim did a double take. "You're *twenty-four?*"

She blinked overly made-up gold eyes at him. "How old did you think I was?"

"Twelve."

"Twelve, huh?" She took off her leather jacket, revealing a little black crop top that told him she indeed was far older than twelve.

She laughed at his expression. Tish laughed, too, and dropped her lollipop. In Tim's lap.

Tim removed it before Tish could and mentally tossed his nap right out the window.

"Tish, sit down," her mother called.

*Yes, Tish, sit down.* He stared at his companion. She smiled. He did not. He'd liked it better when she was twelve.

A different flight attendant came through the aisle, tossing each passenger a pathetically small bag of peanuts.

His hungry companion wasn't quite quick enough on the uptake and took hers in the face. She stared down at the bag of peanuts that landed in her lap. "I hate commercial flights."

But at least she'd forgotten her fear. That left him in the clear. Hoping for a little sleep, Tim settled back, confident she'd be okay now.

And quiet.

Hopefully very quiet.

"I can't sleep while flying," she said, sounding a little dejected as she played with the bag of peanuts.

*Crinkle. Crinkle. Crinkle.*

With a sigh, he reached out and put his hand over hers.

"Thank you," she whispered, entwining their fingers and holding his hand. Amazingly, she said nothing more.

And that's how he ended up holding a crazy juvenile delinquent's—no, not a delinquent at all, but a woman's, a crazy woman's—hand.

# 2

In Natalia's world, everyone knew she was a princess, no matter how much she tried to disguise it. And try to disguise it, she did. Mostly to avoid being compared to other recent and far more popular princesses. But there was a part of her that simply enjoyed shocking people. It was an unusual hobby, but it kept her amused.

Yet, here in the U.S., she was a no one, and the American expression "royally pissed" was taking on a new meaning.

Of course, according to Amelia Grundy—ex-nanny and current friend and companion to Natalia and her two sisters—a princess never lost her temper, not in public anyway.

She'd blown that rule several times today alone. She wouldn't do it again. It was easier, and far more fun, to get a rise out of the gorgeous cowboy next to her.

Not exactly politically correct, but Princess Natalia Faye Wolfe Brunner of Grunberg wasn't known for following the rules. Never had been. It wasn't that she didn't like her world, but more that she didn't like having to conform. Not for anyone or anything, including her heritage. So she was different. It worked for her. Her family loved and adored her whether she wore silver and leather and blue makeup or played nice little princess, which she did once in a while to please them.

But today...ugh. She'd been traveling all day from Europe, and still, the utter lack of...politeness among the American people in airports shocked her. She hoped it was just the airports, otherwise this was going to be a very unpleasant visit indeed.

Hadn't Amelia warned her of the good old U.S. of A., land of pop-up minimalls, Hollywood divas and Wild West cowboys?

If truth be told, Natalia had a secret passion for old westerns. Both her sisters felt she watched too many Clint Eastwood movies, and maybe she did, but they fascinated her. Logically, she knew modern American men didn't wear hats and carry six-shooters, but it was a good visual, and she appreciated a good visual.

There was a *real* good visual sitting right next to her; all long, leanly muscled and wearing the requisite Stetson hat. And he was holding her hand. How sweet was *that?* She hadn't imagined a cowboy could be sweet on top of being tough as nails—and she had no doubt that this man with his rugged looks and low, authoritative voice *was* tough as nails. She looked him over, thinking Hollywood had missed the mark by not using him in movies. "You don't, by any chance, carry a six-shooter do you?"

He lifted his hat and stared at her. "Have you been drinking?"

"No, of course not." Another thing princesses didn't do in public…indulge. "I was just wondering. So do you? Carry a gun?"

He put his hat back over his face, which was a crying shame given how amazing his face was. Not pretty-boy amazing—she got enough of that at home—but amazing in the way the Marlboro man would look without a cigarette hanging out of his mouth. A tanned, lived-in face, so arresting she couldn't look away, paired with a body that would make any woman drool.

"I left the six-shooter at home," he said. "With my talking horse." He yawned and stretched that tough, coiled body, bumping his knees on the seat in front of him. Swearing beneath his breath, he tried to fold himself back up, but oddly enough, he did it while leaving his large, warm hand in hers.

Not a woman easily touched, Natalia nearly melted. He wore a dark blue T-shirt. And denim. Let's not forget the denim, which looked incredibly soft and perfectly worn. She'd bet all the earrings in her left ear that he hadn't bought them that way, but had worn them in with years of work.

Contrary to what one might imagine a princess's wardrobe to contain, she herself had several pairs of jeans, none of which were with her now, as she preferred stirring things up, and leather seemed to do that nicely.

It was a middle-child thing. When she'd been ten years old her mother had taken her to a "specialist" to find out why she had to be the center of attention all the time. All it had netted her mother was a big doctor's bill, though Natalia could still fondly remember the cool candy he'd handed out after each session. Anyway, her mother had never discovered Natalia's problem, but Natalia figured she knew. She *loved* attention.

Which was why she was here, alone. On her first solo trip sans attendants on her way to a royal friend's wedding, where she planned on representing her family and making them proud. For once. But she hadn't counted on good old-fashioned nerves.

She was sandwiched in between the once-again prone cowboy and a three-hundred-pound woman who'd fallen asleep with her mouth open. Her snores had gone from loud to off-the-sonic scale, even over and above Blink-182's latest CD blaring out of her earphones.

At least the cowboy slept utterly silently, though he still proved quite the distraction because he had such a commanding presence she couldn't seem to stop sneaking peeks at him.

But unfortunately, she'd sipped too many glasses of water and needed to visit the facilities. Badly. She looked at Ms. Snoring-Loud. *Please, someone just shoot me dead if I ever fall asleep in public with my mouth open wide enough to catch flies.* "Excuse me," she whispered, gently nudging the large woman. "I need to get up."

The woman jerked awake with a loud snort and glared at her. "I was sleeping."

"I realize that. But I must use the facilities."

"The facilities?"

*Did they have no class in this country?* Natalia pointed toward the front of the plane, past first class where she should have been seated.

"Oh, you mean the pot?" This was said loud enough for the people in the Republic of China to hear. "You have to pee. Well, my goodness, you should've just said so." She cocked a brow. "Or isn't a princess allowed to say the word *pee?*"

Oh, amusing. Wasn't she amusing? "Can I please get out?"

"Yeah, yeah." The woman heaved herself out of the seat and into the aisle. "Far be it for me to keep the princess waiting."

Once Natalia was finally in the "pot," she stared at her harried face in the mirror. Pale and sickly. She tried splashing her cheeks with water, but succeeded only in making her hair look like the Bride of Frankenstein. Very nice.

The cowboy stirred when she sat back down, and slowly tipped back his Stetson, prying one eye open. One green eye. One amazingly forest-green eye, which looked her over before closing again.

Unlike everyone else she'd ever met, he didn't comment on the makeup, jewelry or clothing. "Are we there yet?" he asked.

"No."

"Hmm." He settled back in the seat, his long, built body far too big for it. His arm bumped hers off the armrest, and she stared at him, shocked he didn't immediately fall all over himself and apologize as most people did when they accidentally touched her.

He didn't even look at her!

Because he was obviously squished, and because she didn't want to draw his attention again, she let it go. But even as rude as Americans were, she had to admit, they sure made their men quite magnificent.

"Are you watching me sleep?" he asked in a low, rather husky voice.

She jerked her gaze off him. "Of course not."

"You're watching."

Not anymore. Not if her life depended on it. Refusing to so much as look out the window—heaven forbid he mistake *that* for her watching him—she eyed the woman next to her, who was once again snoring.

With a sigh, Natalia turned straight ahead and gave her best imitation of a royal at utter tranquility, even when the plane dipped unexpectedly. It was the hardest thing she'd ever done.

And a very small part of her wished the cowboy would give her his hand back.

WHAT SHE HADN'T REALIZED during that hideous plane ride was that things could get worse.

Far worse.

The plane landed on schedule. Natalia got off on schedule.

And that's where, unfortunately, the worse part came in.

The flight attendants waved goodbye to everyone as they exited the plane, smiling and looking like parade commissioners. When Natalia got to the front, they all promptly stopped waving. On cue, they bowed and cried "farewell thy princess."

Funny. Ever so funny.

She thought maybe her Clint Eastwood look-alike, standing behind her, laughed. The sound was low and rough, just like his voice, but when she whirled to glare at him, he was simply looking at her with those intense, see-all eyes of his. No smile at her expense on his mouth, but there was a very little hint of it in his gaze, she just knew it.

She stared at him for another long second, during which he patiently endured her scrutiny.

Then someone behind him nudged him forward, and he pressed against her back for a brief moment before widening his stance to better brace himself.

Her spine indelibly imprinted with the feel of his warm, hot body, Natalia rushed forward, in a desperate hurry to...

Get lost.

She had to find her next flight in this monstrous airport in...where was she? Oh, yes. Dallas. Dallas, Texas. Where all the women had huge hair and the men wore belt buckles larger than—

Well. No use going there.

Not when she had herself to feel so sorry for. She stuck out like a sore thumb and felt people staring every time she so much as moved, which of course made her thrust up her chin and give everyone hard stares back. Funny, but she'd never felt like an atrocity before. Distracted by that, she somehow ended up in Terminal C instead of Terminal B.

Uh-uh. No way was she going to miss her connection. Not when she had two perfectly good legs to get her there. She had her sights on first class this time, and she would accept no less. But with only a few minutes to spare before the flight, she was afraid she'd be told that ridiculous overbooked story again. To avoid that, she started running. Not easy in an overcrowded airport full of people and wearing heavy boots meant for looking good, not sprinting a marathon. Dodging left and right, she hustled on, her carry-on banging against her thighs with every step she took, her toes screaming against the steel front of her boots. But damn it, the boots looked good.

It took forever to make progress. Old people walking too slowly, kids in the way…. At this rate, by the time she got to the right gate, she'd be a very unprincesslike sweaty mess. She already felt so out of breath she had to stop, drop her purse and carry-on, and bend over to suck in some serious air.

*This is it,* she decided, gulping air like water. *I need an exercise regime. Pronto.*

But first she needed an oxygen mask.

"Hey, there. Move it."

This from a uniformed man driving a golf cart. A golf cart! To save her lungs, she'd get on a damn skateboard. "Oh, thank God." She stopped to gasp some more. "I need a ride to gate…" Huffing like a choo-choo train, she glanced down at her ticket, trying to figure it out.

"Sorry, no rides."

"What?" She looked at the cart. It was huge. More than enough room. "What do you mean no rides? I just need to get to—"

"Nope."

"I realize you don't know who I am, but—"

"Look, I don't care if you're Santa Claus, I ain't giving you a ride. I only take senior citizens."

Then, unbelievably, he zipped away, leaving her standing there, hair slipping, arm ready to pop out of its socket from her carry-on, toes still screaming.

With no choice, she started running again, and got to her gate with a full two minutes to spare. Heaving herself to the counter, she held up a finger to the woman behind it, signaling she couldn't possibly speak until she caught her breath.

The unsympathetic woman impatiently tapped her pen against the counter.

"I'm here…to check…in." Natalia added a smile for good measure. A royal smile. A royal don't-you-dare-turn-me-down smile.

"Ma'am, this flight has been canceled due to weather."

Soon as she got home, she'd have to have her ears checked. "What?"

"Thunderstorms over New Mexico."

"But that's where I need to go."

"Yes, you and two hundred others."

Okay time to pull out the cell phone and hit auto-dial for home. Home sounded good. Home sounded great. Her father, her assistants, even Amelia—especially the know-it-all-see-it-all Amelia—would get her out of this mess. Amelia Grundy had been getting her out of messes all her life, and as always, that brought a sense of wonder. It was as if Amelia were a modern-day Mary Poppins the way she always instinctively knew when Natalia needed her. Natalia and her sisters had long ago just accepted strange things could and would happen when Amelia was involved. Magical things. Wondrous things. And, in the case of one sister or another causing mischief, terrible things.

Truth was, Natalia needed Amelia now, and Amelia probably already knew it. Chances were she wouldn't even get an "I told you so" out of it.

Chances were.

But she *would* get that knowing tone, the one that would have the I-told-you-so all over it. No one, especially Amelia, who always knew when trouble was coming, had wanted Natalia to come here alone.

But all Natalia's life she'd been sheltered and over-protected. All her life she'd chafed at the restrictions. Hence, being stranded in Dallas. "So what happens now?"

"Well…" The woman's fingers flew across the keyboard as she decided Natalia's fate. She had hair teased up like a Dolly Parton wig, and earrings as big as saucers hanging from her poor lobes. And they thought *Natalia* dressed strangely. "The next flight out is tomorrow," she said.

Natalia stopped comparing hairstyles. *"Tomorrow?"*

"Tomorrow."

Natalia resisted the urge to thunk her head on the counter and have a good cry. "What about my luggage?"

"I'm sorry, you're going to have to meet up with it at your final destination."

"You're kidding."

The woman didn't crack a smile, not even a sympathetic one.

"You're not kidding."

"Ma'am, kidding isn't in my job description."

Natalia shook her head. "This isn't happening."

"If you'd like, you can check the bus schedule.

The shuttle to take you to the depot is outside the terminal.''

"Bus?"

"Bus."

*Bus.*

WHICH WAS WHERE Natalia found herself forty-five minutes later. Sitting on a bench outside waiting for the shuttle bus in the soggy, muggy, disgusting heat, with clouds surging overhead, waiting.

For her bus.

There was no lunch service on a bus, she was fairly certain. She removed her leather jacket, setting it on her carry-on at her feet. No pretty but huffy flight attendants. No bags of peanuts.

But there was, she'd been told, a "pot."

Goodie.

At any rate, it was the lack of food that got to her now.

Given how out of shape she was, she could probably stand to skip a meal or two. Since there was no one around—apparently everyone else had been smart enough to stay inside the airport and wait for a flight—she looked down at herself. Definitely, being on the plump side of average, she could stand to go without lunch.

But being on the plump side of average gave her good breasts, she reminded herself.

Not that breasts mattered when she was as chaperoned as she had been all her life.

*You're not chaperoned now.*

At that thought, a good amount of her tension faded away. She even smiled to herself. She was alone, just as she always had wanted to be. And come hell or high water, she was going to make her family proud.

She was well aware of how wonderful her life was. But there was more to life than mugging for the press and charity parties.

And with all her heart, she wanted to experience some of it.

Hard to do with two sisters, bodyguards, an ex-nanny, an entire country and a protective father hovering over her night and day. But it was past time for her solo flight. An adventure. Okay, so the wedding of one of her mother's oldest friend's daughter in Taos, New Mexico, wasn't exactly an adventure, but it would be a start, even though her older sister would also be attending. But as Andrea—being the oldest— had been asked to be in the wedding and would therefore be quite swamped with wedding stuff, Natalia had demurely suggested she meet her there.

Demurely, ha! She'd leaped at the chance.

Her father had agreed, reluctantly. *Be careful* he'd told her a million times. *Call often.*

Natalia had promised, in good humor because it would be worth the entire trip to see her older, tomboy sister in a dress. Just thinking about it now had her letting out a quick, sharp grin that she knew would make Annie pounce on her.

Thunder hit, and Natalia jumped, suddenly wishing Annie was here for a good diversion. Or even Lili— the baby of the family at twenty-three. But Lili was coming straight from another obligation, and was to meet them in Taos.

A breath later came a flash of lightning. Not good. She grabbed her phone, clutched it to her chest and stared up at the sky. It wouldn't hurt to call home. Just to assure everyone that she was fine, of course, because they worried about her.

Another crack of thunder and lightning, and she dialed, hoping she wouldn't be electrocuted before she heard a familiar voice.

A strict female voice answered. "Tell me everything, Natalia."

Not her father, but Amelia, and nearly as good as her father, even if the woman had the strangest and most disconcerting ability to read her mind. "What if there's nothing to tell?" Natalia asked, keeping a wary eye on the sky.

"Natalia, sweetness, you always have something to tell. Now spill it. You're okay, of course. I'd know if you weren't."

Yes, she would. Amelia had that inexplicable way about her when it came to the princesses. When they'd been young, Natalia and her sisters had been convinced Amelia was a fairy godmother. Complete with fairy dust.

Sometimes Natalia was still convinced. Mostly, she had accepted and was just grateful. "I'm okay," she agreed, looking around at the flattest landscape she'd ever seen. And in case Amelia had grandiose ideas of sending escorts, Natalia hurriedly added, "More than okay." Another clap of thunder shook the ground beneath her feet. "P-p-perfect, in fact."

"Hmm." There was a long pregnant pause, in which, clearly, Amelia expected Natalia to spill her guts.

Tempting, but she managed to keep her mouth shut—barely.

"We're here if you need us, Natalia."

"You mean if I've screwed up."

"'Screw up' is not a very princesslike term." Amelia's voice was diplomatic, and contained the hint of an indulgent smile. "But if you need anything, anything at all, I'm just a phone call away."

Natalia knew that. Probably she wouldn't even

have to make that call, Amelia would just know. What a comfort that was. Her throat tightened just thinking about how much she was cared for. She cared for them in return, and making them proud was her biggest goal here. She could do this, she could do anything. After all, she was a princess. And maybe, just maybe, she would have a little adventure while she was at it.

"Natalia? This week you wanted all alone, it's a long time for someone like you. There's no shame in that."

"You mean someone inexperienced in the real world."

"If you need anything…" Amelia repeated calmly, refusing to be baited.

"I won't. You understand this, Amelia, don't you?" Natalia needed to hear her say it. More than she'd known.

"Yes, sweetness," Amelia said, her voice softer now. "I understand. This is a way to prove yourself. You'll do great. Just keep your head."

"I can do that. See you soon."

"See you soon, lovely."

Natalia hugged the phone close to her heart, as if she could retain the warmth and love. And she could, if she closed her eyes and concentrated—

"Do you have the time?"

Natalia nearly leaped out of her skin at the voice. It was a young man, in his early twenties, looking like he'd skipped far more than just lunch. His face was gaunt, his head and hair—if he had any—were completely covered in a knit beanie despite the humidity. And his eyes...sparkled with malice.

Uh-oh. Her heart started a rapid tattoo. Why hadn't she told Amelia where she was?

Because she could handle this, that's why. And besides, as irrational as it sounded, Amelia probably already knew.

Much calmer than she felt, she said, "The time? Why, yes, I do..." *Please, go away.* She twisted her wrist to check. "It's just after three— *Hey!*"

He snagged the carry-on, the jacket over it and the purse she still had on her shoulder.

And tugged.

"Oh, no you don't. Those are—" She stopped shouting at him to get a better grip on her purse. *"Mine."*

"Let go!" he growled, playing tug-of-war with her.

But her fear turned to temper. Clearly, he had no idea who he was messing with and how much she'd already faced in one day. It gave her an unbelievable strength. "I'm not letting go, you...you *miscreant!*"

"Hey, I'm robbing you here."

"No you're not!"

He looked so utterly surprised, she nearly laughed. And held on like a pit bull.

"You're supposed to freak out," he grated. "Cry. Scream. Not fight back! Jeez, haven't you ever taken a self-defense class? They don't advise you to fight back!"

"I'm not going to freak out, I'm going to fight, and then I'm going to turn you in! Now *you* let go!"

For what seemed like forever, they grappled with her bags, until, with a loud screech, Natalia lost the game and her grip. Freed, she promptly toppled backward over the bench, ass over kettle, landing incongruously in the dirt.

Meanwhile, her thief, who took the time to stop and grin triumphantly in her face, took off with her beloved carry-on, her purse and her bus ticket.

And her pride.

# 3

By the time Natalia—sputtering in a very unprincesslike manner—scrambled to her feet and jerked down her skirt, the young man was but a blur on the horizon. All she could do was watch in disbelief as he ran away, her bag banging against his thighs as it had banged against hers all day long.

She hoped it left one hell of a bruise.

"Idiot!" she yelled. "Moron! *Jerk!*" Sagging back to the bench, she wondered who she was calling names, the thief or herself.

A drop fell from the sky, hitting her on the nose. The storm that the airline had been threatening her with all day had finally arrived.

Another drop. Then another. The sky lit with a long jagged flash of lightning.

And Natalia stood there, stunned stupid by the events of the day. She was out in what felt like the middle of nowhere, with no identification, no money and even worse, no makeup, not even a brush. She should call on the credit cards, but then again, at this moment, even that seemed like too much effort.

Rain fell. Leather wet was a whole new, uncomfortable experience. Lightning flashed again, punctuating the disaster her life had become.

Perfect. Now she was going to get struck by a bolt and get amnesia. That would top things off nicely.

*You'll do great. Just keep your head.*

At Amelia's words, spoken in her wonderful British accent, Natalia whipped around, but of course, Amelia wasn't standing there.

It was just that her voice had sounded so…real.

But Natalia was alone, utterly alone. It must be the self-pity, she decided, causing her to hear things. Because surely, not even Amelia could be that… magical.

She should just call home with the cell phone still in her pocket. But that put a sour taste in her mouth because darn it, she wanted to do this.

Her hair was beginning to unspike, and her clothes were plastered to her like a second skin. She had no idea what should come next. Maybe a hero on a white steed. Wouldn't that be handy.

A rumble sounded. Not a white steed, but a truck, rumbled up the street. It nearly passed her, until, with a quick brake, it came to an abrupt halt right in front of her.

Her heart leaped into her throat, but she reminded herself she had nothing left for someone to steal.

Except *herself,* came the dismal, unhelpful thought. Fear bloomed again, and she might have started running regardless of her combat boots, until the window rolled down and a man leaned across the seat. Beneath his hat, piercing green eyes landed right on her.

Her Clint Eastwood look-alike from the plane.

"Problem?" he asked in that slow, Southern drawl that somehow sent a warm shiver down her spine, when just a moment ago she'd been chilled from her fight with her thief.

"Problem?" she repeated as casually as she could, cocking a hip and trying to look like the badass princess she was known to be. "What makes you think I have a problem?"

"Because you're standing out here in a downpour looking like a drowned rat."

*A drowned rat!* "The bus hasn't come yet." But even if it did, her ticket was sitting all nice and cozy in her purse. The purse that was right this second gracing the neck of a thief. But she couldn't tell this man that, not when her pride was sticking like crow in her throat.

He put his truck in Park and rested a forearm on his steering wheel. "So what's a princess doing riding a bus?"

With her self-esteem at her feet, there was no way she could tell him.

"Ah, hell," she thought she heard him mutter. And then he'd turned off his truck and got out in the rain, moving with the easy grace of a man who wasn't in a hurry to be anywhere other than where he happened to be.

Standing in front of her, he seemed bigger than he'd been on the airplane, bigger than life. He was over six feet, all broad shoulders, hard muscle and about zero body fat. Certainly bigger than any man she was used to standing so close to her, so she took a little step back. But she left her chin thrust high into the air, because she'd choke on all that pride before admitting defeat to anyone.

"Here." He shrugged out of his jacket to set it on her shoulders. She didn't know if his caring enough to want her warm helped or made it worse. "So what happened to your stuff?" he asked.

"It was just stolen. And before that, my second flight was canceled. Having a hell of a day here."

He had a way of looking at people, of tilting his head back and gazing at her with deep green eyes that made her stomach flutter. "Are you hurt?"

*I'm fine,* she almost said. But she wasn't. There was a strange, slow, unfurling in the pit of her belly, and it didn't come from the horrid day or the rain or the theft. Or even from the way her makeup was starting to run down her face.

It came from his hands on her shoulders. From his easy grace and confidence.

"Princess?"

She gazed up at the man towering over her, at his unfathomable gaze and the lock of brown hair falling over his forehead. It was streaked with light gold from what she imagined were long days in the sun. On his horse. Being a cowboy. The unfurling in her belly ignited. "Do you really believe I'm a princess?" she whispered.

He frowned, then bent down a little to look into her eyes. "Maybe you hit your head? Is that it?"

He thought she was crazy. And she was.

Because he was a stranger, a one-hundred-percent-male stranger who made her want to drool, made her want to stand straighter with her breasts thrust out and check her makeup all at the same time. She felt as if she'd known him all her life even as she wanted to know him even better.

*How stupid is that, Amelia?*

TIM SCOOPED the woman's tangled, soggy hair back from her forehead, frowning as he looked her creamy skin over for a bump. Somehow the black smudged eyeliner beneath her eyes made them look ever bigger. More vulnerable.

"I didn't hit my head," she said quite clearly, stepping back from his touch. "And I really am a princess. Your Serene Highness Natalia Faye Wolfe Brunner of Grunberg, to be exact."

Stepping back, he scratched his jaw and studied her, but she didn't crack a smile. "That's a mouthful," he said.

"Which is why I go by just Your Serene Highness Natalia Faye."

"Still a mouthful."

"My things have been stolen, or I'd show you identification."

"Want to go to the police and make a report?"

She frowned. "No. The thief is long gone, and my family would just insist I come home. All I need is a ride to Taos, New Mexico. I'm going to a wedding."

This was said in a hoity-toity voice, her chin thrust high in the sky and eyes flashing, as if he were her servant. So he stared at her for one more beat, then tossed his head back and laughed.

"I'm not finding the humor in this situation," she said, crossing her arms across her chest.

Oh, boy. Nutcase alert. Despite her superior airs, he could tell she was cold, all covered in goose bumps. Suddenly she looked twelve to him again. Or she would if she didn't have the most mouthwatering, curvy body he'd ever seen. Damn it, she was the prettiest nutcase he'd ever seen, and any bastard could come along and take advantage of her. Tim wasn't into pretty nutcases himself, but he couldn't just leave her here.

He wished he could. He had enough to deal with, but he knew this woman and her expressive eyes would haunt him tonight if he didn't try to do something for her. "Look, you're obviously a little down on your luck."

"A little today, yeah."

It made his gut clench. "So let me call someone for you—"

"No!"

"But—"

*"No,"* she said so firmly, he almost believed she could really be royalty. She ran a hand down her wet, clingy leather and thrust her shoulders back. "As I've said, I'm fine."

Terrific. She was fine and he was...delayed. And yet he couldn't just drive away. Maybe it was his save-the-wounded-bird heart. Hell, it was *definitely* his save-the-wounded-bird heart. "Where are you off to, then?"

"Nowhere at the moment."

"I could take you with me to my ranch."

Her eyes narrowed. "Why?"

Why? Because he was an idiot. Because clearly he didn't have enough to worry about with his grandmother refusing his help and his sister sleeping with his new ranch hand. "You'd...be safe there."

"At your ranch."

"Yes." Where he already had a corral full of rescued animals he couldn't bring himself to get rid of. Not that he'd put this woman in the corral, but the rescue efforts weren't much different.

Which was exactly what his grandma had told him when he'd tried to convince her to come back with him this weekend.

*You're just trying to save me from old age, Timothy. But I like old age. And I like it here. Now I love you, but go home and save a cow or something.*

He sighed. Instead of a cow, he supposed he'd rescue this drowned-looking woman. "So...is it a go?" He shielded his eyes from the now even heavier rain soaking them. "Are you coming with me?"

A gold eyebrow vanished into her hair as she regarded him with mistrust.

"Not for whatever you're thinking," he added quickly.

Another sharp jag of lightning lit the sky, with thunder too quick on its heel for comfort. "You can clean yourself up," he said, wanting out of the damn rain. "Get some food and sleep. Then maybe...I don't know...look for work."

"Work," she repeated, as if the idea had never occurred to her. "Hmm. Interesting. Do you have a job opening?"

"I'm hiring right now for a cook and a ranch hand." To replace the ranch hand he planned on firing if he—Josh—was still boinking his baby sister.

Which reminded him to wonder if Sally was still mad at him. Actually, that particular worry was just a waste of time.

Knowing Sally, she was still mad.

Too bad. His parents had wanted him to take care of her, and loyally bound, he would, even if she'd be twenty this year. He would take care of her, or die trying.

Which was a far more likely result of his efforts.

Impatient to be home, he looked the woman over. She appeared to be in good health, other than her general inability to face reality. Her gold hair now clung to her face. Her leather had shrink-wrapped itself to her very curvy body. Not that he was noticing.

Much.

"A job," she repeated, tapping her lower lip. "You know, that might work just fine."

He tried to picture her in denim. "Ever been on a ranch?"

"Oh, of course."

Of course.

"Once on holiday we stopped at a petting farm."

He blinked, then shook his head. "How about cooking? Can you cook?"

She swiped at the water running into her face. "You mean, for other people?"

"No, for the queen of England."

Her mouth tightened. "Now you're making fun again. Why does everyone use poor Elizabeth as a joke?"

"Can you?"

"Cook? Of course."

There was that "of course" again. Ah hell, she probably couldn't cook. He tipped up his hat. "It's raining pretty hard," he said, hoping to rush things along a bit.

"I don't have a change of clothing," she said, brow furrowed. "I like to have lots of things with me."

He pulled his wet shirt away from his body with a suction noise and winced as it slapped back against his skin. "I'm going to get back into my truck, princess. Down the road is a store. If you'd like, you can borrow some cash and make some purchases. But I doubt they have black leather."

"I can try something new. I like new."

"Yeah? Well, you *might* have a choice between blue denim and dark blue denim."

"I know how to wear jeans."

"Then let's go."

She cocked her head. "You *are* like the cowboys from the old West. Chivalrous. Kind."

"No," he said, backing up. "Anyone would do this."

"You're wrong. I think you're special. Different."

Different as insane. "Are you sure you're not hurt?" *Or on medication?* "Or that there's no one I can call for you?"

"Nope. I just wanted to do this one thing, travel by myself. It's a first and I've bungled it horribly." She scooped back fistfuls of her hair and it stuck straight up again. "I'll earn my own money this time."

She was going to come with him. He opened the passenger door, put his hand to the small of her back and touched bare skin. Not wanting to feel the odd shock of awareness, he gently nudged, not knowing whether he was unnerved or relieved that she climbed in.

"You're not an ax murderer, right?" she asked.

Unnerved, he decided. Definitely, he was unnerved. "No."

"I've never hitchhiked before." She looked around

inside his truck, probably searching for something obvious. Like body parts. "Contrary to what you must think of me, I don't take this lightly."

"You're safe."

"I bet that's what all the bad guys say."

"But I'm like Clint Eastwood, remember?"

She actually laughed. *Laughed.* A sweet, bubble of a laugh, that in return made him grin like an idiot.

She carefully settled in as if she was indeed a little princess, and hooked up her seat belt, dripping water everywhere. "You wouldn't, by any chance, just take me to Taos?"

"Sorry, princess. Do you know how far away that is? I've got a ranch that needs my attention. I've been gone for a few days myself." God only knew how his sister had fared in his absence. *Forget Sally.* How had everyone *else* fared? "But say the word, and I'll call someone for you. Anyone, anywhere."

"No, thank you. I'll be your cook, at least for a few days."

"Not just my cook," he corrected. "But for all the ranch employees as well."

She put a confident smile on her face he wasn't sure was real or forced. "So…how many people is that?"

*Forced,* he decided. Great. "Depends on how many

people quit while my sister was in charge,'' he said grimly, and drove.

FOR SEVERAL YEARS Natalia had been having dreams. Dreams wondering what the real world was like. Dreams about being a woman first and a princess second.

She was quite certain Timothy Banning didn't believe a word she'd said about herself or her heritage, but that was fine. She didn't need him to believe.

In fact, his disbelief worked in her favor, because for the first time ever, her dream could come true, if only for a few days.

She could be a woman first.

And a princess a very distant second.

''How much farther is your ranch?'' she asked, avidly soaking up the landscape. She appeared to be stranded in a desert of grass, grass and more grass. North-central Texas was, without a doubt, one of the flattest places she'd ever seen. So different from her home, which was nestled high in the mountains, between Austria and Switzerland, surrounded by incredible vistas and wild forests.

She thought she'd miss home, but this land was beautiful, too, in a stark sort of way. The terrain was broken up by a few trees here and there, pecan and oak, it appeared. Very different.

She liked it.

"About forty-five more miles." They'd already made the requested stop at the store, and he'd been right. No leather. But she'd borrowed against her wages and on top of the jeans and T-shirts, had managed to find some interesting wild-apple-green lip gloss, so the whole thing hadn't been a waste. Now her cowboy looked suddenly tense, as if he regretted taking her with him.

"I'm not crazy or dangerous or anything," she said. "Just so you know. I wouldn't hurt anyone on your ranch."

That made him grin, and oh, my, it was a very appealing one. Slow and easy. Sure and sexy. His teeth were white and straight, except for a crooked eyetooth, which somehow made him look mischievous when he showed it. His face, lean and angular, looked tanned and rugged. He had laugh lines fanning out from his eyes, assuring her he shot that grin of his often. Then there was his body, all long and muscular, and she'd bet it wasn't any sort of a gym-made body either, but one finely honed from hard physical labor.

And let's not forget his hands, which were big and sure of themselves on the wheel, tanned and work roughened. Tough. Oddly enough, the most wicked thoughts ran through her head at the sight of those hands.

No doubt, Amelia Grundy would shake her finger and warn her about a man like this. And yet Amelia wasn't around. For once it was just Natalia.

A woman first, princess second.

Dangerous thoughts. Dangerous but fun. She wondered if he knew how to use those long fingers on a woman, wondered if—

"You're looking a little flushed there, princess." He flicked her a glance. "You okay?"

"Of course."

But she wasn't okay. She was as crazy as he suspected if she was really daydreaming about this man. She didn't know what she expected from her Clint Eastwood, she'd never taken the fantasy that far. But behind those green eyes and easy smile was an obvious intelligence that went beyond cow-wrangling abilities.

She sat and wondered about him for a good long while. Until he pulled off the highway onto a road with a sign that said Banning Ranch, 1898.

"Your family has been here a long time." She liked that. In her life, traditions and family pride meant something. Apparently, it meant something to this man, too.

"Yeah, ever since my great-great-grandfather won the place in a card game over a century ago."

She shot him a look of horror, which only made him laugh again. "The Wild, Wild West. The good old days."

"Your great-great-grandfather should have been ashamed of himself."

"And he might have been," Tim agreed. "But since my great-great-grandmother's father shot him a few years later for cheating on his only daughter, we'll never know."

She narrowed her eyes at him but he only smiled guilelessly, that slow, easy smile that tended to leave her feeling like jelly. "You have quite the colorful history."

"*I* have the colorful history?" He laughed. "Hey, I'm not the princess."

She had no idea if he was teasing. "I really am," she said. "A princess."

"Like I said. Colorful history."

He still didn't believe her, but that he had been so easy about it, so nonjudgmental...she could really fall for that alone.

As if she'd ever really fall for a cowboy.

Or he for a princess.

"Almost there," he said, then nodded toward a

ranch house at the end of the road. "That's the main house."

Home was a freshly painted two-story ranch house, with flowers in the flower beds and neat rows of trees lining the driveway. It was bigger than she had imagined, much bigger, and behind the house she could see several more buildings, corrals and a tower of hay.

"What are you thinking about?" he asked as she stared.

"That I'm grateful I didn't agree to clean for my bed and board."

He laughed.

Natalia didn't. She'd taken gourmet classes, *foreign* gourmet classes, to please herself, and as a result, she was pretty good at froufrou party food—when she kept the ingredients straight and didn't mix up the measurements. But she'd never cooked regular food, and certainly not for a bunch of hardworking, rough and tough ranch hands.

She really should have thought of this sooner.

But as she'd been doing all her life, she sucked up the fear and put her badass-princess face on. She'd do this. And she'd do it right.

Hopefully.

# 4

NATALIA GOT OUT of the truck and looked around. She was used to people. Used to being the center of attention, sought out and acknowledged. It came with the whole princess thing. People loved royals.

But out here, with the vast sky and even vaster landscape, she wasn't the center of attention. There were no crowds to wave to. No movie theaters, no tattoo parlor, no dry cleaners…nothing but space.

She felt as though she'd stepped foot on another planet.

Which brought her to another point. Tim had been nothing but sweet and compassionate, taking in what he seemed to think was a crazy woman, all to get her off the street.

What kind of man did that?

And what kind of woman let him? Was she simply acting on impulse—*cruel* impulse, in fact—wanting that time to herself at Tim's expense?

Today was Sunday. The wedding wasn't until next Saturday. She'd originally figured on an expensive

Taos hotel, lots of room service and time alone to enjoy a good book and the pool.

But after today's fiasco, something else had taken root. The need to do this, to prove herself, both to her family and herself. To be *normal*. A normal woman.

With all her heart she wanted that, and part of being a woman, she told herself, would certainly include taking care of the people she cared about.

Stupid as it may be, she cared about this man who'd stopped for a perfect stranger. She could help both him and herself.

And still make the wedding.

"Take until tomorrow to acclimate," Tim said, coming to stand beside her. His arm brushed hers, a simple, uncalculated touch, yet her pulse kicked up a gear. She stood still to be sure, but yep, those were lust hormones racing through her veins faster than the speed of light. Bad, bad princess.

It was also bad how much she enjoyed following him during his tour, watching his very watchable behind and thighs in those jeans nearly worn through in the most interesting of places. He showed her the main house, the bunkhouse where some of his ranch hands lived, and pointed out the two barns; one filled with equipment, one filled with animals. He offered to show her inside those barns, but she hadn't yet figured out how to mention one little detail she'd forgotten until now.

She was afraid of animals.

So she declined the tour of the barn.

"Why don't you change out of your wet clothes, then relax until morning?" he suggested when she stood on his porch looking over the vast, open land.

It was quiet here, very quiet. Except for this little eventful trip, there hadn't been many times in Natalia's life when she felt as quiet. Alone.

Suddenly all her bravado and swagger deserted her, and she wished she knew this man better, because weak as it sounded, she would have liked to set her head on his very capable-looking shoulder. Let him shield her from the unknown. Curl into his body and be protected.

But she *didn't* know him better, and she would do this by herself. "I'll change," she said. She'd purchased clothes during their stop at a general store. With his money. *An advance,* she'd told him. To be paid back. Now she had jeans and T-shirts, just like Tim.

Somehow she doubted she'd look as good in them as he did. "But I'll start work now."

"That's not necessary, Natalia."

"You'll all need dinner, correct?"

"Well, yeah." He looked right into her eyes, in a

way few others did, completely uninhibited by who she was. "You sure about this?"

Sure? Ha! She hadn't been sure of anything since she'd stepped on the plane a tough princess and had gotten off a regular, unsure woman. "Point me to the kitchen."

He led her through the house, which was as open and spacious as the land around them. The wood floors were scarred but clean, the furniture oversized, just like everything else in Texas appeared to be, and surprisingly warm and inviting.

At home in Grunberg, there were rooms for guests, and rooms for children. Never the two shall meet.

Not so here. Everyone would be welcome in any room, as there were no precious antiques to destroy, or priceless paintings to breathe on. Here would be an incredible place for a kid to run free. Literally. "It's beautiful," she said, meaning it.

He laughed as he headed toward a set of white, double swinging doors. "You sound so surprised." He stopped and turned so fast she nearly walked right into him. Heat radiated from his big body as he lifted his hands to her waist to steady her. She hadn't closed his jacket. Beneath she still wore her wet leather skirt and top, which didn't quite meet. As a result his fingers slid around her bare waist, his thumbs brushing her belly. "Do I look that uncivilized to you?" he asked.

He was teasing her again. She could see the smile tugging at his lips, but with his hands on her, she couldn't react. Couldn't even open her mouth to retort.

Then a stream of vulgarities erupted from the kitchen in a very furious, very female voice.

"Who is that?" Natalia asked, stepping back so that his hands fell to his sides.

"My sister." Tim stared at the closed door with dread. "Please, don't let her have set anything on fire or killed anyone," he muttered, and with a weak smile to Natalia, he pressed through the swinging doors.

At the huge table sat a small group of rough-and-ready men, all of whom brightened considerably at the sight of Tim.

But at the refrigerator, wearing low-slung jeans, a tank top and scuffed boots, stood a woman, swearing at the rather sparse-looking shelves. "I am not going to face the grocery store," she said. "No way, no how, not again. I don't care how hungry you all are, you'll make do with whatever is in here." She picked up something moldy. "Well, f—"

"Sally," Tim said quickly, with his hand low on Natalia's spine as he guided her into the room.

"Hallelujah." She whirled with a wide, anticipatory grin that perfectly matched her brother's.

A grin that vanished at the sight of Natalia, who stood next to Tim in her wet leather covered by Tim's jacket.

"Sally, meet—"

"Oh, great. Just great. I get in trouble for kissing Josh in the barn and you—"

*"What?"* asked a man from the table, where all the men had perked up.

"You were kissing Josh?" another asked.

*"Wow."*

"Damn, you didn't tell us that."

Sally ignored all of them. "—and now you're flaunting some new biker chick right under my nose. Nice, Tim. Real nice."

Natalia's jaw dropped. "I am not the...*new biker chick.*" Just the idea made her want to laugh. Made her want to stomp her foot in anger.

Made her wonder what it would be like to be Tim's "new biker chick."

"Well, then who are you?" Sally demanded.

"I'm trying to tell you who she is," Tim said mildly, though there was a definite warning in his eyes for his sister. "Now try to behave. Natalia's the temporary cook."

"Uh-huh," Sally said. "And I'm the queen of England."

"My God, you people and the queen of England!" Natalia exclaimed, baffled. She instantly pitied Tim for having such a horrid sister, and decided to kiss Annie and Lili the moment she saw them next.

Tim laughed and shook his head. "Okay, let's start over. Natalia, forget Sally, she's just being bad-mannered and equally bad-tempered, which happens... oh, every few moments or so."

"Anyone related to you would have the same problem," Sally muttered.

Tim ignored her. "Natalia, these guys at the table—Ryan, Pete, Seth and Red—they're my head guys."

All four men smiled.

She smiled back.

Tim turned her toward the refrigerator, and the woman who was standing there scowling. "And this is my sister, Sally, who is going to try very hard to be kind and sweet. Sally, this is Natalia. The woman who's going to relieve you in this very kitchen, so be nice."

Sally eyeballed Natalia up and down.

Natalia eyeballed Sally up and down right back.

"Sally," Tim warned.

"I'm always nice," Sally said with a sniff, but she

at least came forward and gave her brother a great big bear hug, resting her head on his shoulder as if she was very happy to see him.

"I'm always nice, too," Natalia said, oddly touched by the obvious show of affection between siblings.

"Good. We're all nice. No problem." Tim pulled back and gave an extra long look to his sister. "So, I guess you're still mad about Josh."

"Gee, give the man a prize."

"Where is he?"

"Outside eating. Like you said he had to."

"Yeah, let's hear more about Josh," Seth said from the table. "Details."

"In your dreams," Sally said, then turned on Tim. "So if she's only the cook, why do you have your hand on her?"

He did, it was still on Natalia's back, lightly. He didn't remove it. Instead, his thumb brushed her spine as his green, green eyes gazed down at her from beneath the brim of his hat. "I was protecting her from you."

The men laughed heartily, while Sally sent them daggers with her eyes.

"If this is going to cause problems..." Natalia started. "I can—"

"No problems," Tim said with another pass of his

thumb, which in return, caused most of the thoughts to dance right out of Natalia's head.

But she wasn't some silly teenager, run by racy hormones. She wouldn't get all flustered and tongue-tied over a sexy-as-hell cowboy whose jeans should be registered as an illegal weapon. "I don't want to be the cause of any bad feelings."

"Well, don't leave on my account." Sally smiled sweetly and held open the kitchen door. "Unless you feel you must. How about I call you a cab? You can take it to the nearest body-piercing saloon. In say, California."

Tim reached out and shut the door.

But Natalia stepped forward. She spoke for herself, always, and had since the age of two. "I'm—"

"Staying," Tim interrupted again.

*He was going to have to stop doing that.* Natalia frowned at him.

He frowned right back.

Sally frowned at the both of them. "No cook wears black leather and shows belly button," she said suspiciously. "Not in Texas, anyway."

"I'm not from Texas."

"Hmm." Sally crossed her arms, clearly stating with that one little rude "hmm" that if one wasn't from Texas, one wasn't worth her time. "I thought you were going to hire someone old and ugly," she said to Tim.

Tim had the good grace to look embarrassed. "I said old and ugly when you wanted to hire Nick the Sleaze, remember?"

"Well I'd stay away from *whoever* you hired if you hadn't told Josh that if he touched me again you'd cut off his—"

"Sally, you're driving me crazy."

"Yeah, well. It's a short drive. Speaking of crazy, how's Grandma?"

"Crazier than even you."

Natalia watched this exchange between brother and sister with fascination. Not because she'd never fought with her siblings, because she had. A lot. Mostly with Annie just because Lili being the baby— quite literally sometimes—wasn't as much fun to wrestle with. And she was a tattletale.

But Natalia could never in a million years have pictured cool, calm, collected cowboy Tim Banning acting like an obnoxious older brother.

"So, where is Grandma, Tim?" Sally asked with a false sweetness. "I'm sure with all your charm, you managed to kidnap her away from the life she loves, all in the name of family duty."

"Ouch," said Seth from the table with a wince.

"She didn't come with me," Tim admitted.

"Probably because she knows you'd ruin her life, too."

Tim looked tense again.

Natalia, the middle child and therefore a peacemaker at heart, stepped forward and smiled. "How about I cook dinner?"

"Good plan." Sally strutted across the kitchen and sat at the table with the men. "Though you should know, if you hurt my brother I'll have to kick your butt. So…is your tongue pierced?"

Natalia blinked. Good Lord, Americans were certifiable. "Hurt your brother? Why would I do that?"

"Just a friendly little warning."

"Friendly. Right." Like Tim, Sally Banning was tall, lean and muscular and also sported a crooked eyetooth. Somehow it wasn't nearly as attractive on Sally as it was on Tim, but Natalia had to admit that it was probably because Sally was looking at her as if she was a bug on her windshield.

Natalia had felt like that a lot today, and she was getting mighty tired of it. She opened her mouth to say so, but Tim neatly cut her off.

"Sally, do you have an extra coat you can spare?"

Sally's eyes narrowed. "What happened to *her* coat?"

"It was stolen," Natalia said. "I'm visiting the States for a royal friend's wedding."

Sally lifted a single brow. "Royal friend?"

"I'm a princess."

Sally lifted the other brow now and looked at Tim. "What have you done?"

"I was going to ask you the same thing," he said lightly. "Everything still in working order around here?"

"She won't fit in the stockade with the others."

"Others?" Natalia asked.

"My brother collects the weak, the weary. The pathetic."

A funny feeling started in the pit of Natalia's stomach. She didn't want to be someone Tim felt sorry for, and it was a tribute to her own privileged upbringing that it hadn't occurred to her until now that he might see her like that. In a way she didn't fully understand, she wanted to be someone he liked and respected.

But who in their right mind would like and respect a pampered princess who'd never lifted a hand to help herself in her entire life?

Good question, and right then and there Natalia became even more determined to become her own woman, successful in her own right, not her birthright. "I'm not weak or weary." She'd leave pathetic out of this.

Sally gestured to the kitchen window. "See that

stockade out there? The one filled with the three-legged pig, the ancient horse and the blind goat?''

''Um…yes.''

''That's Tim for you. He collects the needy.''

And the pathetic.

Natalia got the message loud and clear. She'd just been added to the save-the-world stockade.

TIM CALLED a friend of his, who happened to be a cop. No one matching Natalia's description had been reported missing. Tim didn't have him run a criminal check, that would have been wrong. But at least his beautiful crazy cook hadn't walked out of a halfway house or insane asylum. Good. He didn't have to feel bad about letting her stay.

Now he had to face what he *did* have to feel bad about, the fact that he wanted her to stay more than he'd wanted anything in a long time.

DINNER WAS something so fancy Tim couldn't pronounce the name of it. Since Natalia looked so utterly pleased with herself, Tim tried to like it. So did everyone else.

But the moment she turned her back, they stared at each other in horror.

''What is it?'' Red mouthed.

Sally shrugged and fed it to Grumpster, Tim's thir-

teen-year-old mutt lying hopefully beneath the table.
Everyone else quickly followed suit.

Grumpster, who routinely licked his own parts for
hours on end, sniffed once and turned his head away.

Which left everyone scrambling to stuff their nap-
kins with the rest, making it appear as if they'd eaten.

Tim wondered at all of them—including himself—
at the length they went to not to hurt Natalia's feelings.

When she saw their empty plates, she beamed with
pride. Tim's chest hurt just looking at her, and he
smiled back through the pain. So did his men, while
Sally rolled her eyes and looked disgusted.

"Goners," she said sadly. "Complete goners."

BREAKFAST THE NEXT DAY was more of the same.
They were served some wildly foreign-sounding thing
that involved very little food and far too much sauce.
But because Natalia had obviously tried so hard, and
was waiting with bated breath at the side of the table,
hands clasped, eyes hopeful, no one said a word.

They all just smiled at the woman now in denim
and a T-shirt, hair still spiked, earrings still in, but
face void of makeup except for green lip gloss. The
moment she turned her back, they made gagging faces
at each other.

They couldn't even bribe Grumpster with the stuff

because he'd refused to come inside with them for the first time ever. They were on their own.

AFTER BREAKFAST, Tim entered the barn and found Seth handing out chocolate bars from his personal stash. Five bucks apiece. Highway robbery, but Ryan, Pete and Red were all digging into their pockets for the cash.

Sally lifted her head from where she was taking care of her horse and shook her head in disgust. "Hey, here's an idea. Tell her the cooking sucks."

"Don't even think about it." Tim's stomach growled with a gnawing hunger, and with a grimace, he pulled a ten from his pocket. "I'll take two," he said to Seth.

"Unbelievable." Sally leveled her annoyed gaze on him. "Did she call her so-called royal family yet?"

"No," he admitted.

"And do you know why?"

"It doesn't matter."

"Oh, I think it does. She hasn't called home because she doesn't have one."

"I couldn't leave her at the bus stop, Sally. And you know what? You couldn't have, either."

"This isn't about me, but, yes, I could have." Her eyes softened. "You can't take care of everyone."

Tim let out a sound of frustration and ripped into the chocolate. "Look, I know she cooks a little strangely."

"She lied about knowing how to feed a large group."

"She never claimed to know how to do that."

Sally's mouth dropped open. "You're telling me you hired without asking? Damn, Tim."

"She's trying hard, and that counts. And anyway, she's only going to be here a few days, just enough to earn her way to New Mexico."

"So you're really not going to tell her everything she touches in that kitchen turns to lead in our guts?" She sighed theatrically. "It's going to be a long few days. Damn it, someone front me a five and hand over the chocolate."

Tim waited until her first bite, then nudged her away from the others. "I need you to go to the grocery store today." He spoke cautiously, because sure as the sun came up every morning, coaxing Sally into doing this was going to cost him.

"No way."

"If you do, I'll…"

"You'll what?" She cocked a hip and crossed her arms, shooting him the universal irritated-sister-to-idiot-brother look. "Let me date Josh?"

"Is that what you call what you were doing with

him?'' She just lifted that brow of hers, making him sigh. "Do you really like him?"

"I like how he fills out his jeans, and that's all that matters right now."

Tim cringed. "I don't want to hear this."

"Then don't ask."

"Please? Go fill up the refrigerator?"

"Because your new cook can't be trusted with your truck?"

"Because she's just learning the ropes, I don't want to dump that chore on her right now."

"But you have no problem dumping it on me." She rolled her eyes, swore beneath her breath. "Fine. But I'm going out with Josh on Friday night."

"What if he doesn't ask?"

"Oh, he'll ask." She took another bite of her chocolate bar.

So did Tim. "You being smart?" he asked.

"I know how to have safe sex, if that's what you're asking. You made sure of that when you gave me the birds and bees talk, remember? I make him wear a party hat."

Tim groaned.

"Would you rather I use the word condom? Or better yet, multipack?"

Tim shut his eyes and covered his ears, making Sally laugh as she dug into her chocolate.

For a long moment there was no sound in the barn except the rustling of paper as everyone continued to fill their empty bellies.

"I'll make a store run," Seth promised. "Tomorrow I'll sell something more substantial."

"Like Jelly Bellys?" Josh asked hopefully.

Seth laughed. "Maybe."

Then the barn door opened.

With the sun pouring in, Tim couldn't immediately see much, except a very memorable silhouette of a body in jeans and a T-shirt. A real woman's body— lush breasts, curved hips, long legs. How had he ever mistaken her for a jailbait juvenile delinquent?

She stepped closer, eyes locked on their hands, and what they were eating. When it registered, she went still. "Well."

There was a wealth of things in that *well*, with hurt leading the pack. Damn it. "Oh, this?" He looked at the chocolate in his hands. "It's…a morning ritual." He stepped on Sally's foot as she was about to open her big, fat mouth. "Eating chocolate together before we head out for the day." He nodded and smiled. "Yep, we do it every morning."

Seth, Pete, Ryan and Red's heads all bobbed up and down in collective agreement.

"Yessiree," said Seth.

"Yeppers," echoed Red and Ryan.

"Perfect dessert to your breakfast," Red added.

Natalia visibly brightened, her smile becoming full. "Really?"

Tim's gaze lowered to her lips, and allowed himself to imagine she tasted as good as she looked. "Really." She looked so different today. She looked real. And he wanted, quite suddenly, to bury his face in the skin in the crook of her neck and inhale like a bloodhound.

"But," she continued in a sweet, soft chastising voice, "you should have just said you were still hungry." She smiled. "Never mind. I'll cook more at lunch."

"M-more?" Seth glanced in horror at Tim.

"Oh, yes." She laughed and headed out. "Can't have you going hungry!"

"Can't have that," Sally said through her teeth, and shot Tim a look to kill.

# 5

LATE THAT AFTERNOON, Tim rode back to the barn. He dismounted Jake, who immediately began searching his pockets with his warm, wet muzzle.

"Stop that." Tim hoisted off Jake's saddle. "You've already had your goodie today."

The horse snorted and looked pouty, and behind them a soft laugh sounded.

Natalia stood there wearing a smile that shot straight through him, a smile that got to him when he hadn't planned on her getting to him at all. "You make it look so easy," she said. "Getting on and off. Riding. All of it."

Which meant she'd been watching him. He wondered if she watched him as much as he watched her.

"My mom loved horses." A flicker of sadness touched her eyes as she looked at Jake, though she carefully stayed back from him. "She, um…died in an avalanche twelve years ago."

"God. I'm sorry."

"It was a long time ago."

"Yeah." He stroked Jake. "Let me guess. You'd be rich if you had a penny for every time someone told you it'll get easier, you'll see her again someday, she'll live on in your heart forever...right?"

She lifted her head. "You've lost someone, too."

"My parents. In a car accident."

"So you know."

"I know," he agreed. "I also know the only consolation that works is to say that it sucks."

That got a laugh out of her. "Yeah. Sucks."

He smiled at her, thinking she looked good standing there in her new casual wear. The jeans clung to her hips and thighs, the T-shirt to her breasts. The wind ruffled her hair and had put color into her cheeks. She looked different here, far more earthy than wild, and though he knew that was because her makeup had been stolen, he liked it.

Too much.

"So that's why you put up with your sister," she said. "You're raising her."

"Someone has to."

"You love her."

He sighed, even as he smiled. "Like I said, someone has to."

She smiled back, then shifted when he just stared at her. "What?"

"I was just thinking you don't look anything like the woman from the plane."

Immediately she lifted a hand to her hair and looked regretful. "I know, I—"

"I like it."

"Are you saying you don't miss the leather?"

"No." He grinned. "The leather was good. But I like seeing your face."

"Which is why I was fond of the makeup."

"You liked hiding."

"I liked hiding. I didn't realize how much, or…"

"Or?"

"Or that I wouldn't miss the hiding at all."

They stood there, smiling at each other stupidly, until Jake shifted his weight, moving between them, ready to get back to his stall for his feeding if there were no goodies to be had.

Eyes wide, Natalia nearly tripped over her own feet in her hurry to back up.

At her sudden movement, Jake snorted, this time stomping his front hoof for emphasis. *Feed me,* he said with a toss of his head.

Natalia took another step back, and this time she did trip over her own feet, and would have fallen if Tim hadn't grabbed her.

"Hey. You okay?"

"Oh, sure." She forced a smile. "Just fine—"

Jake's large head swung around, and he leveled Natalia with a baleful stare. *Food!*

Natalia staggered back from both man and horse, until the fence was at her back. "He's…uh, really huge, isn't he?"

If he didn't know better, this outwardly tough woman was trembling in her boots. "Not a horse person, I'm guessing?"

Her eyes didn't move from Jake. "Not an animal person."

Jake, oblivious, thrust out his neck and nosed at Natalia's front pockets, which earned him a petrified shriek.

Tim stepped between the nose and Natalia. "You must smell good." *Fact.* "Don't worry, he won't hurt you."

"I'm…fine. I'm not afraid."

Uh-huh. She was only holding her breath. Trying to soothe, he ran a hand up her arm. "Natalia? Honey, breathe."

"Yes." She gulped air. "Of course. Breathing."

He smiled at her attempt to be cool and calm. "What kind of pets did you have growing up?"

"Actually, where I'm from, there are plenty of horses and cattle." She managed to tear her gaze from Jake. "It's me. My failing. It's a silly little phobia."

"Nothing to be afraid of with Jake. He's just looking for a snack. He thinks everyone loves him. Watch.'' He turned to the horse and let out a soft whinny noise.

The horse repeated it, and affectionately rubbed the side of his face on Tim's arm. Tim looked at Natalia. ''Want to try?''

Before she could say no, before she could so much as let out a shriek, Tim had slipped an arm around her waist, pulled her against his side and let out that soft whinny again.

Jake mirrored the noise and rubbed the side of his huge face against Natalia's arm. It felt warm and damp. And terrifying. In fact, she would have screamed if she hadn't just swallowed her tongue. She would have shrunk away, but she was plastered against Tim, and—

*And she was plastered against Tim.* Oh my God. Heat, confusion, more heat. A noise escaped her and it had nothing, absolutely nothing to do with fear.

''Okay?'' he asked quietly, staring into her eyes, completely focused on her.

It was the oddest thing—she'd been surrounded by people all her life, and yet for the first time she really felt as if she had someone's one-hundred-percent-undivided attention focused on her. Totally and completely on her.

It was intoxicating. *He* was intoxicating. ''Not sure,'' she whispered slowly.

His gaze slid to her mouth, which fell open, just to get air to her suddenly deflated lungs.

At that, his eyes darkened, and his arm tightened around her. ''And now?'' he whispered across her cheek.

Senses on full alert, she leaned toward him, unable to resist his big, solid, warm body. Standing so close like this, feeling him react to her, surround her, it felt like coming in from the rain.

''Natalia?''

In anticipation her entire body tingled. She even licked her lips and…

A sound escaped him, a near groan, and her eyes fell closed.

Here it came…a kiss…a perfect kiss…

Only it wasn't a man's hard, demanding lips that met hers. It was a horse's demanding whinny in her ear, as Jake once again thrust his head between theirs.

Her eyes whipped open just as Tim let out another groan. ''Nice timing, Jake.'' He pushed the horse's big head away, but Jake was persistent, and finally Tim had to laugh. ''Sorry, but the big lug here thinks he's my baby.''

Heart still pounding, Natalia pulled back. ''Yeah.

Baby.'' The biggest baby she'd ever seen. ''I...have to get back to work.''

Tim looked at her, an easy smile on his lips, as if it was the most natural thing in the world to stand so close, to have blood racing through her body, to want him with all her being.... Unless he didn't feel it.

Of course he didn't.

''See you at dinner,'' she managed, then walked out calmly, sedately, as if she had near-miss kisses every day of her life.

Alone in the kitchen, she sagged against the sink and drew a deep breath.

And wondered at the fact that she wished they hadn't missed at all.

THE NEXT DAY after breakfast, Natalia stepped out into the sunshine. Everyone had been in a huge hurry to be out and gone. Though they'd all smiled—well, except Sally—at what Natalia thought had been an incredibly inventive casserole dish made from bread, eggs and sausage, they'd still vanished the moment she'd turned her back.

They were busy, she understood. It didn't matter. She was having a great time. It felt almost wrong, this lovely rush of joy she got piddling around in the kitchen, and she didn't want it to end.

Feeling good and nice and sure of herself, she

moved off the porch, lifting a hand to shield her eyes from the bright sun. She would have denied it to her dying day, but she stood there, a kitchen full of work to do, secretly hoping for a peek of Tim.

Just a peek, mind you, just one, of his tall, built, wildly sexy self. She hadn't been able to stop thinking about him since yesterday, when he'd touched her.

Nearly kissed her.

She hoped to catch him working, which meant she'd get a good look at all those muscles in action, stretching taut beneath his shirt. Maybe he'd be hot— hot enough to have removed said shirt, for an up-close-and-personal view.

Something deep inside of her pitter-pattered at that, and she moved off the porch. When she did, the animals in the side stockade, the "pity pets" Sally had called them, all came to hopeful attention.

Her heart stopped. Her palms went damp. It was ridiculous, this terror, and she knew it. She even knew where it came from. Every year in her hometown the royal family rode in the Christmas parade. When she'd been five, her father had deemed her old enough to sit on a pony by herself. How proud she'd been, forgetting to hold on to the reins so that she could wave to one and all.

But then a pack of Labrador retrievers from the float behind her had broken loose, and startled her pony into rearing. In her velvet Christmas finery, Natalia had slid off the back and to the ground. She had still been sitting there when the pony had decided to let go of all it had eaten for a week.

Covered in pony dung, which stuck nicely to her dress, the dogs had run in circles around her while the entire town…laughed.

Yep, nearly twenty years and she still harbored this irrational fear of animals.

She took another couple of steps and so did Tim's animals—toward her. Actually, the little three-legged pig came running. Well…*hopping,* but he was good at it, moving as fast as three short legs would take him, his snout quivering with such velocity it nearly took him off the ground into flight. At the fence that separated them he pressed his snout against it and let out a series of frustrated snorts.

Startled, Natalia stopped short, her heart pounding. But there was a fence between them. A good one. She was safe. Determined to get over herself, she took another step, even closer.

The goat came, too, but it wasn't until it bumped right into the pig that Natalia remembered the thing was blind. Which didn't stop it from lifting its head over the fence and sniffling, searching…for food, she realized as she nearly fell backward to get out of the way.

The ancient horse shuffled forward, too, stepping over the pig until all six eyes—four good and two not—waited expectantly.

"But...I don't have anything," she told them, lifting a hand to her racing heart. "I'm sorry."

Still, they pressed against the wood, putting out whatever they could, which in this case was a very muddy snout, a set of teeth surrounded by a goat's beard and a soft, searching muzzle.

They cried, each looking so unexpectedly adorable she had to laugh. "I'm telling you, I'm not carrying food." She lifted up her hands, which turned out to be a bad idea as it started a wave of enthusiasm on their part.

They looked so hungry, her heart tugged. "Hold on," she said, then raced back to the house and grabbed the first thing she found in the fridge.

Back at the stockade, her three new friends were now making a huge ruckus. Oh, boy. They looked ready to rumble for the three carrots she'd brought, and not nearly as adorable as she remembered. "Don't eat me," she begged, and bravely handed one to the old horse, who in its excitement, dropped the carrot to the ground.

It snorted at the food, but couldn't seem to pick it up out of the dirt. Then, to the great consternation of the old horse, the pig started toward it.

"Oh, no. That's not yours—" She went to her knees to reach through the fence, trying to help the horse.

But the goat got a hold of the hem of her shirt and started to eat it.

"No," she cried, the terror gripping her by the throat, trying to pull back, but the goat wouldn't give up.

Then the pig got into the act, wiping its dirty snout down her trapped arm, looking for another carrot, and Natalia nearly had a heart attack, imagining herself without a limb or even worse. With all her might she wished for lithe, toned, strong Annie, who could handle these animals with her eyes closed.

With one hard tug, Natalia freed herself…and fell to her butt in the dirt, ripping the shirt. But she was free! Frantically, she checked all her limbs. After careful inventory, she decided that the only thing damaged was her pride and the T-shirt. "It could be worse," she told herself. "I could have been pooped on. Someone could have seen it all."

"Oh, it's worse."

*Sally.* Great. Natalia sighed and craned her neck, finding Sally standing behind her, arms crossed, a spiteful smirk on her face. "Hey. I was just…"

"Feeding the goat your shirt. I know. I watched." With a shake of her head in disgust, she walked on.

Natalia got to her feet and told herself it didn't matter. Sally didn't like her whether she was an idiot or not, and surprisingly, when she went back into the house and changed her clothes, she felt even lighter of heart than before she'd made a fool of herself.

In fact, she felt so good, she hadn't thought about New Mexico for at least a couple of hours.

A slight amount of joy faded as she remembered now.

This was all temporary. Very temporary, as in one day left temporary, so no use getting attached in any way.

But she had a sinking feeling it was far too late.

"It's never too late."

Natalia jerked at the sound of Amelia's voice and whipped around, but she was alone in the kitchen.

"Amelia?" she whispered, feeling ridiculous, and yet Amelia's beloved and very British voice had sounded so real.

No one answered.

With a little laugh at herself, Natalia turned back to the task at hand. Lunch. Good God, she was really losing it here.

*Never too late.*

What did that mean? That she could stay if she wanted, just a little bit longer? She fingered her cell phone in the pocket of her jeans. What if she called ahead to New Mexico and said she couldn't make it for some reason? She wasn't due back in Grunberg until next Monday.

She pulled out the cell phone, and before she could change her mind, called information for the hotel in Taos where she was to meet up with her sisters on Saturday morning. It was chicken of her to do it this way—calling and leaving a message that no one would get until Saturday—but then she wouldn't be missed until it was too late.

She finally got through to a hotel representative. Perfect. "Just say I've come down with..." Natalia wracked her brain trying to come up with a viable, believable excuse that wouldn't bring the entire royal family to Texas in arms. "Poison ivy," she said brilliantly. That would keep people away, right?

"Poison ivy," the woman said. "Tell her Your Serene Highness has poison ivy. Ma'am, is this some sort of a joke?"

"No." Not a joke, just a little white fib. *Sorry Annie. Sorry Lili.* "Be sure to tell her I'm covered with this horrific rash, terribly contagious and smell to high heaven from all the oatmeal baths I'm taking." Yep, that would do it, and she hung up feeling far too excited for someone who'd just sentenced themselves to cooking for ranch hands for another week.

Luckily for her, lunch was fairly simple. Hors

d'oeuvres that she'd whipped up from the night before and oddly had some left over. No sense in wasting food.

It was the iced tea she had a hard time with. Caught up in the hors d'oeuvres and an approaching thunderstorm that made the sky so pretty she couldn't stop looking out the window, she let it brew too long.

But cowboys liked things strong, didn't they?

She'd have to learn to multitask better. She had it down pat in other aspects of her life. She could, for instance, spread treats out on a tray while gazing out the kitchen window at Tim, working with his horses.

He'd just come into her view. Already her heart was drumming as it had when his horse had frisked her, but it wasn't simple fear making it nearly leap right out of her chest.

It was him.

He took off his hat, and swiped at his forehead with his arm. Then he shoved the sleeves of his shirt up to reveal forearms corded with strength.

Such a large man, and yet he appeared so utterly gentle with the young horse he was currently whispering sweet nothings to.

In response, the horse playfully bumped his chest, causing Tim to toss back his head and laugh.

The low, husky sound of it carried across the yard and through the window to her ears.

"Ridiculous," she muttered, but she kept her nose plastered to the window all the same. Maybe he'd get hot and rip off his shirt. She didn't want to miss that.

*Get hot,* she mentally transmitted. *Really hot.* Instead, he bent down, scooping up the front right hoof of the horse in his big hand to inspect the bottom.

She got busy inspecting, too. *His* terrific bottom.

"Oh, jeez." From behind her came Sally's groan. "What the hell are you doing *now?*"

# 6

NATALIA WENT FOR cool and calm when she turned to Sally, who had apparently come into the kitchen and walked right up behind her while she'd been staring at Tim. "I'm—" *What had she been doing?* Blindly, she stared at the knife in her hand. "Um…"

Sally's brow disappeared into her hair.

"Making lunch."

"You mean you're starving the men again."

"No, I'm—" Natalia blinked. "What?"

"Oh, nothing, for God's sake." Sally leaned against the counter and crossed her arms. "You might want to wipe your chin."

"Why?"

"You were watching my brother's ass and drooling."

Natalia managed a laugh that didn't fool either of them. "Don't be ridiculous. That would be…" *A definite spectator sport.* "Insulting."

"You were."

Natalia busied herself fixing the large tray in front of her. "Is everyone ready to eat?"

"Oh, yeah."

She sounded so sarcastic Natalia turned, but Sally just sent her an innocent look. She grabbed a stuffed mushroom off the tray, turned it this way and that, carefully inspecting it, then finally took a tentative bite. "Hmm," she said in lieu of a thank you.

Okay, that was it. Natalia crossed her arms. "Is that 'hmm' good or 'hmm' bad?"

"No comment."

"You can do better than that."

"No, really. I can't."

"You know, I'm trying here." She watched Sally wolf six more down in half as many bites.

"Yeah." Sally swallowed and brushed her hands over her thighs. "Which brings me to another point. Why?"

"Why am I trying?"

"Why don't you just go on welfare, or hit a shelter, or better yet, get a job you're equipped for, like cooking for a bunch of people who like weird food."

"First of all, I do not need welfare."

"Uh-huh."

Carefully, Natalia set down her knife. No need to tempt herself. "And second of all, I'm not even a citizen. I'm a princess, which I know your brother already told you. I suppose, as it does sound outlandish way out here in the middle of nowhere, I can forgive you not believing it. But as far as why I'm here and what I'm doing..." No. She couldn't share it, because the need to be a woman first for once, and a princess a distant second was strong. How could a woman like Sally, who did what she wanted, when she wanted, without a care to her duties, understand? "I'm afraid it's none of your business."

"Fine. But if you're here to snag my brother, think again. He's not into body piercings or spiked hair."

No, but he'd been into the leather. "*Snag* your brother? What does that even mean?"

Sally uttered a one-word adjective that perfectly conveyed what she meant. It was a word people didn't often utter in front of a princess.

"And," Sally continued, "if you harm one little hair on his head, I'll rip out your fingernails, one by one. So stop staring at his ass."

Natalia actually gaped. Was this woman for real? Knowing it was rude to respond to her host in such a manner didn't stop her. She hadn't been raised with sisters for nothing. Thanks to Annie being so tough and forward, she knew how to fight back. "You're kidding me, right?"

Sally didn't so much as blink.

"Wow." Natalia shook her head. "It's clear the American reputation of being crass and rude is completely undeserving. Because really, you're all so sweet and caring."

"Just remember what I said," Sally said.

"Tim is a big boy."

"Yes, but he's also a softie, with a heart just waiting to be stomped all over." Sally took another mushroom and headed toward the door. "I'll be watching you. Waiting for an excuse to kick your pretty little butt." The door slammed.

"I guess this means we won't be polishing each other's fingernails tonight at the slumber party, right?" Natalia called out after her, then kicked the refrigerator.

TIM FORCED himself to take another bite of dinner, but only because Natalia was watching, her forehead puckered in a line of worry. He swallowed, hard, and managed a smile. "What is it?"

"An old family recipe." She clasped her fingers together. "Do you like it?"

"Uh…" Everyone looked at him. "Well…I've never tasted anything quite like it."

Sally snorted.

Natalia bit her lip.

Sally pushed her plate away. "Nick would have made chili."

"Sally—"

"And looked damn good while doing it."

"Nick?" Natalia asked.

"The guy *I* would have hired for the job," Sally said.

Natalia looked down at her plate. "Chili. I hadn't thought of that. Or that I'd taken a job from someone who needed it."

"Nick has another job already," Tim said.

"Oh, okay then."

Seth leaned forward eagerly. "You know, chili is really easy, Natalia. I bet you could do it."

Pete nodded hopefully.

"Well, it's not really a gourmet thing, chili." Natalia tilted her head and considered. "But…"

Tim poked at whatever was on his plate. "Is that what this is? Gourmet?"

"Of course." Natalia set down her fork. "What did you think it was?"

He looked into her eyes. What did he think? That she looked very anxious, and not very tough, as she clearly wanted to be. That she was incredibly appealing looking at him like that.

That he couldn't tell her everything she touched was inedible. "I..."

She pushed her plate away, looked aghast. "You didn't know." When he winced, she shook her head. "Oh my God. You didn't know. You thought I couldn't cook."

"Well—"

"No." She stood up, looking mortified. "You thought...you just chalked it up to my craziness. Right? Oh, let poor Natalia alone. She thinks she's a princess, she thinks she can cook, she thinks..." She shook her head again, covered her mouth. "Excuse me."

She rose and stalked from the room in her denim and combat boots.

At the table, the men all turned accusing gazes on him. "Now you did it," Pete whispered. "You hurt her feelings."

"Yeah. Go fix it." Red pointed to the door. "Go tell her it's only you. Tell her *we* love everything she made."

Sally rolled her eyes. "Oh, jeez. You guys are as pathetic as she is."

"Hey, now, she never did anything to you," Pete said. "Except maybe try hard."

Tim sighed, tossed aside his napkin and stood. "I'll talk to her."

"Yeah, you'd better," Pete said. "Go make it right."

Everyone but Sally nodded, and Tim might have laughed if it wasn't so damn touching. Every one of them was willing to eat the inedible, just to save Natalia's feelings.

"Bunch of softies," Sally muttered.

Tim had to agree. And with the exception of a certain of part of his anatomy that was rarely "soft" around Natalia, he was the biggest softie of all.

HE FOUND HER on the back deck, watching the moon. She leaned back against one of the wood posts, her hands behind her on the wood, her face hidden by shadows. But not her body, which was illuminated by the glow of the moon, appearing all long and curved and gorgeous.

It made no sense. In the jeans and T-shirt, covered now with an old opened flannel shirt of his, she should have looked ordinary. Plain.

But she took his breath. "You okay?"

"Sure. For a crazy lady."

"Natalia—"

She didn't look at him. "I know what you guys think of me."

He moved into her line of vision, standing in front of her so that she had no choice but to take her gaze from the moon and look at him. "They care about you," he said. "And so do I."

"Like you'd care about a blind goat."

"I don't think you're a blind goat, Natalia."

She let out a rough breath and turned away, but not before he caught the glimmer of a sheen of tears in her eyes.

"I don't," he said softly. "I just—"

"—think I'm a three-legged pig who needs a stable."

She moved fast, and might have gotten away if he hadn't grabbed her hand, might have fought him if he hadn't held on.

"I have to go," she whispered.

"Hold on." Her breath sounded funny as she struggled for control, and his heart slipped. "No, don't..." He took her shoulders and gently pulled her resisting body close. For comfort, nothing more, but he realized the mistake instantly, as there was far more than comfort at work here. She was soft against him, so soft, and she burrowed close, burying her face in his shoulder as she struggled with composure.

So strong. So alone. To soothe, he stroked a hand over her hair, down her slim spine.

*You're asking for trouble, man, in a big way.*

It didn't seem to matter, not when she sniffed and burrowed a little closer, pressing her face into the crook of his neck.

"I was trying too hard." Her words whispered against his skin. "You'd probably would have rather been eating peanut butter and jelly."

"No." Her soft, warm lips against his flesh were killing him slowly. "We just didn't know what you were dishing out, that's all."

What she was dishing out now, with just this one embrace, was going to give him a king-size heart attack any second now.

"I'm sorry," she said on a sigh. "I'm just ever so tired of making a fool of myself." But she snuggled closer, heating his body. "I was just having so much fun being needed for a change. At home, I'm important, but not *needed*." She sighed again, still against his skin, and he nearly went to his knees. "You have no idea how nice it is. To be needed."

Needed.

*Whoa.* Big mental step back.

When had it gone from her needing him to *him* needing *her?*

With a good amount of shock, he lifted his head.

She lifted hers, too, and for one moment they hovered like that, their lips a fraction of an inch apart, until one of them—he had no idea which one—closed the gap.

Then they were kissing as if their lives depended on it. And in that moment, his did.

# 7

_____

COMING UP FOR AIR, Natalia pulled back a fraction. Her mouth was wet, her eyes slumberous, her fingers entangled in the hair at the back of Tim's neck. The look on her face nearly undid him.

"Don't take this wrong," she murmured, sending delicious shivers down his spine with her fingers, "but I've been wondering what that would be like."

The admission was as big a turn-on as her kiss had been. He slid his hands over her hips. "Yeah?"

"Did you wonder, too?"

No. He hadn't wondered. He'd been too busy. Hadn't he? "After that kiss, I can think of little else other than doing it again."

"Again would work for me."

He was smiling when he kissed her this time. _Smiling_. He couldn't remember ever doing that while kissing a woman before. Her body against his felt good, and he pressed closer for more of it, sliding his hands beneath the flannel and over the soft curves he'd been thinking about all day—

He *had* been thinking about her all day. About *this*.

At his low, surprised laugh she pulled back. "What?" she asked suspiciously.

"Nothing." He leaned in for more kisses but she slapped a hand on his chest.

"You stopped to laugh."

"No, I—"

"Let me give you a hint about women, Tim. Laughing at their kissing technique is bad form."

Uh-oh. "I wasn't laughing at you. Honest. Now come here."

"For what? More kissing? You'd still be doing just that if you hadn't laughed."

"I laughed at me. Okay? I didn't realize until now that I *have* been thinking about you all day."

"And this is funny because…"

"It's not funny, believe me." He held her hands when she would have turned away. "It's distracting."

"Not exactly a compliment."

"No?" He stepped close again. "How's this for a compliment? You're making me hot. All the time. I fantasize in the middle of a workday about you, about this, about us. About things I've convinced myself I don't need."

"I don't need them, either."

"Okay." He took a breath. "So we both fantasize, but…"

She sighed. "There's always a but."

"But my life isn't exactly laid out for this."

"And mine is?" She laughed and shook her head. "No, it is not. Believe me."

"Natalia, everything I am, everything I do, is this ranch. Women have tried to fit in here with me before, but they get tired of playing second fiddle to this place, and...well, I'm left alone and disappointed."

"I'm sorry for that, *more* than sorry, but I'm temporary."

"Exactly. So what the hell are we doing?"

"I don't know. Scratching an itch?"

"Scratching an—" Shocked, he stared at her. "Where did you learn such a thing?"

"Oh, I see." Her eyes chilled. "It's one thing for a man to suggest an affair. But if a woman...if she has..."

"An itch?"

"Never mind! Just forget it."

"Wait." His head was still spinning. "Now I've insulted you."

She sputtered, then laughed. Then, before he could so much as blink, she shoved away from him and turned her back, staring up at the moon, her arms wrapped tightly around the body he'd been molding with his hands only a few moments ago.

"Natalia." A little wary, he came up behind her,

set his hands on her shoulders, which she promptly shrugged off. "Let's try this again."

"Okay." She drew a deep breath. "I'm sorry I brought it up. It was stupid."

"No," he said, looking at her beautiful profile. "It wasn't."

"But just because I thought about…scratching that itch, you should know, it wasn't a declaration of undying love." She dropped her gaze from the moon and landed those huge, dark gold, expressive eyes on him. "I wouldn't expect you to love me."

His heart twisted. "Natalia—"

"It's a one-night stand, Tim, that's all. Only technically, I have several nights, not just one."

His body responded immediately, but it took his brain a moment longer. "You deserve more than that. You deserve time, and a man taking it to get to know you."

"You want to know me? How's this? I'm the middle kid. I'm usually pretty easygoing, that is when I'm not in Texas. And contrary to what I've shown you, I'm known as being pretty damn tough and fearless. And though you might not believe that by looking at me at the moment—" she broke off to glance down at her plain jeans and T-shirt "—I'm into clothes. I also love to ski. Unfortunately for me, Texas doesn't seem to have many hills." She smiled, but when he just looked at her, it slowly faded. "And I'm a princess, which brings us back to the delusional crazy woman thing. I'd nearly forgotten. I'm just another one of your pity hires."

"Natalia—"

"No." With dignity, she backed away. "In a few more days I'll have earned myself enough to get where I need to go, which is all I really wanted. To see what it was like to be just me, without any expectations or preconceived notions. To support myself. Without the title. End of story." She reached the gate. "I appreciate all you've done, but I think we should get back to the boss-and-employee relationship." And with her head high, shoulders extremely straight, she walked toward the house.

Looking every bit like a princess in denim.

NATALIA MANAGED to avoid conversation with Tim before breakfast the next morning. She was no longer mad. Or even hurt.

But she did feel wiser. Apparently, in this so-called modern country, no matter what the men claimed, they didn't want to be come on to. She'd remember that the next time her hormones kicked into overdrive.

She baked a dish she remembered from school, similar to the American quiche, which despite its plain ingredients, was quite spicy and exotic. It came out excellent, if she said so herself.

But Tim stared down at the plate she served him. "You, uh…didn't decide to poison me for last night, did you?"

Sally lifted her head. "What happened last night?"

Natalia took a bite of the delicious, hot meal.

*"Hello?"* Sally said. "Last night?"

Tim looked at Natalia.

Natalia took another bite.

Sally frowned. "Oh, man." She pointed at Tim. "You. You're an idiot."

He didn't take his eyes off Natalia. "I'm well aware of that, thank you."

Sally turned to Natalia with a questioning look.

Natalia simply continued to eat.

Until Sally leaned close. "Stop messing with his head or I'll mess with yours."

"So charming in the morning." Natalia took another bite and smiled sweetly at the men. "Isn't she? Are you always that way, Sally, or is it just me?"

"It's you." Sally lifted her fork, sniffed at the food, then set it down with a clatter. "You've never heard of simple scrambled eggs?" Shoving away from the table, she pulled a five out of her pocket and tossed it toward Seth. "I'll expect you in the barn. Come supplied." She left without another word.

Natalia left the table, too, and went into the kitchen to check on the bread. When she came back out, the food was gone. So was everyone else.

At least she was doing something right, she thought with a spurt of satisfaction at the empty table. Just because Tim and Sally obviously had no taste whatsoever meant nothing.

Back in the kitchen, she turned on the sink faucet. Contrary to what most people thought of a day in the life of a princess, she did know how to do dishes. She could also do her own laundry, bathe and feed herself. Shocking.

She looked out the window at the great day. She was up to her elbows in greasy dishwater, she was exhausted from getting up before the crack of dawn, but she wouldn't have traded any of it for the world.

Not even the kiss.

Nope, no regrets. Besides, she'd be gone before she knew it. Back to her life, her very busy, fulfilling life, where she'd never look back—

Oh, who was she kidding? She *would* look back. She'd smile and get misty all at the same time, because she'd had the time of her life here.

All in spite of one gorgeous, sexy, stubborn Timothy Banning.

She stared out in the yard, yearning for a quick

sight of him, maybe working his horse. Riding. Walking. *Breathing*.

She could watch him breathe all day long.

He didn't feel the same.

How was that for humility? Amelia always said she needed more of that in her life. Well, she had plenty now, didn't she?

In the pen in the yard, in front of her, the blind goat walked into the three-legged pig. The pig fell over and then struggled to get up, but he did get up.

Only to have the goat do it again. Now the pig was squealing like a...well, pig. He was stuck on his side, his three little legs peddling the air ineffectively, like a bug on its back, while the goat nudged at it as if in apology.

Natalia's heart tripped at the sight of the pig struggling. "Damn it." She watched another moment. "I'm not going out there," she said to no one. "I'm not."

But the pig continued to struggle. She grabbed a bag of leftovers she'd been saving and went into the yard. For a long moment she stood in front of the pen, trying to breathe normally. This was a perfectly easy thing to do, she told herself. Perfectly easy. Just open the pen and walk in.

Slowly, she let herself into the pen and...stepped into something brown, squishy and distinctly stinky.

"Uck!" She lifted her foot until it came free with a terrible suction noise, and with considerable less enthusiasm, stepped toward the still-thrashing pig.

"Hey."

It didn't respond. "Slow down," she said. "Have you tried that?" Actually forgetting her fear, she hunkered at his side just as he got traction in the mud.

Coming to a stand at a run, he plowed into her on his way to run circles around the blind goat. Not for the first time, Natalia fell to her bottom, right in the muck.

Towering over her, the goat chewed on something green. Then suddenly the pig charged it, charged her, and her fear reinvented itself with a scream as she dived out of the way chest first.

The goat, still being charged by the pig, waited until the precise moment to nudge its head into the oncoming animal.

Who once again fell to its side.

"You." Natalia pushed up to a sit. "Stop that." Struggling to her feet, she tried not to feel the gross, icky stuff that was now on her hands as well as her bottom.

The pig was up now, and running circles around the goat, who bleated noisily, over the obnoxious squealing of the pig. The horse, old and crickety, just stood and watched the entire circus, slowly rotating her jaw as she chomped down on grass.

Fear had to take a back seat to the fact that Natalia couldn't hear herself think. *"Order,"* she demanded in her most royal voice, but all she heard was very male laughter from behind her.

Tim, of course. Because apparently she hadn't experienced quite enough humility.

He stood just outside the pen, his forearms resting on the wood, one leg bent at the knee, his boot on a fence rung. His eyes were crinkled with good humor at her expense, his mouth curved wide.

She refused to acknowledge the way her pulse tripped at the sight of him. "Did you know your goat is a bully? And she's a fake blind? She's torturing your pig, poor little guy."

"First of all, he's a she. And she's a he. Should I show you how you tell?" He grinned that unbearably sexy grin of his. "And by the way, they're the best of friends. They're just playing. Pickles loves—"

*"Pickles?"*

He looked a little chagrined as he scratched his head. "Not my choice, the goat came with the name. And he's *nearly* blind, but not completely. Mrs. Pig likes him, trust me."

"They're trying to kill each other."

"No. Watch—" He opened the gate, and sure

enough, Mrs. Pig gently nudged Pickles in the right direction, making sure she came out first.

"Want to pet them?" Tim asked as they mobbed him for attention.

"Of course not."

"Right." He managed to pet all of them equally. "Because you don't like animals."

"That's correct." Better he think she didn't like them than to know she was afraid of them.

"Ah," he said with a secret smile.

She put her hands on her hips, then remembered what was on those hands and hastily dropped them to her sides. "What does that mean?"

"It means you're a big, fancy liar, Princess." He leaned close, too close, so that she could smell soap and hay and horse, and warm, clean man.

"I never lie." Rarely, anyway.

"Which is why, of course, you've been feeding these guys. Because you don't like them."

She glanced down at the bag of leftovers sticking out her pocket, but he just laughed softly, in that low, husky way he had that made her insides go all liquidy. "Is there a point to this conversation?"

He just lifted a brow, while her entire body had become so hyperaware of him that she had goose bumps and nipples standing at attention.

This attraction was getting the best of her.

"The point is," he said patiently, "you act tough, you dress tough, but inside you're just as soft as the rest of us."

She tried to come up with some retort and failed.

"I can tell you're not used to this world," he said softly. "But you don't seem big city, either, despite yourself." From the other side of the fence, he slid a finger up her ear and all her silver hoops, then touched her hair, which she hadn't spiked in two days. "Who are you, Natalia?"

Wasn't that just the problem? She no longer knew. She'd been happy with her life, but these past few days, hard and difficult and different as they'd been, had showed her all she'd missed with her rather sheltered existence. "I've got to get back to work," she said. "Nearly lunchtime." She was out the gate and halfway across the yard before he called her name.

She stopped, but didn't turn to look at him, afraid she'd weaken and let him do whatever he wanted, which a very bad part of her hoped was something sexual.

"Might want to wash your hands first," he said. "Before you put lunch together."

She looked down at her hands. So much for what he wanted, and so much for it being sexual. "It would serve you right if I didn't," she muttered and kept going.

BY DINNERTIME, it was raining. Natalia had discovered that the weather in Texas, whether sunny or raining or thundering or whatever, was…big.

Squinting out into the yard while shaping meatballs, She could see Pickles standing in the downpour. Alone. Looking wet and miserable and lost.

"Oh, you damn fool." She set down a meatball and willed the stupid goat to find his way back to the others, who stood protected beneath a tree.

But no. The goat just stood there and let out a pathetic little bleat she could hear all the way in the house.

She shaped some more meatballs, refusing to look. "Not looking," she said out loud. But she couldn't help it.

He was still there.

More rain fell.

Pickles slowly tipped his head up and bleated louder. Sadder.

"Oh, for God's sake, get under the tree!" she yelled out to him.

He didn't budge.

Natalia washed her hands. Turned off the stove. Waited for the mentally challenged goat to get a clue. Finally, she stepped out into the pouring rain. "What do you think you're doing?" she called from the porch. "Get under the tree! Scat! Run! Get moving!"

He lifted his head and stared blindly in her direction.

Damn. She ran toward him. "Go on!"

He just blinked in her general direction.

"Good goat," she said, patting him awkwardly. "Don't eat me." She tried to pull him in the right direction. "This way."

Instead of being grateful, he dug in his heels and refused to be moved. But at least he didn't try to eat her. "I'm trying to help you here!" Under the drenching rain, she moved behind him instead, and shoved. "Pickles, move!"

"Bullying goats now, huh?" Sally, fully protected in rain gear from head to toe, tipped back her hat enough to reveal her amused face.

"I'm not bullying him, I'm going to kill him." Natalia was already muddy again, and drenched through to the bone as she gave up and straightened.

"Oh, well, if that's what you want to do why don't you just feed him some of your cooking? That should kill him in record time."

Natalia stopped with the goat and stared at her. "Talk about being a bully!"

"Girlfriend, I never bully."

"Ha!" Natalia was cold, wet, muddy and very, very tired of Sally's holier-than-thou smirk. Furthermore, she'd physically wrestled with Annie enough to know she could hold her own. And she *was* going to hold her own. Right here, right now. "You're the rudest cowboy, cow chick, *whatever*, that I ever met." She jabbed her finger into Sally's bicep. "You know that?"

Sally's eyes blazed, too, and perfectly dry and comfortable in her rain gear, she let out a tight smile. "Jab me again and you'll be sorry."

"Really?" Natalia, goaded on beyond help, did as a princess never would. She jabbed at her again. "There. Make me sorry."

Sally retaliated with a jab of her own.

"Is that all you've got?"

Sally laughed. *Laughed.* "You can't handle what I've got."

"Try me."

"No way."

"Chicken."

Sally jabbed her back, harder. Much harder, and Natalia found herself sitting in the mud. Again. Without hesitation, she went for Sally's feet, pulling them out from beneath her, until Sally screamed and hit the mud.

"You got me dirty," she said in disbelief.

"Yeah, and you know what?" Natalia sank her fingers into the mud at her sides. "You're still too clean." She flung a handful. It hit Sally square in the chest with a satisfying splat, then slowly ran down her body. "Oh, yeah. *Much* better."

"You're dead," Sally said calmly, and lunged for her.

AFTER A LONG, hard day of work, half of which was spent in the rain, Tim stopped to watch Jake eat. His horse was enjoying his hay in a way that made Tim's stomach growl. He hadn't enjoyed his food since... since Natalia. "But she means well," he told Jake.

Jake eyeballed him.

"She wanted me. And I actually talked her out of it. Can you believe it?"

Jake let out a soft nicker that was either a snort of sympathy or a smirk of disgust.

"Yeah." Tim sighed, then headed across the yard in the rain, ready for something hot in his belly and not sure he was going to get it.

Halfway there he came across a group of his men standing in the rain watching...a mud-wrestling match? To his shock, Natalia was holding her own with...*his sister?*

Yes, that was definitely Natalia and Sally rolling around on the ground. Startled into running, he pushed his way to a front-and-center view. Covered from head to toe in mud that molded every nuance and curve of her hot body, Natalia pulled free. Breath heaving, she came to her knees and looked at him. "What are you staring at?" she asked, not very friendlylike.

He knew it was wrong, very wrong, but his body responded like a caveman to the gorgeous sight of her shining with mud. "You."

"Oops. Wrong answer." She scooped a handful of mud and flung it at him.

The caveman inside him leaped to hopeful, quivering, primal attention. *Mud Fight!*

But she stood, and with amazing dignity, given she had mud dripping off her nose, walked away.

# 8

NATALIA STALKED to the side of the house, past the gawking men, past the blind goat and three-legged pig. Past everyone and everything, while mud fell from her, hitting the ground in little ping-pings as she went.

Since her luck sucked, the rain had stopped and the sun came out, which had the mud drying on her so that when she bent to turn on the hose at the side of the house, she felt like a candy-coated chocolate.

Naturally, the water was ice-cold, but she hosed herself off anyway, figuring it would work on the hot fury bubbling beneath her skin.

"So."

Sally. Gritting her teeth, Natalia kept her back turned. She bent at the waist and let the cold water run over her head until she felt her brain freeze. "Want to go another round?"

"Actually, no." Sally sighed rather regretfully. "I don't suppose you'd believe I suffer from PMS?"

"Pretty crappy apology."

"Yeah. Look, I'm a little protective of my own."

Natalia let out a little laugh and kept hosing off, and was tempted to hose off Sally, too. "No kidding."

"And maybe I went a little too far, okay? Like with all the comments about your food and stuff."

"Hmm." The mud was really sticky. Hard to wash off. She concentrated.

"Are you listening?" Sally asked, coming around to face her. "I'm saying I've been...well..."

"Rude? Obnoxious?" Natalia shot an uncomfortable, mud-slathered Sally a long look. "Is that what you're saying? Because if you are, and if you're also saying you're going to back off, then great. I look forward to it."

"Good." Sally smiled a muddy smile. "So...we're okay?"

"Sure. Why not?" Natalia shrugged and tossed the hose aside. "After all, we both know I could take you any day."

Sally's eyes narrowed.

Natalia's mouth quirked. "Kidding."

"I still don't like you," Sally warned, fighting off her own smile.

"Good. I still don't like you, either."

Her work done, Sally nodded, and still dripping mud, walked away.

Natalia looked down at herself, saw more mud and groaned. She picked the hose back up. How could she have let them get to her like this? Had she so effectively forgotten this was temporary? That she could, at any moment, pick up her cell phone and put an end to it?

At the thought her heart lurched. "Oh, perfect, I've gone ahead and started to fall for this place."

She couldn't imagine why.

Or why, when she turned around and found Tim watching her with a mixture of heat and humor and wariness, that her heart lurched again.

"What was that about?" he asked.

"Well…" She lifted a shoulder as nonchalantly as she could with freezing water running over her limbs. "Sally and I had some…issues."

"Issues?"

Bringing the water over her torso and arms made inhaling a detriment. "I'm pretty sure we have them worked out now." Especially since she'd be leaving soon.

Temporary, she reminded her heart. Temporary.

Tim's eyes followed the hose running water over her body very carefully. "She can be difficult. I'm sorry."

"Not your problem. So." She smiled through blue lips and wondered if he could see every single goose bump riddling her body. "I guess you've seen me wet a few times now."

His eyes darkened. "Have I?"

Wildly, she wondered if she was only imagining the possible sexual context of what she'd said, or the heat in his eyes.

He stepped closer and she retreated, lifting the hose up as a weapon. "Stay back."

Stopping short, he lifted his hands. "Staying back."

"Good. Because you're looking at me funny again."

"I am?"

"I nearly threw myself at you before," she reminded him, still wielding her weapon. "And you didn't take me up on it, so—"

"Clearly, I was not in full use of my faculties at the time. Natalia, put down the hose."

She didn't. "You're in use of your faculties now, do you think?"

"Oh, yeah." He lifted his gaze from the hose in her hand and ran his eyes slowly over her, from her wet head to her wet toes, then back again, touching on every place in between. "You look good all wet and dirty, Natalia."

"Obviously, you need your eyes checked."

"My eyes are fine."

She looked at him then, *really* looked. He was no longer devouring her body, but looking right into her eyes, and it was clear he was thinking he liked what he saw. Natalia the woman, not the princess.

Her dream come true.

So why then did she take another step back? And suddenly, oddly, wish with all her heart that he wanted both the woman *and* the princess? "I think I'm going to get a hot shower and change," she said slowly.

He stepped forward. "I need a hot shower, too."

Lord, all that heat and hunger in his gaze. Once again she lifted the hose. "I can arrange a cold one."

"You wouldn't do that."

A dare. He didn't know her well enough, or he would never have said such a thing. She was the middle child. A born hellion. Never had she let a dare pass unanswered.

The adolescent in her warred with the woman. The woman who wanted to be noticed. Wanted. Held. *Kept.*

None of these things were a really good idea. Not when the princess within her suddenly reared her head and demanded equal time as the woman.

Truth was, she was this whole, complicated human being, and she wanted cowboy Timothy Banning to see it.

Would he?

Maybe if he could ever stop "rescuing" her for long enough to really *see* her. She glanced at him from beneath lowered lashes and realized...he was again looking at her body. Her wet body.

And there was nothing in his expression that signified he wanted to do anything but devour her.

On the spot.

She shivered in delight and reservation at the same time.

"Natalia? Put down the hose."

"I can't do that, Tim," she said softly, wondering how he'd look all drenched with water. Probably pretty darn breathtaking.

"Why not?" he asked, just as softly.

"Because I find I'm still a little mad." Not really. Hot, yes. Very hot.

And it was mostly his fault. Given that, no one could blame her for what she wanted to do. Not a single person.

He was looking at her, focusing all his attention on her in a way that made her feel indelibly female. And powerful. The powerful part was a definite mistake on his part. "Natalia—"

"I'm sorry," she said ahead of time, and leveled him in the chest with the hose.

But the joke was on her because as the droplets

slid down his chest and absorbed into the waistband of the soft jeans hung low on his hips, her mouth watered. Her body overheated. And ached.

Damn it, all she'd done was reawaken those pesky lust hormones.

THE NEXT MORNING Tim still couldn't get over it. He was miles from the house on his horse, checking fences, and already he needed a shower.

A cold one.

It wasn't the weather making him hot, though it was an unseasonably warm day. It wasn't the torn fence he'd just found. Nor the missing cattle. Nor the fact he had a sick calf.

It happened to be his cook. The woman he'd hired only to help *her* out. The woman he'd brought home intending to give her a leg up, a place to regroup.

Instead she'd knocked him for a loop. And it wasn't about how she'd pushed him flat on his ass into the mud with the cold water from the hose the day before.

It was how she made him see things. Food for instance. Watching her eat and enjoy her food was pretty much a mind-blowing experience, even if they obviously had very different ideas on what good food was.

Bottom line, he'd had no idea how little passion he'd put into his life lately.

She made him smile, too, at every turn. When was the last time he'd wanted to kiss a woman stupid and laugh at the same time?

And then there was how she made him feel when she looked at him as if he were the greatest man on the face of the earth. Why did she do that? Didn't she know it cut right through his heart and made him want things he was better off not wanting?

She was leaving, possibly today. Tomorrow for certain. He'd paid her daily, expecting every morning to wake up and find her gone, but she was always in the kitchen ahead of him, no matter how early.

Cooking.

The food had been awful. He swiped his forearm across his forehead and pulled his shirt away from his body, wondering how many candy bars and other snack foods he'd consumed with the guys in the past few days trying to ward off starvation.

But he'd miss her.

The thought was sudden and strong. Which was how he found himself heading back to the house in the middle of the day, with no real reason except to see her.

The house was quiet. Too quiet. Damn, he was too late. She'd gone, just like she'd come.

Then a sound came from the kitchen, a horrible sort of caterwauling, and he moved through the house with growing urgency. Someone was hurt. Someone was dying.

Bursting through the double doors from the living room, Tim took in the sight of Natalia, her back to him, wildly gyrating as if she had a bee in her pants.

"Natalia?"

She didn't answer, and that's when he saw the earphones on her head, attached to his portable CD player hooked on her belt.

And the noise? It was singing. *Natalia's* singing, and it was beyond horrible.

She had a large bowl tucked under one arm, the other hand whipping whatever was in it into a frenzy. Her entire body shook and shimmied while she sang at the top of her very untalented lungs.

Leaning against the wall, he shook his head as a big grin split his face. Oblivious to his presence, she continued singing in her godawful pitch, wailing with pure, passionate abandonment. She danced better than she sang—slightly. Her moves were decidedly late eighties, but the wriggle she had going was enough to make his eyes cross with lust. Definitely he liked the wriggle.

Then she slowed with the music as it came to a halt, and thrust a *Saturday Night Fever* finger into the air. She had one hip out, legs straight, passion on her face and he couldn't contain his laugh.

With a screech, she whirled around, whipping off the earphones. There was a rim of chocolate around her mouth and a spot over her left breast.

"You just took five years off my life." She put a hand on her chest. "Maybe ten."

"Don't stop on my account." He pushed away from the wall, still grinning. "Come on. Dance for me some more."

"I wasn't dancing for you." She took in his ear-to-ear grin and narrowed her eyes. "And you know what? I think any employee whose boss who sneaks up on her when she's making him a truce dessert deserves a raise."

"Do you?" He tried to remain casual and cool, but her tongue darted out and licked the chocolate off her lips.

Oh, man, did his body leap to attention at that, and he stared at her, hoping she'd do it again.

She said something to him, but he was a man—a very weak man at that—and he'd lost his train of thought. And his ability to hear.

Looking amused now, she opened the top of the blender on the counter and poured in the contents from the bowl. "Are all men as easy as you?"

He followed her like a puppy, watching her every move. "What?"

She dipped a finger into the chocolate mix. Brought it to her mouth and slipped it between her lips. Closed her eyes. Moaned a little as she sucked off the chocolate.

He groaned out loud.

She opened her eyes. "See? Easy."

He cleared his throat. "Yeah."

She put the top on the blender and contemplated the buttons. "I wanted this to be a surprise."

What she said slowly sank in. Was it a goodbye dessert? God. All the heat vanished—well, a good chunk of it—as the protective feelings he'd had for her from the very first moment reared up and bit him again. "About your leaving…where will you go after the wedding?"

"Well, what do you know. Progress." She was still studying the buttons on his machine. "You admit you believe I was going to go to a wedding in New Mexico the day after tomorrow."

*Was going to go.*

"Which means," she said, lifting her gaze and meeting his, "that you must believe I'm a princess. When did that happen?"

"Uh…"

Her gaze shuttered. Just like that. "Oh, I see. You don't. Not really."

"Natalia—"

"No. No biggie." She slammed down a button and sent the blender whirling. "Please go away," she said over the whir of the machine. "I'm busy working here and don't need any distractions."

"Natalia—"

She put the earphones back on. "Sorry. Can't hear you."

"Look, let's talk about it. You came from... Grunberg, right? Near the Alps?"

"I'm trying to concentrate."

He lifted the right earphone and spoke in her ear. "You like to ski. What else do you do for fun, Natalia?"

"Cook." She pulled away. "Believe it or not, some people think I'm quite good at it." She took her hand off the top of the blender to tuck a stray strand of hair behind her ear, purposely not looking at him. Then she hit another button sending the blender into high gear. "Now go away."

"But I just wanted to—"

Which was all he got out before the top of the blender blew off, sending chocolate spraying across the room, over the counters and floors.

And all over them.

# 9

THE BLENDER sprayed its contents across the room and over the two flabbergasted occupants, whirling with a high-pitched hum.

Then Tim moved, pressing in front of a shocked Natalia, going in blind to switch the machine off as the dark goo hit everything, including, it seemed like, the inside of his eyelids.

The sudden, complete silence was deafening.

Well, not quite *complete* silence, as there was the occasional drip from the ceiling, the table, the chairs, the counters…them.

Tim swiped at his eyes and looked over at the chocolate-covered Natalia.

She made a sound of bafflement and spread her arms wide, staring down at herself.

Tim stuck his tongue out and caught a drop off the edge of his nose. "Mmm."

"Oh my God. It's everywhere." It was dripping off her own nose, her chin, and was plastered across the front of her shirt and down her jeans.

She looked very edible, and immediately he started salivating.

As if she could read his mind, she pointed a finger and glared at him. "This," she said in a very royal voice, "is all your fault."

"Mine!" He put his hand to his chest—his chocolate-splattered chest—and had to laugh. "How do you figure that?"

"You distracted me! I was trying to work and you wouldn't stop…you just…"

He liked where this was going. "Yes?"

"Oh, never mind. It's just all your fault."

Oh, no. Not good enough. He wanted to hear it. "Because I distract you."

"I just said so, didn't I?"

"Because you're attracted to me."

"*That* I never said."

"I'm attracted to you back, Natalia."

She lifted her face and studied his. "Really?"

"You know I am."

Her eyes closed. "Yes, but you hate to take advantage of a crazy woman." She reached for a towel, wet it and started wiping her face. Her expression was a war of things, with annoyance topping the list, and for some unknown reason, it made him want to hold her.

Kiss her.

Because now it was in his head; the taste of her, the feel of her, the little murmur she made deep in her throat when he used his tongue. Taking her wrist, he pulled the towel out of her fingers. "Let me."

"Don't."

"I want to help." But he dropped the towel as he moved his mouth down just a little, to beneath her lobe. Then with his tongue lapped at the spot, taking in chocolate and the sweet taste of woman.

Natalia's eyes fell closed. "Wait."

"Why?"

"I'm still mad at you. I can't stay mad at you with your mouth on me."

"Oh, well, then." He kissed his way down her throat to the pulse beating wildly at the base of her neck. "Good dessert."

"Tim." Her voice sounded satisfyingly weak. "I mean it."

"Yes, you want to stay mad. Go ahead…" Another nibble. "Go right ahead."

Her low moan aroused him, so did the way she tilted her head to give him better access, and he smiled against her delicious skin.

"I'm…famous for holding a grudge," she warned breathlessly. "Ask…my sisters. Annie and Lili."

"Ah, classified family information." He wanted more, wanted to know everything. "I'd love to ask your sisters all about you. Tell me more.'' His mouth had worked its way down to her collarbone, a very sexy spot that made him want to tear off her clothes and start the blender again, all over her naked body. Now that would be a worthy food fight. ''Tell me, Natalia, about you.''

''You may not believe this, but people actually look up to me. Value my opinions.'' Her eyes shuttered closed, her breathing still shaky, but she managed a smile. ''My cooking.''

''And yet you didn't want to call anyone.''

''I needed a break.'' He blew on the spot he'd just wet with his mouth, and she sucked in a big gulp of air. ''They like to smother me.''

''Your father?'' His hands slid from her waist to her back, to just beneath her shirt where he could play with the soft skin at the base of her spine.

''Yes, my father.'' A sound escaped her that managed to perfectly convey her reluctant arousal at what he was doing, but what really turned him on was the way she'd fisted his shirt in her hands, as if she couldn't quite stand on her own. He wondered if she even realized how tightly she was holding him to her.

''He worries about me.'' She tossed her head back, eyes still closed. ''Thinks I'll get taken advantage of in the real world.''

He lifted his head to look down into her face. Her

eyes were still closed, her mouth opened slightly, as if she needed more air. On her cheeks where she'd scrubbed the chocolate off was the blush of arousal that he'd put there. Of their own, his hands tightened possessively on her, but suddenly he couldn't take this any further. Couldn't take advantage, no matter who the hell she was.

She was only here because he'd wanted to help her. He wasn't sure that still applied, as he'd never met anyone more capable of handling herself—mud wrestling came to mind—but that didn't change things.

Or did it? Even if she was who she claimed to be, did he really want to follow through with this crazy attraction? No doubt his body did, quite badly.

But his brain held things up. She was worth so much more than what a one-night fling would give them, and what more could he offer? What more would she want? Women hadn't exactly clamored for what he could offer before, and he couldn't say he blamed them.

In any case, he'd kept his mouth off of her too long, and she pulled back. "This is such a mess." Hands on her sticky hips, she looked around with a stern expression completely overridden by the spatters across her face and entire body. "I can't believe you did this."

He grinned and she narrowed her chocolate gaze on him. "You laughing at me?"

"No ma'am."

"This is going to take forever to clean up."

"I guess you'll have to stay longer."

In the act of reaching for a sponge, she went utterly still. "How much longer?"

*How much time do you have?* "That would depend, I suppose."

"On?"

"Well, you have that wedding to attend, for one."

"I'm not going to the wedding. I tried to tell you the other day, but..." She lifted a chocolate-covered shoulder. "I called ahead, told them I was..."

"Covered in chocolate?"

"Something like that."

She was looking at him, searching for something in his eyes, only he didn't have a clue what she saw when she looked at him.

"Why didn't you tell me?"

"I wasn't sure about it."

"Because you wanted to go."

"Because I wanted to stay."

Something deep inside him reacted at that, and instead of panic, he felt a surge of yearning. "There's nothing wrong with that," he said carefully.

"So now I have a few extra days…if you still want them."

Oh, he wanted them. "And then?"

"And then I go home." Averting her face, she busied herself at the sink, wetting towels. "And that's that."

"Sounds pretty final."

"It is."

Did it have to be? What was so wrong about seeing this thing through? Hell, if *he* was willing to try, why couldn't she? "Natalia…" He took a step toward her, then hit a particularly slippery puddle of goop. Before he could blink, he was sliding, backpedaling…and bouncing on his butt.

*"Tim!"* Natalia dropped to her knees, wrapped her arms around him and pressed his face to her chest. Specifically to her breasts. "You okay?" she demanded.

He opened his eyes to take in the soft, lush curves cushioning his head. "I think I'm a little dizzy," he said truthfully, and she pulled him closer, close enough to feel her nipple in his ear. He could have turned his head, opened his mouth, stuck out his tongue and licked it. Even as he thought it, the nub hardened, pressing against the material of her shirt as if perfectly in tune to his thoughts, making him groan.

"Tell me what hurts, Tim." She bent a little so

that her hair fell all around him like a silk curtain, tickling his face, poking him in the eye. She held her body—a chocolate-covered body, he might add— against him so tight he could feel her every curve and nuance. Her flesh was hot, her hair—still poking him in the eyes—sweet scented. And he wanted to haul her close, shift their positions until she was beneath him, until he was buried deep—

"Tim?" She leaned closer, bumping their noses together, her eyes wide with concern. "Talk to me."

"I—"

"Yes?" Worried, she blinked, and her eyes were so close he could feel her lashes over the skin of his cheek.

"Butterfly kiss," he whispered inanely.

"You need a doctor."

He thought about the erection threatening the buttons of his Levi's. "I doubt he could help."

Brow furrowed, she ran her gaze down his body. At the juncture of his thighs, that gaze widened briefly, then narrowed. "You're not hurt."

"No."

"You're…"

"Yeah. I'm…"

She didn't move for a long moment, still staring, during which time his condition worsened.

"Is it because I'm…you know, touching you?" she

whispered, as if it were a state secret she made him hard by just being.

"Well...partly."

"What's the other part?"

"You've got your breasts in my face, for one."

"Oh!" Startled, she pulled back so fast, withdrawing her arms from around his neck, that he fell back and hit his head on the tile floor.

Flat on his back, he stared up at the ceiling. "Okay, now I'm hurt."

At his side, her hand covering her mouth, her eyes dancing, she let out a sound that came suspiciously close to a laugh.

He cranked his head to the side and stared at her, into her sweet, smiling face and thought *you're it for me.*

"I'm sorry," she said behind her hand.

"Now who's laughing at who?" he wondered, wincing as he sat up. "We're still covered in chocolate."

She took her hand off her mouth and put it on his chest. "It was going to be a great dessert."

It still could be if he licked it off her. Which brought the next thought...which one of them really needed rescuing here?

He was starting to think it was his own heart.

"I could make another batch," she offered. "After I clean up."

The kitchen door opened. Sally took a step in, then stopped short. "What the hell?"

"We had a little accident," Natalia said.

Sally took in all the mess, then Tim prone on the floor with Natalia all cozied up to his side, her hand still on his chest. "Uh-huh. *Accident.*"

Tim sat up and rubbed the back of his head, eyeing his sister. "You're not feeling the need to start another mud-wrestling match, are you?"

"No, I'm feeling the need to load the shotgun and have you put out of your misery." She walked up to Tim, swiped a finger over his cheek and inspected it. "Do I want to know why you're covered in chocolate?"

"No."

"I miss all the fun." She stuck the finger in her mouth. "Hmm."

"Good?" Natalia asked.

Since their little tussle, there had been a definite shift in his sister's bad attitude toward Natalia. It was almost as if she was forcing it now, as if she wanted to hide the fact she'd accepted Natalia. Respected her. Even…she'd probably deny this to her dying day… liked her.

"It's…okay," Sally decided.

Natalia shook her head. "Liar."

"Hey, it's *okay*."

"It's perfect. Or it would be if wasn't on the floor."

"Stop acting like such a princess."

"I *am* a princess."

"Whatever." Sally rolled her eyes at Tim and took another lick.

Natalia came to her feet and cocked a hip. "Why do you keep eating it if it's only okay?"

Sally took another finger swipe. "Well...maybe it's slightly better than okay."

"It's way better."

"It's better than the stuff Seth supplies me with, that's for sure."

Tim quickly stood, not ready to explain to Natalia how they were all slowly starving to death, not when she'd actually forgotten she was mad at him. "Sally—"

"Seth's supply?" Natalia asked very quietly.

"Yeah. Make more of this and I might not feel the need I've felt all week to supplement my meals with outrageously priced candy bars and junk food."

Oh, damn, Tim thought, and turned to Natalia. "Nat—"

"What are you talking about?" she asked Sally.

"Oh...nothing. Right, Tim?"

With four eyes on him, Tim could have cheerfully strangled Sally. He didn't want to lie, but how could he tell the truth without purposely, cruelly hurting Natalia?

"Tim?" Natalia turned and looked at him.

"Did I mention I hear my horse calling me?"

Natalia stared at him, then reached for a sponge. "And you guys think *I'm* crazy."

"Yeah." Sally grabbed Tim's hand and pulled him toward the door. "Don't get too close. It's contagious."

NATALIA FOUND herself watching Tim often. And though she didn't catch him at it, she felt him watching her back.

He did nothing about the yearning shimmering between them, which was fine. She could resist him, too, and still enjoy being here. And enjoy it she did. Cooking was her greatest pleasure.

To her shock, Sally had come back into the kitchen after the dessert fiasco, right after Tim had left. Without a word, she'd helped clean up.

Then, casually as she pleased, had asked about Natalia's family and background. This time, as Natalia talked about her father, the Crown Prince, and her sisters Annie and Lili—both princesses in their own right—Sally didn't scoff or scorn.

Now Natalia sat on the porch swing watching Tim feed his menagerie of pity pets by moonlight. He'd had a long, long day, and still he didn't stop, not until everyone and everything was taken care of. She knew he had to be tired. Misty, the horse, kept drooling on him while Pickles knocked him flat trying to get to his food. And Mrs. Pig…she stood at Tim's feet and put up a fuss, bouncing as high as she could on her three good legs, looking like a Mexican jumping bean.

Natalia couldn't figure out what the thing wanted until Tim scooped her up and held her like a puppy, stroking her belly.

In ecstasy, the pig's head rolled back.

Propelled by a force she didn't try to fight, Natalia got off the swing and walked to the gate. "You don't have to feed them," she said.

Surprised at her voice, he looked up. Then smiled a smile that warmed her. "I'm late. They're starving."

"No." She shrugged, embarrassed to have been caught in a chore that had been pure pleasure. "They looked hungry, so…"

He put down Mrs. Pig, who promptly started wailing at his feet. "So…you what, Princess?"

Oh, wasn't he ever so smug. "I go by Your Serene Highness, thank you very much."

His grin widened, and damn him but he looked good enough to eat. "You're changing the subject. What did you do with the animals?"

"You know what I did. I fed them. I admit it, I feed them when you're not looking."

He picked Mrs. Pig back up, who immediately stopped her ruckus. "Why?"

"Because they're there, okay? Because I've..." *Lost my fear. Somehow. I've become attached.*

God, it was going to hurt to leave. Maybe she should rethink these extra few days and hightail it out of here right now. Right this minute, in fact. She had enough for her bus fare. But she'd given up on that idea from the moment she decided to forgo the wedding in order to have this adventure.

She should still leave. All she had to do was pick up the cell phone and call Amelia, and she'd be out of here within the hour.

But she was afraid of the strange, and oddly new, tugging on the strings of her heart.

Texas—the huge, wide-open place—had grown on her. So had the people, and the wonderful ranch hands who were so hardened on the outside, but sweet as kittens on the inside. Even Sally, the tough female cowboy she'd never forget.

But most of all it was Timothy Banning; also rough and tough, and able, and...staring at her with a heat in his eyes and a three-legged pig in his arms.

# 10

---

"WHAT ARE YOU LOOKING AT?" Natalia whispered
by moonlight, her eyes large and luminescent.

"You," Tim said, and once again set down Mrs.
Pig.

When he straightened, Natalia took a step back.

It made him smile grimly, for he knew exactly how
she felt. She didn't want to feel anything for him any
more than he wanted to feel something for her. But
it didn't seem to matter. They'd tried to ignore it, but
this…this *thing* was far bigger than that.

"Stop it," she said. Since it was dark all he could
go by was the tone of her voice, which was saying
"back off" loud and clear.

But he knew her now, or at least he wanted to think
he did. She was scared, and he of all people understood that, too. He'd never really felt this way about
a woman, had never worried about getting her out of
his system. The women in his life had always washed
*him* out of their systems first.

Natalia didn't seem eager to wash him out of her system.

It was incredibly arousing. *She* was arousing.

"You're still staring," she pointed out.

"Yeah." He smiled. "You're so beautiful. I know that's not very original, and you've—" He started to say she'd probably heard it a thousand times before, but suddenly her eyes misted, threatened to spill over. "Natalia?"

"No." Clearly embarrassed, she stepped back, not anticipating Pickles, who'd come up directly behind her. Her foot came down on the blind goat's front hoof, startling the thing into a noisy riot.

The other animals pitched in, as well.

"Oh!" Natalia turned, held her hands out. "I'm sorry." Awkwardly she stroked the goat, trying to reassure it, and also, face averted, swiping at a few tears glistening on her cheek.

"Hush, Pickles," Tim said, stepping around the animal who didn't hush at all. He took Natalia's shoulders in his hands. "Talk to me."

"Your horse is frisking you."

Misty was indeed attempting to get into his back pocket with her soft mouth. He batted at her, but couldn't have made himself heard over the amazing decibel level Mrs. Pig and Pickles had created. "Come on, we're out of here."

She had her hands over her ears. "What?"

"I said— Oh, for Pete's sake." Grabbing her hand, he led her out of the pen. Instead of heading back toward the house, he took her on the path toward the barns, only he didn't turn in there, either. He led her behind them, to a slight rise, where they could sit on a grassy knoll in peace and relative quiet, and look over his land.

It was inky dark, but the moon, hung in the sky like a glowing beacon, lit the way. So did the stars, so many they were nearly on top of each other. And as they sat, their shoulders and arms brushing, he slid his arm around her waist and drew her slightly resisting body a little closer. "Better." He cupped her face and looked into her troubled eyes. "Tell me. Do you want to leave now? Is that it? Do you miss home? Is my sister being a pain again? What?"

"You…really think I'm beautiful."

Her nose was running, her eyes red. Her hair was loose about her face, framing it. She had a streak of dirt on her jaw, probably from one of his animals, the ones she said she didn't like, but fed at every opportunity. His chest tightened. "You *are* beautiful."

"You mean me, as a woman."

"Yes." Who did she think he meant? "Surely you've heard that about yourself before."

"Only as a princess, and then, not so often really."

She sent him a watery smile. "But never as a woman."

He'd nearly forgotten the princess thing. Had nearly convinced himself she'd forgotten, too.

"It's why I did this," she said. "Why I wanted to come here. I wanted to see what it was like to be an independent woman. Nothing more, nothing less, and..." Her voice hitched a little. "I have to tell you, Tim, I've never had such a great time."

He thought of how hard she'd worked, of how much crap she'd taken from Sally. Of how she obviously had never lived in a world like this before, and yet she'd done it anyway, even after she'd earned enough to go where she wanted to go. "I figured by now you'd be running for the highway. This isn't an easy life."

"No. But it's lovely. Here nothing matters, not what I look like or what I've done to stir up the press, nothing. It's...real." From somewhere behind them a cow let out a long cry. An answering cry came, then another.

And then the distant squeal of Mrs. Pig, which made them both laugh a little.

"*Real,*" Tim repeated with a shake of his head, relieved to see the smile on her face. "This life is definitely that, Natalia. For what it's worth, I don't care how you dress, either, or what you've done."

Her eyes misted again. "I know. But I'm leaving tomorrow, Tim." She took a shaky breath. "I have to. I want you to know, though, I'll miss this. And you."

He wasn't sure how it happened, but one moment he was staring down into her face at her lovely mouth, parted slightly, and the next moment he'd put his right over it. Just a little kiss. Just a comfort kiss. A you're-not-alone kiss.

A goodbye kiss.

Only she made the sexiest little sound from deep in her throat. Grabbed his hair in her fists and held him close.

What could he do but keep kissing her? He couldn't pull away, not when she threatened to pull the very hair from his head.

Her tongue against his ignited all the heat he'd been attempting to hold back. She made it impossible to remember he wasn't going to do this, wasn't going to take advantage of her in any way—

But she made that sound again, and pressed closer so she practically sat in his lap, her breasts against his chest, her nipples drilling holes into his skin.

Then she was in his lap, her bottom pressing against the part of him begging for more. His hands moved to her hips, gripping, shifting her back and forth over his hard-on until his eyes were crossed with lust.

And again she made that rough sound, the one that assured him she was feeling as needy as he.

Good. That was good.

No, wait. It was bad, very bad. One of them had to be in control, one of them had to be able to pull away.

But, God, it wasn't him.

With a little whimper, she plastered herself against him, rotating her hips back and forth in a telltale sign that made him groan. Apparently, it wasn't going to be her in control, either. "Natalia," he said thickly, trying to pull back. "We need to stop."

She tightened her grip on his hair, angled her face the other way and kept kissing him. She also did something pretty amazing with her tongue and his body jerked, getting aroused to the point of pain from just a kiss.

Just a kiss. What a joke. This was no "just a kiss." They were practically sucking the air right out of each others' lungs, letting out dark sounds into the night that were earthy and needy and arousing all in itself.

"Natalia," he said again. Valiantly.

But then she twisted, straddling him. Which meant that her thighs were open, her legs around his waist, the hottest, most neediest part of her was rubbing against the hottest, most neediest part of him.

"I wish I was wearing my skirt," she said, coming up for air. "Because then I could just lift it and…"

Just the image made him tremble. "Natalia, we need to get a grip." He had a grip, two luscious handfuls of her perfectly rounded butt, but that's not what he meant. "This is getting out of control."

"I want to take this with me, this memory of you and me. What's so wrong about that?"

"Because it's not enough, not for you. One night isn't enough."

"It is."

"It shouldn't be."

"Here, in this miraculous place, with you, I'm a woman, and I want to feel like one." Her eyes were wide and dark on his. "Please." Then she rocked against him until he could hardly remember why he resisted. "There's no one else who makes me feel this way."

Which pretty much made him feel like a superhero. "Be sure, Natalia. Be sure."

Lifting his hand from her hip, she placed it over her breast. "I am."

His heart nearly stopped. Beneath his fingers, her nipple was a hard, pouting point, and when he stroked it, he elicited a sweet little whimper from Natalia. His other hand got into the game, too, so that both were filled with her. She sighed and pressed against him some more, her head tossed back a little so that her throat was exposed right at mouth level.

He couldn't help but lean forward and nibble at it.

She gasped and rocked to him. "You have no idea how good that feels."

Tim felt good, too. And in spite of the very sexual nature of the moment, he felt a rightness of it all that came from his heart, not the hard-on currently making sitting a challenge.

Then Natalia reached down and pulled off her T-shirt.

If he'd thought his heart had stopped before, he was sorely mistaken. Her breasts were barely contained in a white, lacy little demibra with a front hook, her nipples dark and thrusting against the material.

She reached for his shirt, too. "Lift," she demanded, and when he obliged, lifting his arms, she tossed his shirt over her head and slid herself against him. "I've always wanted to be like this, skin to skin with a man." With a frown, she suddenly sat straight up, unhooked her bra and tossed that over her shoulder as well. He caught a quick glimpse of the most beautiful breasts he'd ever seen before she plastered herself back against him with a heartfelt sigh.

"There." Her breasts were pressed to his chest. "Yes, there. Much better. Yes?"

If he so much as moved, he was going to actually come in his pants. A fact he'd so far managed to avoid all his life, even during high school horn-dog make-out sessions.

"Tim?" She lifted her head, which sent her hair sliding over his jaw. With each breath she took, her breasts lifted, which meant her nipples tantalized and teased his bare flesh, as well.

She was driving him crazy, and he gripped her hips. "Hold still."

Against his fingers she managed to still move, managed to arch and writhe, and he let out a rough groan.

"Natalia...Wait."

She froze, then removed her hands from his hair and put them over her breasts. "I'm sorry."

"What? No, I—"

"I pressed myself on you. Again. It's just... inexcusable, really."

She made to move off him, but he grabbed her, rolling her beneath him so that she was flat on her back in the grass with him sprawled out over the top of her. Taking her hands off her breasts, which he wanted to see again, he pulled them over her head and held her still. "Don't move," he said gruffly. "Or I'll be a goner. Do you understand? I'm saying you're going to make me come right this second if you move another inch. Now I need to touch you, quite badly. Is that okay?''

She blinked. "I thought—"

"You thought wrong."

She stared at him for one more long moment before slowly relaxing.

"There," he whispered encouragingly, dipping his head to taste her jaw, her throat. "That's better." He nipped her collarbone. "Much better."

Natalia had to agree. Tilting her head back, eyes open to the dark, starry night, surrounded by nothing but wide-open space, she absorbed his weight and when he nibbled at her again, gasped.

"Where's the nipple ring?"

"I don't have one. I'm...too chicken."

He lifted his head. "Know what I think? That you're tough as tough can be on the outside, where you've needed to be, and yet soft as soft on the inside, where no one can see." He smiled a very sexy smile. "But I can see, and I like it."

He rocked against her, then rained hot, open-mouthed kisses to her shoulder, down her arm and yes, finally, over her breast. She tried to remain cool, tried to act as if she'd done all of this before, but when his tongue swirled over her nipple, she jerked and nearly sobbed out loud. She couldn't help it, she was burning up, from the inside out, and couldn't stay still. Her hips rocked, her heart pounded, the blood roared in her ears, and she thought she would die if he didn't hurry up and touch her everywhere.

"Mmm. You like what I'm doing." He kissed and tasted and sucked his way to her other breast. "Don't you?"

This time she did sob out loud and nearly bucked him off her in her haste to get more.

He let out a low chuckle as he took that talented mouth back to her first breast.

She amused him. While she was on her deathbed, dying from this…this unbearable, shockingly consuming need, she amused him. "Don't stop," she demanded, shameless, and she didn't care. *"Don't you dare stop."* She fought with his hands to get hers loose, and when he let go, she gripped him by the ears and held his head to her breast. Who would have thought sex would feel so amazingly good? She'd have tried it long ago if she'd had any clue, any clue at all.

But while she was wild, he was…not. Somehow he'd regained control, and was just fine while he nearly drove her out of her mind. Unacceptable, really. She'd let go completely, and he would, too. Together. She ran her hands down his sleek, strong and oh-so-delicious-feeling back. He was amazing, no doubt, but she was getting sidetracked. Determined to make him as out of control as she, she danced her hands down farther, to his very nice bottom, and squeezed.

Obliging, he thrust against her. Oh, yes, that was very nice, and before she could help it, she'd spread her legs, further accommodating him. It made her whimper for more, but no. She was not going to lose it.

At least not until he did, not even if she had to calculate complicated math problems to keep her thoughts together. She worked her hands around his sides to the button on his jeans, which she popped open. "Off," she demanded, tugging on the denim.

"Yes, ma'am." He obliged her, then kneeled at her side, sliding hers off, too, running his hands down her bare legs while he stared down at her with a hunger that made her arch off the grass.

"Is it too itchy?"

She blinked, then realized he meant the grass beneath her. "I can't feel anything but you touching me."

"Good." Her panties sailed over his shoulder the way their pants had gone and he bent, kissing her, long and deep and wet, just the way she'd discovered she'd liked it.

No one had ever kissed her this way, though it was

fair to say many had tried. She just hadn't seen what all the fuss was about. Sex had seemed sweaty and rather nasty, and a lot of work. And, according to several of her friends, unsatisfying.

She hadn't bothered to find out for herself. She wasn't a prude, or even shy. She knew how to pleasure herself. She just hadn't let a man do it.

She would let Tim.

His hands glided over her body, paying special attention to her breasts, before he replaced his fingers with his mouth. That left his hands free to dawdle lower, and dawdle they did, dancing down her belly, which quivered at his touch. *Oh, good.* Down, down...*oh, please to the right spot*...but...no. He passed the goodies and swept his fingertips over her thighs and down her legs and...*yes.* They were coming back!

"Please," she whispered without meaning to, thrusting her hips toward him in an attempt to help him find the right spot.

He missed it again.

Instead, he played with her thighs while he stretched out at her side, leisurely, as if he had all the time in the world. His mouth played at her ear, at her throat, and those fingers—the center of her world at the moment—came...very...close...but...*no.* "Tim."

"Mmm, you're so sweet." He nibbled his way to a nipple while he continued to tease her with that barely there caress. Now his tongue brought a new sort of tension, making her arch and writhe.

She was wound up, no doubt, her every muscle tense, shaking. She was starting to sweat, too, and if she didn't get some sort of…*more,* she was going to scream. *"Tim."*

"Right here."

Maybe he didn't know what to do. That was all right, she was a new-millennium type of woman. She could show him.

She spread her legs. Wide. Rocked her hips. And when his fingers skimmed up high on her thigh, she moaned her encouragement. Rocked some more. Tried to give him a clue.

"Ah," he murmured in a silky voice that brought shivers to her heated skin. "You're getting ready now."

"I *am* ready! I'm really, *really* ready!"

"Are you? Let me see…" And finally, oh, finally, his fingers caressed the spot, the *right* spot, over the *ohmigod* spot, and as a result of that one very slow, very sure caress, she let out a sound that might have horrified her in its neediness if she'd had any modesty left at all.

She did not.

Then he did it again, moaning when his fingers came away wet. "Yeah. You're right. You're just about ready."

"Not just about," she panted, because he did it again, that just oh-so-perfect glide of his fingers. "I'm there!"

"Well…" He deepened the touch, in just the right rhythm, assuring her he'd known what he was doing all along.

This was no ordinary orgasm she was currently on the cusp of, that much was certain. Her toes curled, her eyes rolled back in her head, and she lost all ability to think as her body hovered on the edge. Hovered and hovered, while he held her there purposely, then finally, finally, did something amazing with his thumb while his fingers—

And she exploded. Burst right out of herself. Saw stars, a kaleidoscope of colors, the whole shebang.

When her senses returned, Natalia found herself still on her back, still in the grass, blinking up at the stars glittering far overhead.

"You okay?" he asked.

She'd just had her first man-made orgasm. A *screaming* orgasm. And lying there, her skin sheathed in a fine sweat, slowly being cooled off by the lovely night, she laughed.

"I'll take that as a yes." Tim's face came into her view as he leaned over her, also wearing a grin.

His seemed a bit tight, though, and she remembered. She'd lost control after all, damn it, and he hadn't. Not yet. "I believe there's more?" she asked. *Please let there be more.*

He arched a brow. "When you speak like that, you do indeed sound like a princess."

"More," she repeated.

"Well, yeah, about that." He grimaced. "We seem to have a little protection problem."

That she could handle. "In my back pocket."

He gaped at her. "*You* have a condom?"

"Amelia always insists I carry one."

"Amelia?" He went to her pocket and shook his head. "Never mind. I don't want to know right now." He opened the packet and removed the condom.

Natalia sat up, reached for it. "Can I?" She'd always wanted to try this part, but when she took it from his fingers, she nearly dropped the thing. "It's…slimy." But gamefully, she held it up to the moonlight. "Uh, Tim? This isn't going to fit."

With a rough laugh, he took it back. "It'll fit." He started to roll it on. "See?"

She could hardly breathe, and certainly couldn't tear her eyes from the sight of him stroking the condom down his own length. "That's a very sexy thing," she decided. "Do men like to watch a woman touch herself, too?"

"A man would *die* to watch a woman touch herself."

Something in his eyes made her bold. Whether it was the plain hunger or the even more obvious affection shining there, she didn't know, but she lifted her hands and stroked them down her own body. She was about to ask "like that?" but before she could open her mouth, he'd growled low in his throat and tumbled her back to the grass, running his hands down her arms, her sides, down her thighs and up the backs of them, spreading them wide so that he could—

"Oh!" she cried when he slipped an inch inside her. She'd had no idea how perfect it would feel—

Then he bent over her, his forearms flat on the ground on either side of her head, sinking his fingers into her hair, kissing her long and hard. "You feel good," he whispered against her lips.

He felt good, too, but she wanted more, she wanted all of him.

Especially before he figured out she hadn't done this before.

# 11

"MORE," NATALIA SAID so politely Tim might have laughed if he wasn't on the very edge, barely holding on to any semblance of control.

"Tim?" She wrapped her legs around him and tried to pull him inside her. "I said more."

"Yes. More," he promised, and thrust into her.

By the time he figured out the truth, it was too late. She'd arched to meet him at the exact moment of resistance, and then stared up at him in startled surprise at the bite of pain.

"Oh, my," she said a bit tearfully.

Buried to the hilt, he went utterly still. Not easy when his body had started the happy dance toward orgasm. "Natalia. My God."

She blinked, sending a tear dancing down her cheek. "Don't get mad." She wriggled, just a little, and he clenched his teeth trying not to plunge again.

"Don't move," he managed. "I'll hurt you."

"You're going to kill me if you don't move."

"What?" This couldn't be happening. He was

hurting her. His worst nightmare. "Sweetheart, I'm sorry. Let me—" He started to pull back but she grabbed his butt with both hands and dug her fingernails into him, but good. She wriggled some more and panted at the same time.

"Tim, wait. It's good. It's..." Her breasts were flushed, her eyes glossy as she tossed back her head, pulling back her knees, everything within her power to make him understand.

"Natalia—"

*"Please."* Grabbing his hand, she thrust it between their bodies.

And he finally got it. She was good. She was great. She was rubbing herself against his fingers and pushing him in and out of her body, driving them both toward the finish line.

She got there first, but only by a fraction of a second as the sight of her lost in her own pleasure totally and completely undid him.

He was still shuddering when he felt it, something cold and wet nudging against his bare butt.

Mrs. Pig.

Her snout, to be exact, and when he craned his neck and peered over his shoulder, she nudged him again, less politely this time. "Oh, for the love of—"

*Oink.*

"Damn." If he didn't know better, he'd think that

pig was grinning. He must have left the gate open in his hurry, which meant both Pickles and Misty were wandering the countryside, as well.

Still deeply embedded in Natalia, he turned back to her.

"Problem?" she asked.

"Oh, yeah." First, he was never going to rescue another ungrateful animal again. Second, why had she had been a virgin? Why hadn't she told him?

And damn, that was her blood on his thigh.

"Tim?" She turned her head to the side and came face-to-face with Mrs. Pig. "We seem to have an audience."

"I know. Natalia—"

"Wait." She cupped his face. "You're not going to mess this up by saying something stupid right now, are you?"

"I just might." He pulled out of her and discovered the third major issue. "Uh…Natalia—"

"Because a speech right now would really be annoying."

*"Natalia."* He swallowed hard and tried not to panic. "I really need to make a speech."

"No."

"Yes. The condom broke."

"Oh. *Oh.*"

He groaned and rubbed his face.

"Uh...Tim? Do condoms expire?"

He dropped his hands from his face. "Tell me that condom wasn't old."

"Okay, I won't tell you."

NATALIA WOKE UP with the sun streaming into her bedroom. Stretching luxuriously, she froze as three things hit her at once. Okay, four, but really, the condom thing didn't count. No use panicking this early, right?

Anyway, first, she was sore. Strange, though, how it was a good kind of sore, if there even was such a thing.

Two, for the first time since she'd arrived, she'd failed to get up before Tim and get breakfast together.

And three...and here was the shocker...she'd fallen hard for the cowboy.

She was in love with Timothy Banning.

Not just a little in love, either, but the something-old-something-new-something-borrowed-something-blue type of love.

She couldn't tell him. He was one of the good old guys, a man she hadn't realized still existed. He'd feel honor bound to do something stupid, like offer to marry her.

She was a lot of things, but one thing she was not, was a woman willing to trap a man into a lifelong commitment, no matter how much she'd suddenly discovered she wanted one.

Damn, she should have gotten up this morning, just like always, so he wouldn't know anything had changed, but it was too late now.

He'd tried to talk to her last night, between catching Mrs. Pig—who didn't want to be caught—and Pickles, who had delighted in playing the game of running off into the night every time Tim had gotten close.

When he'd realized Natalia was escaping, too—she'd tried to sneak off to her bedroom so she didn't have to answer the obvious questions he'd have—he'd immediately stopped catching animals and caught her, instead.

She'd begged off, promising him a talk today before she left.

*Before she left.*

She had no idea which was worse, the thought of that, or facing Tim with all his questions. Neither appealed. Not when she just wanted to be alone to bask in her new knowledge.

Which was being a woman far beat being a princess any day of the week. God, she wished for Annie. Annie, so tough, so strong, would know what to do.

Still in her borrowed nightgown from Sally—which was a big, old, ragged, cut-up T-shirt she suspected had come from Tim's throwaways, she threw herself backward on the bed, arms and legs spread out and grinned up at the ceiling.

Oh, yeah. Today she was all woman.

Now all she had to do was figure out how to combine the best of both worlds. To do so, she'd have to say goodbye, and make her arrangements. Then actually leave.

Her grin vanished.

Leaving was going to be next to impossible. Worse than she could have ever anticipated. It wasn't just the affection she'd developed for Texas. Or even the odder affection she'd developed for the people here, including the fiercely proud, protective Sally.

No, there was far more she'd miss.

With all her heart, she'd miss Tim. She'd miss his smile, his voice, how he made her feel.

And no doubt, being forced to go back to her own battery-operated pleasure, she'd miss the wild, screaming orgasms he'd given her.

Just thinking about them, and how incredible last night had been beneath the stars and Tim's hard body, she tingled. Her body ached. Her nipples hardened.

Oh, definitely, she could lie here for a while and think of all those delicious things he'd done to her.

But a knock came at her door. She leaped up, then

stood still, her heart racing, even before his unbearably familiar voice came.

"Natalia."

Just the sound of him had her thigh muscles clenching together.

The handle jiggled, then opened to reveal Tim, looking larger-than-life and unusually subdued. His gaze ran over her, from the top of her rumpled head to the ragged old T-shirt slipping off one shoulder, to her bare legs and feet. "I woke you. I'm sorry."

"No," she said, oddly breathless. Had his voice always had this effect on her? This trembling, got-to-have-his-hands-on-me effect?

Or had it just been since last night?

"I'm sorry about breakfast," she said. "You must be starving."

A funny expression crossed his face. "Starving? Um. No. Natalia, last night—"

"I feel so bad, letting you down like this. Here, I'll hurry and throw something together." She was talking, talking, talking, a nervous habit. "Maybe the men can take a break and eat, too." She couldn't stop. If she did, she'd break down, because he looked so good, he looked so hers, and how was she ever going to go? "Tim, who's going to feed you after I'm gone?"

"It doesn't matter. But Natalia, about last night—"

"I should have been helping you train someone." She couldn't do this, couldn't get normal, not when it was all over. "Maybe I should try to extend my stay, you know, just until you place an ad and get someone in here—"

Eyes glittering with sudden knowledge, he stalked forward, slid his fingers around her jaw and tipped her face up.

Bad. She was so close to losing it, her breath hitched. She studied the ceiling.

His other hand slid to her waist and gently squeezed. "Look at me. Please?"

As a reward for getting lost in his deep green eyes, he sank his fingers into her hair and massaged her suddenly aching head.

She nearly melted against him. Not a good plan, as she needed, desperately, some distance. This weak and clingy thing, it was unacceptable. "I'd better…" What? Fall apart? "Shower."

"You're avoiding me, Natalia, and we need to talk."

"I've found talking overrated." She would have moved away but he held her still.

"You were a virgin," he said. "You let me take that from you. Why, Natalia?"

"What's a little inexperience between friends?"

She tried to smile, though her throat was so tight she nearly choked. "Anyway, I've got to—"

With a gentleness that nearly broke her, he slid his hand over her throat, as if he knew it ached so much that she could hardly breathe, much less talk. "Being with you was different. Special. Even with Mrs. Pig interrupting the big finale." He sent her an apologetic smile. "But it can't have been a decision you made lightly. Why didn't you tell me?"

"I didn't know how."

"How about... 'Hey, Tim, I'm new at this.' Or better yet, 'Virgin alert.' Either would have done the trick just fine."

"You're angry."

"Are you kidding?" He shook his head, tipped up hers and kissed her. "I'm incredibly touched, Natalia. I just wish I'd known, that's all. I would have done things differently."

"You were perfect."

"I would have given you a bed. Made sure there were no pesky pigs watching." His eyes conveyed so much affection, she felt her own well up again. "Now talk to me."

"Oh, Tim." Talking hurt. *Looking* at him hurt. "What can I say? Princesses are fairly heavily protected as a rule, you know? I was a virgin because I never really had the chance to...not be one."

Some of his open expression became not-so-open. "So, it was a convenience thing?"

"No." She put her hands over his. "*No.* Until last night, there was never anyone I wanted to...well, sleep with."

"There was no sleeping involved."

She felt her face heat. "You know what I mean."

"Yeah." He watched her for a long moment. "Which brings us to the bigger problem."

"The condom."

"The *broken* condom."

She envisioned herself with child. Tim's child. Living on his ranch forever because he couldn't bear to part with his son.

Her heart beat hard and heavy against her ribs at the thought. *Could I get so lucky?*

"Natalia?"

She blinked away the image of sharing his life forever. "Yes?"

"Promise you'll tell me. Contact me. From wherever you are. I want to know."

"Tim—"

"Promise, Natalia."

So intense. So absolutely fierce. "I promise."

"Okay." He relaxed slightly, and smiled. "Okay."

*What about us?* she wanted to cry.

But there was no us. If she was pregnant, he wanted

to know. If she wasn't, then there was no need to write or call or visit.

She was free to go, no regrets, nothing.

Now she really was going to lose it. Pushing past him she went into the bathroom. As she shut the door, she said, "I'll make an early lunch. Then…"

Then she'd go.

From the other side of the door, Tim didn't say anything.

He'd probably already walked away. Pathetically close to tears, Natalia stripped and stepped into the shower, which hadn't yet heated.

But there was one good thing about freezing off her vital body parts. She didn't have the breath left for tears.

STRENGTHENED IN BODY if not spirit by her unintentionally icy shower, Natalia went down to the kitchen and made lunch. Actually, she improvised, as she had an unusual amount of dinner left over from last night. Basically she just reheated her first attempt at American chili and flagged down Sally, thinking they wouldn't mind eating such great fare two meals in a row, right?

Besides, this way Sally could take it out to the men, and Natalia could dwell on leaving. On not seeing these people ever again.

Especially one Timothy Banning, who apparently couldn't wait to get rid of her.

After Sally left, pretending to gag over the smell of lunch, Natalia sat at the empty kitchen table, her heart heavy.

And knew. She couldn't do it. Couldn't leave without seeing them, if only one last time.

She walked out of the house and to the barn, thinking this life should have been hers. She'd have loved it.

In fact, she'd better not look at Tim too closely, or she might mistake a simple smile for a sign that she was meant to stay.

Opening the barn door, an anticipatory smile on her face, she stepped forward.

And froze.

There, in front of her, were Tim and Red and the others. Huddled in front of a little plug-in heater, staring with hungry-looking eyes at five frozen burritos sitting on top of it.

"Highway robbery, I'm telling you," Red said.

Seth shook his head. "I think five bucks apiece is fair, and if you don't, someone else will pay it. Now who wants chips? A buck a bag, which is a good price, I'm telling you."

Steam rose off the burritos, and the scent of heated beans and cheese filled the air.

On the floor next to the heater was Mrs. Pig, standing in front of several bowls of chili. Her chili.

Mrs. Pig wasn't eating it, either.

# *12*

---

DUMBFOUNDED, Natalia stood there with her mouth open, staring at all of them. "What are you doing?"

Tim, caught in the act of holding out his bowl for Mrs. Pig, who kept turning her head away while making a very clear sound of disgust, straightened. "Natalia."

"That would be my name." She looked at Red, who had his bowl out, too, though Mrs. Pig didn't want anything to do with that one, either.

Peter's bowl was there, as well, full but also ignored, as he devoured not one but two store-bought, individually wrapped burritos. One for each hand. He put them behind his back and sent her a wavering smile. A wavering smile rimmed with hot sauce, if she wasn't mistaken.

Sally didn't try to hide the fact she'd been eating a burrito instead of her chili. She just kept eating. "My jeans are tight, and I believe that's your fault," was all she said.

Maybe a large hole could open up in the earth and

swallow Natalia in one bite. That would work. Or an alien ship could land and kidnap her. Even being probed would be better than facing this. "I thought this was only a morning ritual."

"That's for the candy bars," Red said, "This burrito thing, it's actually new."

"How long have you all been doing this?" Natalia asked.

Pete stared at something fascinating down by his boots. Seth stared at something fascinating on the ceiling. Tim winced, but at least came forward to talk to her, though Sally beat him to the punch.

"Since the beginning," she said cheerfully.

"Sally," said Tim.

"Oh, please. I'm tired of saving her feelings." Sally turned to Natalia. "You know I didn't like you. I resented the intrusion, I resented how great you looked in your leather clothes and your badass attitude. I really resented the way you stared at my brother when you thought you were alone."

"Well." Natalia clasped her hands together. "Why don't you just tell me how you really feel."

"Felt. Not *feel*. Now I think you're okay. It's just your cooking that sucks."

"Don't listen to her," Tim said.

"Really?" Natalia asked. "Then tell me what you were doing. No, better yet, *I'll* tell *you*. You were trying to feed the animals what I'd cooked. And even *they* didn't want it." How humiliating was that? "You know what? I'm thinking it's time to go." She didn't have a fairy godmother to pull out her magic wand and wave it, but she had Amelia, the next best thing.

Tim put a hand over her arm, his eyes regretful. "Wait. You know we'd never hurt your feelings on purpose—"

She did know that, which is what made it all the more embarrassing. "You were paying me to waste your food, Tim. Do you have any idea how that makes me feel?"

"Lucky?" Sally guessed.

"I wanted you to stay," Tim said. Behind him the men cleared their throat. "*We* wanted you to stay," he corrected. "And before I knew you were the most capable, strong, incredible woman I've ever met, I thought I was helping you. I didn't want you to go before you were ready."

Natalia stared at him, knowing this was her fault, not his. "I know I sound like an old record here. But I am a princess. A royal. As in, snap my fingers and have someone come running."

"Dipping in the cooking sherry again, huh?" Sally asked.

Natalia turned on her. "Do you think I need this headache? Believe me, I have enough of my own."

Sally looked at Tim and circled a finger near her ear, signifying Natalia was crazy.

"I *am* crazy," Natalia confirmed. "To have put up with this." She whipped out the cell phone in her back pocket and dialed, her eyes on Tim. "I'm done." With each ring, her heart cracked a little more, shattered a little more, but there was no going back now. She was making the phone call that would change her life.

Their lives.

"Uh, Princess?" Sally stepped closer. "Unless you're calling…I don't know…Siberia or somewhere, you've entered too many numbers."

"Grunberg isn't Siberia." Natalia waited, hoping to hear her daddy's voice. Annie's or Lili's voice. Anyone's voice.

And when Amelia said hello in her cheery British accent, she nearly started crying. "A—A—Amelia?"

"Natalia, honey!"

"I—" Her eyes locked on Tim's, she swallowed.

"You need me," came Amelia's sure voice.

"Yes."

"I'm close by. I'll be there in no time."

Dial tone. Natalia stared down at the phone in her hand. Amelia was close by? How like her to just *know.* Just like the time Natalia had run away from home on a delivery truck, getting herself good and lost within Grunberg's capital city of Spitzenstein before calling home collect.

Amelia had come and found her then, within moments, no questions asked.

Maybe Amelia was better than a fairy godmother after all.

Everyone in the barn was staring at her as if she'd lost her mind. Everyone but Tim. Gaze solemn, he came closer, and right in front of everyone, cupped her face in his hands and gave her one of those soft, melting kisses that made her forget her name. His hands slid down, over her shoulders, down her arms to her hands, which he linked in his. "I'm not sure what to say, Natalia."

Say *don't go.* Say *stay with me always.* Say *you love me back, even half as helplessly as I love you.* "You could just say goodbye," she said in such a fake cheeky, breezy voice he narrowed his eyes.

"I don't like goodbyes." He brought their joined hands up to his mouth and kissed her palm. "I especially don't like goodbyes that involve you."

"Oh. Well." She shrugged and swallowed, hard. Then smiled brightly. "We always knew it would come to this."

"Yes, we did," Sally piped up. "Now we can

move Josh back to the kitchen." She sighed dreamily. "He really knows how to cook."

Tim pointed at the barn door. "Out. All of you."

"But this is just getting good," Pete protested.

"Besides, sounds to me like you're going to need help talking her into staying," Red said.

Sally choked on her burrito.

Natalia managed another smile. "Don't be silly, I can't stay. Heaven knows, you might all starve to death."

"Out," Tim repeated, tugging on Natalia's hand when she started to file out with the others. "Not you."

The way he looked at her, with a mixture of frustration and heat and affection and annoyance made her both want to kiss and smack him at the same time.

"So." He touched her face. "What happens now? You get on a bus? You find another job? What?"

For a moment she just stared at him. "Didn't you hear me make the phone call?"

"Yes, I heard you. I was just wondering where you'll be."

"Why?"

"Why? In case…well, maybe…."

"Why, Tim?"

In the far distance there came a whirling sound. As

it drew closer, Natalia recognized it. "Do you have a helicopter delivering supplies today?" she asked.

"No."

"Any friends who own helicopters, perhaps?"

"No."

"Then that's my ride." And with her throat tight, she walked out of the barn.

TIM WAS IN a state of befuddlement. Nothing new, he'd discovered, when it came to dealing with Natalia. He followed her out of the barn, feeling an assortment of emotions hit him—panic, fear, frustration…but mostly panic.

She was really going. He'd known she would, but he hadn't expected it to hurt.

It hurt a lot. So much so that he put his hand over his heart and glanced down, checking for blood. Nothing, of course, but damn…

This leaving thing, this wasn't going to work out for him.

A helicopter with some sort of royal shield on the side had landed in his yard. In a corner, Mrs. Pig and Pickles were oinking and bleating respectively. His sister was standing there, speechless—a rare event.

"I am Amelia Grundy," came an authoritative voice that managed to carry over the sound of the helicopter, which, probably in reverence, was sud-

denly shut off. "Keep back." Then the door opened.
"I came as soon as I could, dear."

This from Mary Poppins—er, Amelia Grundy. Tim
could only stare, his mouth hanging open, as the tall
and formidable, silver-haired, sharp-blue-eyed woman
who'd alighted from the helicopter hugged his Natalia. She was dressed in tweed and carried a leather
satchel, from which she'd pulled an umbrella as she'd
gotten out of the helicopter, shading both herself and
Natalia from the sun.

Natalia looked a little befuddled herself. "How did
you know where to find me?"

From her satchel, Amelia pulled a pair of wire-
rimmed sunglasses, which she perched on her nose.
"Have I ever failed you?"

"Of course not, but—"

"One week in the United States and you've forgotten all your manners. 'Buts' are better covered and
not discussed, dear, remember?"

Natalia bit her bottom lip, looking suspiciously
close to smiling. "It's good to see you, Amelia." She
gave the woman another fierce hug. "So good."

Amelia's gaze went straight through her light sunglasses, meeting Tim's over the top of Natalia's head,
and it was distinctly...not pleasant. No, she leveled
him with those razor-sharp eyes and he felt pinned to

the spot. Squirming a bit, he squared his shoulders and stepped forward.

"Tim Banning," he said, thrusting out his hand. "Natalia's...friend."

Amelia's stern face frowned, becoming even more stern. "Are you referring to Her Serene Highness? Because if you are, your manners are atrocious. Don't you know the correct way in which to address a royal?"

"Uh..."

"Amelia." Natalia squeezed the woman's hand, her gaze never leaving Tim's. "They don't do royals here in Texas. You're going to have to give these people a break."

"Give them a break?" The woman looked aghast. "Oh, dear. You've been here too long already, you're starting to talk like them."

Two men got out of the helicopter, dressed in black and looking quite commando. At the sight of Natalia, they both bowed.

At that, Mrs. Pig stopped snorting. Pickles went silent. Even Sally stopped sneering cynically and straightened.

But Tim...Tim felt his heart stop. In the back of his mind, he'd known, he'd always known, but he still felt shell-shocked. She *was* a princess. She *was* royal. And if he so much as blinked, she was going to pop out of his life as fast as she'd popped into it. Knowing he had to do something to assuage this terrible feeling that nothing was going to be the same ever again, he reached for her, needing to put his hands on her, needing to feel hers on him.

The two men in black blocked him.

Natalia gave an almost imperceptible shake of her head, and they stepped back, but just barely. He and Natalia were completely surrounded. No more being alone.

Which meant anything he wanted to say would have to be said in front of everyone.

"Goodbye," Natalia said softly, her eyes shining. "I know it didn't quite work out for you, but I want you to know…it was lovely."

"Natalia, I'm not ready to say goodbye."

"Then move out of the way, Ace." Sally stepped in front of him, and with a sort of bewildered, affectionate smile on her mouth, she looked at Natalia. "So. It's true. You weren't crazy after all."

Natalia looked at Tim and made his heart catch. "I wouldn't say that."

"Yeah." Sally caught the glance between her brother and Natalia. "Look, there's a few things you should know. I was rough on you, and I'm sorry for that."

"No, you're not." But Natalia smiled.

So did Sally. "Okay, I'm not. I'm tough on everyone. But I am sorry if I ever hurt your feelings. It's just the way you looked at my brother." She lifted a shoulder. "You scared me because I knew you could hurt him. But then you kept trying hard to please us. You kept smiling. You kept working really hard. For us. I like that, Natalia. And even more shocking...I like you."

"What do you know." Natalia's smile went a little shaky. "You're a big softie, too."

"Yeah." Sally cleared her throat. "So here's the bottom line. Your food is weird. We don't like it. But as I just mentioned, we like you." She startled them both when she leaned in and gave Natalia a hug. "Take care of yourself," she whispered softly.

Tim watched the emotions flicker over Natalia's face. She looked shocked. Overwhelmed. And near tears. His ranch hands looked the same.

Red jerked his chin toward Natalia and tried to tell Tim something. "Keep her" he mouthed.

Keep her. As if it could ever be that simple.

"Stop eating candy bars and snack food for meals," Natalia said as she hugged Sally back.

"I will," Sally promised, stepping aside for her brother.

Tim kept his eyes on Natalia. If she walked away, princess or not, his life would never be the same, not without her smile, her laughter, her constant challenging. She made him a better person, she opened up his heart, and he couldn't let her go. "Natalia."

When he stepped closer, the guards did, too. He glanced at them. "Can we have a moment alone?"

"No," one of them said.

"Fine." He took Natalia's hands. "But there's something I want to say."

She was already impatient to be gone, glancing back at the helicopter. "Yes?"

"Don't go."

Her head whipped back to his, her eyes huge and wide. She shot a quick glance at the two guards, then Amelia, before looking back at him. "What?"

"I said don't go."

"But..." She wet her lips with her tongue, then swallowed hard. "The job was temporary. I've got a ride. That was your whole thing, making sure I was taken care of, and now, you can see that I will be."

He didn't release her hands. "This has nothing to do with any job, or seeing you taken care of."

"What does it have to do with?"

She wanted to know right here, right now, in front of everyone.

"Do it," Red said in a stage whisper beneath his breath. "Suck it up and do it."

There was no sucking it up involved. He *wanted* to do this.

"Go ahead," Seth called out. "Tell her."

Tim tried to block everyone out because they wouldn't be quiet. "It has to do with us."

"Yeah, that's the way to tell her!" Josh pumped his fist in the air. "Take it home, boss!"

"I'm trying." Tim drew a deep breath. "It has to do with us, and the fact that I love you."

A chorus of *woo-hoos* and whistles broke out behind them.

But in the aftermath of the commotion they made, Natalia's uncompromising silence was like a bomb falling.

# *13*

---

"YOU LOVE ME," Natalia repeated in a slow, careful voice she couldn't believe was hers. So calm. So together. No one could possibly know she'd had to lock her knees together to keep from falling. If she didn't shut her mouth, the next good wind would surely tip her right over.

"Yes." Tim smiled rather disarmingly and glanced at their cheering audience. Well, Amelia and the bodyguards weren't cheering, but everyone else was. "Look, do you think we could go inside to discuss this?"

"Most certainly not, young man." Amelia shook her umbrella at him. "She wouldn't be properly chaperoned."

"Amelia, please." Natalia smiled apologetically at Tim. "I've been with him all week."

The uptight looking woman straightened to her considerable height and looked...more uptight. *"What?"*

"Not like that," Natalia said quickly, and most definitely not meeting Tim's gaze. "I've been working here. Cooking. Helping out. Oh, Amelia..." She hugged the woman again. "I loved it. Working for a wage. Earning my way—"

"You don't need money."

"I know, but—"

"Excuse me." Tim waved a hand in front of them. "Hello? We were in the middle of something here." To hell with the guards, he took Natalia's shoulders in his hands and turned her to face him.

Natalia looked into his eyes and everything she'd ever dreamed of were in them. "You love me," she repeated. "Me, the woman."

"I love you, the woman. The one who makes me laugh. The woman who brightens up my day. The woman I want to be with when I'm old and gray and can't find my horse."

"But I can't cook American food."

"No, but there's always chocolate bars and fast food. Natalia, be mine."

"What about the princess thing?" She held her breath. At her side, Amelia made a move. Natalia held her back, afraid her beloved companion would close up her umbrella and beat Tim over the head with it before he answered. "Tim? You love me, the woman—but what about me, the princess?"

"She can come along, too." He cupped her face

in his big, warm hands, just the way she loved. "I want all of you, Natalia. The leather, the denim, even the blue lip gloss. I want every part of your life." He glanced at the men in black. "But them. They won't come along on the honeymoon, will they?"

Okay now she really couldn't breathe. "Honeymoon?"

He tucked a strand of hair behind her ear, stroked her jaw. "Will you marry me? Make sure I don't collect too many geriatric animals or eat too much chocolate?"

"I love your geriatric animals," she said with tears in her voice. "But..."

"There's a but?" He looked nervous now. "Amelia said no buts, remember?"

"I could never ask you to give up all this," she whispered. "It means too much. And my home, my family, they mean a lot to me."

"There has to be a way to compromise," he said a bit desperately. "I could let Sally run this place half the time. Hell, she does it anyway—"

"Hey," Sally said in protest.

Natalia gripped his wrist and stared up at him, truly stunned. "You'd leave this ranch? You'd come live with me in a country you've never even seen?"

Leaning closer, he kissed her. "Natalia, I'd live on

the moon, if that's where you were. I just want to be with you."

She couldn't even blink, for fear this perfect, strong, warm, amazing man would disappear. "I want to live in Texas."

Amelia cleared her throat.

"I do," Natalia said without taking her eyes off Tim. "I'm sorry, Amelia. I love him."

Amelia sniffed, then opened her satchel again and pulled out a purple silk handkerchief, which she brought up to her nose and loudly blew.

Natalia gaped at her. "Amelia?"

*Sniff. Sniff.*

"Are you…crying?" Natalia had never seen Amelia cry, never.

"Oh, dear." Amelia blew her nose again, so loudly Mrs. Pig squealed.

Pickles started in, too, but Natalia could only stare at Amelia. "You're scaring me."

"You have no idea how long I've waited for this event," Amelia said. "It's true love. It's beautiful. You're going to be so happy."

"But she hasn't agreed yet," Tim said quietly. "Or said…*it*."

"No," Amelia agreed, swiping her eyes. "But she feels *it*."

Natalia looked into Tim's anxious eyes. "I feel it," she seconded.

"I want to hear you say it."

She'd never done so before. She'd never even thought it. In fact, before Texas, before Tim, she'd honestly worried about herself, wondering how she'd ever manage to find a man who would love her for her.

That was no longer a fear. In fact, all her fears...gone. "I love you," she said with the most conviction she'd ever felt. "I love you, Timothy Banning."

Amelia beamed at Tim through her tears. "See?"

"A moment ago you were ready to clobber me with your umbrella," Tim pointed out, looking a little baffled by Amelia's easy affection.

"She's fierce, but loyal." Natalia couldn't help herself. Everything was perfect, and she cried and laughed at the same time. "And I don't want you to give up anything for me. I really do want to live here." She looked at Amelia. "You'll come often."

"You know I will."

Tim looked positively flabbergasted.

"But there's one thing," Natalia warned.

"Anything," Tim promised rashly.

"If I'm not pregnant from the broken condom—"

Amelia gasped, then smacked Tim upside the back of the head.

He held his head. "Hey!"

"It wasn't his fault, Amelia." Natalia grinned. "I think he needed a bigger size."

The hoots and hollers from the gang increased intensely.

Tim, beet red, closed his eyes. "She's making that part up," he muttered.

"As I was saying…" Natalia continued. "If I'm not pregnant…" She waited until Tim opened his eyes. "I want to be," she finished softly. "Is that okay?"

Eyes suspiciously bright, Tim reached out and pulled her close. "Nothing has ever been more okay. I love you, Princess."

"Her Serene Highness," Amelia corrected him.

"How about Princess In The Wild, Wild West?" Red called out helpfully.

"How about Pain-In-My-Tushie turned Favorite-Sister-In-Law?" Sally called out, also helpfully.

"How about Mrs. Natalia Banning?" Tim said firmly.

Natalia's heart squeezed. "I like that one best."

# Her Knight
# To Remember

## Jill Shalvis

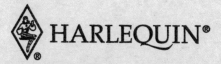

HARLEQUIN®

TORONTO • NEW YORK • LONDON
AMSTERDAM • PARIS • SYDNEY • HAMBURG
STOCKHOLM • ATHENS • TOKYO • MILAN • MADRID
PRAGUE • WARSAW • BUDAPEST • AUCKLAND

# *Prologue*

---

"LOOK, I OWE YOU, all right?"

"Yeah, just don't forget it." Kyle Moore stared at his reflection in the mirror. He was wearing a tux, for God's sake. It wasn't pretty. Neither was being squeezed into a dressing room the size of a thimble—all six feet three inches of him—with his baby brother peeking over his shoulder.

Kevin—some baby at just over six feet himself—took a good look. "Tomorrow that will be me," he said, paling slightly.

"You can still run like hell. In no time you could be out of New Mexico on your way to anywhere. I'll even take you," Kyle offered, in a blatant, desperate, last-ditch effort to get out of being the best man and having to wear the bloody tux.

Kevin smiled and shook his head. "Nah, I'm sort of fond of Taos. And of my life." Reaching up, bashing his elbows on the walls in the process, he attempted to adjust his brother's bow tie. "Besides, I'll look better in the tux than you do."

"No doubt." Kyle still wasn't sure how it had happened, but Kevin had gone ahead and done the unthinkable. He'd fallen in love. It made him do stupid things like sighing dreamily for no reason, or staring off into space for long moments at a time. It made him happy to be trying on a tux.

Insanity.

Kyle shuddered and hoped it wasn't contagious. Not that he had a problem with commitment. Hell, he'd been committed all his life. First, to helping his mother raise Kev, then to spending the last decade being a cop, taking down every scum he could get his hands on.

Truth be told, he was tired. Very tired. In fact, he wanted a nice long leave of absence to…do whatever. Bike across Europe. Sail the Greek Islands. Nap in the Bahamas. Anywhere far from here.

But right now, this tux was starting to itch. "I've got to get to work."

"You just closed a case," Kevin said. "You're entitled to a little personal time after killing yourself for weeks on end for the job."

It was months, but who was counting. "I've got paperwork."

"You work too hard, Kyle."

Yes, but in all these years Kevin had never noticed before. Chances were, he hadn't really noticed until now—he just needed something from Kyle.

Well, too bad. Today was actually a day off, a rarity, and he didn't plan to waste another second of it. But before he could get out of the jacket, Kevin stopped him.

"Don't go yet."

Kyle shrugged him off. "This thing is making me claustrophobic."

"Badass cops don't get claustrophobic."

"This one does." Plus, it was hard to be a tough, badass cop wearing a ridiculously overpriced tux with a pink satin—*pink satin!*—cummerbund. "Who picked this color anyway?"

"Lissa," Kevin admitted. "She has a thing for pink. It's not that bad, really. Squint your eyes a little and it even looks good."

"Yeah, if I squint them closed."

Kevin started fussing with Kyle's bow tie. "A guy only gets married once."

"Not if he's lucky—" Kyle's eyes nearly

bugged out of his head when Kevin cranked the bow tie, cutting off his air circulation. "Hey!" he croaked, waving his hands. "Too tight."

"It looks just right to me."

Kyle shoved his brother's hands away and let in some air. Definitely, he was going to take a vacation. As soon as this was over. He'd go count sand granules in Mexico. Or go castle combing in Scotland. Maybe he'd never come back.

Well, he'd have to, because there was Kevin, who had always needed him.

And suddenly Kyle had to know his brother would be okay. "Hey, Kev...are you sure?"

"Sure?"

"About this."

"Yeah, I think I'll look good."

"Not the style of the tux, Kev. The wedding."

"Are you kidding?" His brother set his chin on Kyle's shoulder and sent him a dopey grin. "Sex every night? Waking up with the woman of my dreams sharing my pillow? Having dinner ready for me when I get home?"

"I don't think women do that anymore."

"Did I mention the sex every night part?"

"That's only if you handle the honey-do list

properly. She's going to tame you, man.'' The thought terrified Kyle.

"Taming wouldn't be so bad, not if Lissa loves me every day for the rest of my life.''

Kyle gave up and sighed. "You've got it bad.''

"Yeah.'' Kevin's grin went wicked as he lifted his pager and studied the message. "Oops, gotta go. Lissa's boss is heading out for a meeting.''

"So?''

"So Lissa wants lunch.'' He waggled his eyebrows. "And I'm the entrée.''

"Oh, jeez.'' Kyle winced at the image. "Don't tell me that stuff.''

"I have to. It's why you have to go back out there right now and do my fitting for me.''

"No way am I going back out there, it's a bridal shop. A three-story bridal shop filled with…bridal crap.''

"Exactly. You need the little dude with the pins sticking out of his mouth to measure you again. For me this time.''

"Once was bad enough.''

"Oh, come on, a guy can never get fondled enough.''

"No. I still can't believe I have to wear a tux, too. You're really going to owe me.''

"I'm begging you, bro." Kevin waved the pager. "I have wild animal sex on the line here."

"It won't work. I'm bigger than you are," Kyle said a bit desperately because damn it, Kevin was giving him the puppy-dog eyes. He'd never, in all his sorry life, been able to resist the puppy eyes.

Some tough, badass cop he turned out to be.

"Not so much bigger," Kevin wheedled. "Come on, please?"

"There are people out there."

"Just a few women from the wedding party coming and going for their fittings, too. Please, Kyle? For me?"

"You want me to wear this tux for another half hour, just so you can get laid?"

"Well, yes." Kevin beamed. "I'd do it for you, in a heartbeat."

"You'll never have to," Kyle vowed, weakening. *Damn.*

"Then I'll do something else. Anything."

"Yeah? Promise me you'll only get married once."

Kevin laughed and slapped him on the back. "Deal. Now get out there and take it like a man. I'm going to sneak out back, and get it like a man."

# 1

---

"DRESSES, and anything pink, should be out-lawed," she muttered while pulling on stockings. She hated stockings, but at least she'd purchased the thigh-high kind.

Her own little defiance.

Princess Andrea Katrine Fran Brunner of Grunberg specialized in defiance. At twenty-six, Annie considered herself a grown-up now, but she was a tomboy at heart, and always had been.

Wearing a dress felt like…wearing a straitjacket. She couldn't run in a dress, couldn't ride her mountain bike. She couldn't plop herself down on the beach and watch the waves. She couldn't climb the highest tower of her castle home and stare off into the neighboring country of Switzerland, contemplating life, wearing a stupid dress.

She couldn't do anything worth doing.

But it wasn't up for discussion on this particular day. A bridesmaid had to wear a dress, and as improbable as it seemed, she'd landed herself a bridesmaid position.

She could put it off no longer. With an anticipatory frown, she straightened, took a deep breath, and turned in the tiny dressing room to face the mirror, much in the same way a prisoner would face an executioner.

"Oh, dear God." She slapped her hands over her eyes.

She shouldn't have looked.

Ignorance had been bliss.

Oh, man, it was bad. But she was strong, looked life straight in the eye, so she lowered her hands and faced her fate. Pink satin hugged her from breasts to hips, then flared out in ruffle after ruffle, all the way to the floor. Pink, pink and more pink.

She'd landed in hell, wearing Little Bo Peep's dress.

She actually felt weak just looking at herself, and she sank to the floor. Immediately her skirts, aided by no less than three hoops, flew up over her head.

The words that erupted out of her mouth were not the words of a nice little princess. Blinded by the horrifying fashion nightmare, she tried to shove down the skirts, but it was a feat of fabric magic and couldn't be done.

Struggling to her knees took all the considerable strength she had, and by the time she managed to get upright again she was huffing and puffing, her irritation at an all-time high.

"So much for losing my misery in champagne at the wedding," she muttered. She'd need all her wits about her to keep from suffocating.

Breath still heaving, she stared into the mirror. Nothing had changed, except now her skirts were crooked and one breast nearly was exposed. Oops. She righted the bodice and swore the air blue again just because she could, which felt good. But facts were facts.

She was still wearing the ugliest bridesmaid dress to ever grace the earth.

At this point, regrets were useless, and a waste of time. She'd come to the United States, to Taos, New Mexico to be exact, to be in Lissa's—the daughter of her mother's best friend—wedding, and that's what she would do.

Even if she'd rather have her fingernails slowly ripped out one by one.

But this dress. Granted, any dress might have given her some qualms, but she wasn't unbendable. She'd made the occasional exception. Hadn't she worn a kilt to Uncle Seany's eightieth birthday party just last winter? Uncle Seany had appreciated the gesture, even if the press hadn't. She'd been highlighted as a big fashion *don't*.

No biggie. She'd spent most of her life being a bit of an enigma to the press, her friends…her family. When all the other good little princesses had been happy wearing dresses and lace and learning their place, Annie had climbed trees and tore her clothing and generally made everyone's life—but mostly her British nanny, Amelia Grundy—a living hell.

Now, years and years later, the tomboy image had stuck. So she was stubborn, strong willed and tenacious. So she knew her mind and wasn't afraid to speak it. So she wasn't likely to catch a husband that way, so what?

She didn't care.

Okay, she cared. She knew she scared men away with her frankness. With her attitude. Or by just by being a royal. But she was who she was, and no way would she be anyone different.

But she did have to wear this dress. No way around that. And though they'd just laugh their butts off at the sight of her, she wished her sisters Natalia and Lili were right next to her.

"Just get it over with," Annie told her reflection.

Knowing Lissa would ask how she liked the dress, Annie attempted a smile. It came out more like a snarl, so she tried again. The glass didn't crack. Good sign.

Lifting her skirts in two fistfuls so she could walk, she pivoted, took a step, put her foot down on her own skirt and...fell on her face.

"Damn it." Struggling, she managed to get up. She grabbed more fistfuls of pink satin and, muttering ungraciously beneath her breath, exited the fitting room without further mishap.

The main room of the bridal store was nearly all mirrors, surrounded by white silk-flower arrangements and built-in closets opened to reveal rack after rack of dresses that Annie wouldn't have been caught dead in.

When she got married, she—*whoa*. Stop the presses. She wasn't getting married. She'd long ago realized there wasn't a man out there for her.

But if she ever did get married—say when hell froze over—there would not be a single pink satin dress in sight.

With all Annie's considerable theatrical talents—she'd been staging temper tantrums since she was two years old—she'd done her best to get out of coming here in the first place. She had work, didn't she? Publishing *A Child Affair*, her monthly magazine on child care and development, took time.

But Amelia Grundy, former nanny, and current friend and companion, had happily stepped in for her, offering to cover until she returned.

Annie had then tried to plan events that only she herself could attend. So Amelia, with her strange and inexplicable ability to make things happen, had cleared those off her calendar with a wave of her pencil.

Damn her efficient, British—and seemingly magical—hide. Amelia always knew best, always.

How infuriating.

While Annie had packed for this trip, Amelia had come into her room and hugged her tight. "Try to keep trouble at bay, Annie," she'd said. "Try real hard."

Annie had laughed. Oh, yes, Amelia knew her well. "I'm grown-up now. Trouble doesn't follow me as it used to."

"No, it leads," had been Amelia's wry reply.

Now Annie took her mind off the home she missed with all her heart and looked around the store. The silence startled her. The place was surprisingly empty. Odd. She'd come from the Taos

Mountain Inn, which Lissa had rented out for the entire wedding party. She'd come alone, but still, there had been customers in here only a few moments ago.

And again, Annie wished Natalia was here. Her middle sister wasn't required to be in the wedding, and therefore didn't have to show up until Saturday morning. Same for her younger sister, Lili.

Not fair.

Then she imagined the look on Nat's face when she caught sight of Annie dressed up like a fairy-tale victim waiting to happen and decided she was better off by herself.

*"Get out of here."*

Annie, startled by the rough command, turned around. Well, *she* turned, but it took the dress a moment longer, and then once it got momentum, it nearly took her in a full circle.

The voice came from her right, where a man in a black tux stood on a white platform in front of a triad of mirrors.

Not just a regular man, either. Oh, my, no. Surrounded by mirrors and the specially contrived lighting to make all brides beautiful, this man... well. He was huge, and built like a Greek god. Tall, dark and incredible, was her first thought.

Probably the most amazing, sexy-looking guy she'd ever seen—even given the handicap of the tux.

Not that an amazing, sexy-looking guy turned her head. No sirree, she wasn't that vain. She required more than a mouthwatering body—which he happened to have in spades—to turn her head.

He needed a brain. A sense of humor. A tough, I'm-in-charge attitude. Definitely the attitude. She'd never denied being attracted to the bad-boy type.

Only problem was, the bad-boy type didn't readily make himself available to princesses. Nor was *she* available. She'd had her fair share of trying, and she was done. Amelia had agreed in relief, saying the male population just wasn't ready for her.

Oh, well. There always were fantasies. And in her fantasy, her main requirement of a man…it was almost too embarrassing to admit, even to herself.

He had to dote on her.

"Get out of here *now*," the man in the tux said through his teeth, his eyes dark with fury.

He couldn't be talking to her. No man would dare speak to her that way.

"Lady, *move it*."

Well, how rude. And he was trying to intimidate her. They'd never even met, so his boorish behavior was completely unwarranted. She squinted to read the name on the piece of paper pinned to his jacket and went still.

*Moore.*

As in Kevin Moore. None other than Lissa's groom. Terrific. It was *this* big lug's fault that she was weighed down with tons of pink satin. That fact made it easier to stand up tall and glare at him in return, because she did not take looking like Little Bo Peep lightly.

"Are you deaf?" he asked.

Annie had many, many faults, the foremost being a rather formidable temper when stirred. It definitely was stirred now. She stepped forward, fists clenched at her side.

"I am most certainly not deaf," she replied with what she thought was remarkable dignity, given what a jerk he was. "I just refuse to listen to rude—"

"Stop right there."

She could hear the danger in his voice, but dangerous, edgy men didn't scare her. Nothing did.

So she took another step and heard something that sounded an awful lot like the sound of the bad guy cocking a gun in a movie.

Slowly, carefully, she craned her neck toward the second man in the room, the man she'd assumed to be the tailor, since he was standing below Mr. Tux. Only, this man looked far more like a thug, with his short, stocky body sporting a badly fitted suit.

And now that she was staring at him, she realized he had no pins sticking out of his mouth.

Didn't all tailors have pins sticking out of their mouths?

Furthermore, he had short stocky fingers to go with his short, stocky body, and she couldn't imagine them being agile enough to thread a needle, much less wield it.

But what he did wield in his hand caught her attention, and everything came to a screeching halt, including her heart.

He held a gun. Pointed directly at her.

She revised her earlier thought. She was afraid of something.

She was afraid of guns pointed directly at her.

# 2

"THAT DOESN'T LOOK like a needle and thread," the woman in pink said slowly. "Because I really need a needle-and-thread person here. Take a look at me in this dress, would you?" She lifted her arms and Kyle had to give it to her, her hands shook only slightly.

"I told you to get out of here," he said beneath his breath.

"I thought you were just being rude," she said beneath her breath right back, her eyes never leaving the gun still trained on her.

"*Rude?*" He might have laughed, if this wasn't a nightmare waiting to happen. "I was trying to save your sorry ass."

"Hey, now, that's no way to talk to a lady." This from the guy holding the gun.

Why had Kyle bothered to get out of bed that morning? It wasn't enough to be forced into a tux. No, he had to be killed while doing it.

Well, damn it, he didn't plan to go easy, and he sure didn't plan to go while looking like a penguin, arguing with an insane lady in the most godawful dress he'd ever seen.

But when Jimmy the thug had turned his gun on her, every muscle within Kyle had tensed. This was *his* battle, and he refused to let anyone else get hurt, especially innocent bystanders. "Jimmy, remember who your target is here," he said in quiet warning.

"I remember." The gun didn't waver from the Lady In Pink. "But maybe I'll take a detour from killing you and have some fun first."

Kyle heard the woman's gasp, but he kept his eyes on Jimmy Tarintino, nephew of Joseph Tarintino, the local mobster Kyle had put away just last week for one hundred and ten years plus three consecutive life sentences. "Don't get greedy now."

"Greedy?" Jimmy's hand shook slightly, making Kyle's heart stop. The idiot was going to pull the trigger without even meaning to. "You're calling *me* greedy?" Jimmy asked incredulously. "You're the one who took my uncle down for the glory of it."

Glory. Yeah, right. Glory was barely making enough money to keep him in a postage-stamp-size condo. Glory was risking life and limb on a daily basis being a cop, only to be taken down in a bridal shop.

Wearing a tux.

Kyle would have given just about anything to have his gun on him right now. But when Kevin had seen Kyle's gun tucked in the back of his jeans, he'd about blown a gasket. *No guns in a bridal shop,* he'd said.

Someone had forgotten to tell that to Jimmy.

Jimmy trained his gun back on Kyle but kept his eyes on the woman. He licked his lips. Grinned. "Just a little detour, I think. You don't mind waiting to die, do you Kyle? I'll let you watch."

Yeah, his gun would be good right about now. "Jimmy—"

Jimmy took a sidestep toward the woman, the gun still on Kyle.

Ah, hell. Blood was not going to go well with his pink cummerbund, but he took a step forward anyway. He was still on the platform, with Jimmy below him. Three wide steps down was where the woman stood. Kyle figured if he could get close enough, he could take a flying leap and tackle Jimmy.

"Come here, pretty thing," Jimmy coaxed the

woman with a lecherous grin that revealed a missing tooth. He'd lost it in an infamous fight with his brother, who'd lost an ear when Jimmy had bitten it off. "Come on, sweet cheeks. Come here and show me your pretty dress."

"If you think this dress is pretty, you need your eyes examined," the woman said in an icy cultured voice. "And if you think I'm going to let you lay one sweaty, beefy paw on me, you need your head examined."

Perfect. A back talker. She couldn't just stand there all meek and compliant-like and let Kyle save the day. No, she had to egg on a crazy man, when anyone in her right mind could see that's exactly the type of fight Jimmy was looking for.

Jimmy's gun hand shook more noticeably now, and his eyes gleamed as he took another step, then another.

Two more and Kyle would be able to leap from the pedestal and jump him. End of crisis. "Jimmy, remember how you let the store clerk and the two other customers go outside? Why don't you do the same for her?"

"No." Jimmy licked his lips. "Look, Pinkie, I said get over here—"

"And I said—" But she broke off with a scream

of outrage as Jimmy tripped off the first of three white satin steps toward her. Then she screamed again as Kyle leaped into the air.

Kept on screaming as she threw herself on top of Jimmy first, fists out and pummeling.

In midair Kyle let out one concise and particularly vicious oath. His original target was now covered with pink satin. He might have landed anyway—he didn't care about crushing her—but he did care about the gun going off accidentally. He cared about that a lot, as he was rather fond of his own hide.

So he pulled back and landed painfully next to the now rolling duo. For a long, terrifying second he couldn't see anything but obnoxious pink satin, so he reached out and pulled it free.

It came with a woman inside of it, fists flailing. Jimmy was coming to his feet and grappling to right his gun, so Kyle was forced to get a better grip on the screaming pile of satin and shove them both behind a counter. He took a fist to the chin for his efforts, and might have taken more if he hadn't manacled her wrists with his hand.

''Cool it, I'm the good guy.''

A gunshot echoed directly above his head, and he swore again—silently this time—before grabbing the fumbling bundle of satin and crawling as fast as he could along the bottom of the counter.

"Let. Me. *Go*," demanded the pink satin. She kicked out, nearly unmanning him.

"If I do, you're going to get yourself killed. Now stop— *Damn it!*" She'd freed her face enough to lean in and bite him on the shoulder. With not a little amount of grim satisfaction, he shifted her, tossing her over that shoulder in a fireman's hold, one hand hard on her backside, the other aiding his crawling efforts.

When she wriggled, trying to get into position to bite him again, he simply tightened his grip on her butt, which he could feel through all her layers, and it was a very nice butt indeed. Finally, with considerable effort, and no thanks to her, he got them to the other side of the room, where he paused, listening.

Dead silence.

Not good. Then, suddenly, another gunshot rang out, halfway between where he held the Lady In Pink and where they had started out.

Good, he thought grimly. Jimmy had no idea where they were. Behind them, and only five feet away, were aisles upon aisles of long, flowing white wedding dresses, behind which he hoped and prayed was a back door.

Crouching down, he dumped his load on the floor, staring in fascination as the satin righted itself and a face appeared. A very furious female face. Her mouth opened, and at the speed of light, he put his hand over it, not wanting her to risk their lives by lighting into him right now.

But oddly enough, she didn't try to speak.

Her eyes however—the most interesting shade of gold he'd ever seen—spit daggers at him. He held her utterly still and looked away, trying to figure out Jimmy's location. He could hear nothing, except Pink's movements. He knew she wanted to tell him something.

Too bad. She could wait.

He cocked his head and listened again. Where could Jimmy have gone? There was no sign of him.

If he lived through this, he was going to kill Kevin.

Then pain erupted in his fingers.

Pink had bitten him! Whipping his head toward her, he fought the urge to bite her back.

She pointed to the opposite side of the store, where he just caught a whisper of a footstep.

Jimmy. Probably figuring they'd gotten all the

way across. He was blocking their exit out the front door, but they weren't going to go out the front door. Ignoring his throbbing fingers, he nudged the woman, directing her with a toss of his head toward the rows and rows of dresses.

She shook her head.

He pointed firmly.

Again, she shook her head.

Unbelievable. Unused to being disobeyed— much less being bitten *twice*—he glared at her and jabbed his finger into the air again. A scary jab. A follow-my-lead-without-question jab. A jab that would have had any of the men he worked with quaking in their boots.

Not this lady.

Instead, she lifted her chin so far he thought she'd get a nosebleed and gave the air her own jab, to her right. Beyond the counter was a discrete elevator door.

The service elevator. Damn, she had a point.

With a stiff nod, he went to lift her to her knees but she shoved him away. Nose still thrust in the air, she pushed back her wild hair and started to crawl under her own steam.

Only to get tangled in the hoops making up her skirt. She would have tumbled to the wood floor, making a racket that would have gotten them both killed, but he hauled her against his side. Suddenly, he was blinded as her skirt raised up like a damn flag, right over both of their heads.

Jerking the skirt down with one hand and holding her tight against him with the other, he made his awkward way toward the elevator, feeling her breathing down his neck the entire way. "I can save myself," she said, her mouth to his ear.

Uh-huh. Right. He'd never imagined it coming to this, crawling on the floor, holding a bossy woman against him, praying for his life. Man, he was tired of this job. Of this city. Of his life.

If he lived—and he intended to live, thank you very much—he was ready, *past* ready, for a new venue. A few feet from the elevator he heard something behind him—or maybe it was just instincts— and one jerk of his head revealed Jimmy, climbing over the counter.

Forget being quiet, it was hustle time. With a last flying leap, he got them to the elevator. "Open, open, *open*," he muttered, hitting the button over and over.

For the first time today, fate was actually on his side and the doors swished open. He tossed Pink into a corner, then followed, reaching for the close button and starting a new prayer.

*Close, close, close.*

"Who do you think you are? Robo Cop?" Pink snapped, fighting to untangle herself from her dress.

"*Gotcha,*" Jimmy cried, falling off the counter to the floor. But he recovered quickly and aimed his gun.

Kyle dove over Pink, covering her body with his. The doors closed.

Several rounds hit the steel doors, leaving an indention, but not quite penetrating all the way through.

"Get off of me!" She shoved at him for emphasis.

Kyle, sweating, sank back against the wall. "You're welcome."

"What for?"

"For saving your life."

She let out a shocked laugh. "Saving *my* life? You should be thanking *me.*"

"Why? I just saved your pretty little hide." Kyle opened his eyes and for the first time leveled them right on her. She didn't look terrified, or in shock, as he might have expected. Just angry.

"You saved my hide." She laughed again, though it was a weak one. Sinking next to him, her head thunked back against the wall. "I saved yours, buster."

"Buster?"

"Who do you think managed to track the gunman?" she asked. "Who found the elevator? Who—"

Another gunshot shut her up. Again, it didn't penetrate, but the elevator jerked to a stop.

"What—"

"Terrific." Kyle tipped his head back. The light for the second floor hadn't come on. "We're between floors. Sitting ducks."

"Why is that?"

He looked at her again, taking in the lightest, most arresting golden eyes he'd ever seen, the most amazing matching gold hair tumbling past her shoulders and the impossibly useless pink dress. No use sugarcoating it. He told her the truth. "We're dead."

"Not until we stop breathing, we're not."

He couldn't believe she wasn't hysterical by now, or in shock. And in spite of the added complication she'd been, he felt a reluctant admiration for her. "Yeah, and we're still breathing, aren't we."

"That's right. Thanks to me."

Okay, she was being a pain in the butt. But now that he'd had a moment to catch his breath, he had to admit she was a beautiful pain in the butt. As disastrous as the pink was on her, the dress did hang nicely from shoulder to low on her hips. And everything in between. For the first time, he saw everything in between. Her slender throat, her breasts thrust up and nearly out by the cut of the dress, her waist...she was pretty damn mouthwatering. He'd give her this, she wasn't a hardship to look at it. "Move back."

She'd come up to her knees, and was inspecting the control panel. "Why?"

"Because I said."

She rolled her eyes and poked at the panel.

Another gunshot rang out, and directly in front of her the control panel buckled out toward her. Clearly not made of the same strength of steel as the doors, the bullet tore through.

Kyle grabbed her and tugged hard, so that she fell back against him.

The bullet hit the back wall, a foot above their heads.

Kyle's momentum had tumbled them both down with a jerk. And though he attempted not to notice, the jarring movement nearly freed a breast.

Until she hit the floor, that is, because that's when the skirt of the dress—buoyed by the hoops—once again flew up and over both their heads.

With a savage sound of frustration, she tugged both of them free and glared at him as if it was *his* fault she had horrible taste in clothes.

"Maybe now you'll listen," he said, gallantly swallowing a cocky I-told-you-so.

"The panel is dust," she said, ignoring him. "We'll have to figure out something else."

She was cool as a cucumber. He'd never met a woman like her.

"I can handle this."

"Really?" Her gold eyes looked him over. "Don't take this wrong, but you're not exactly doing a great job so far." She turned away to inspect their surroundings. "Don't worry," she said in a patronizing voice that made his jaw clench. "I'll figure this out for both of us. Just stay down so you don't get hit."

Not only was he in a tux, not only did he have a mobster trying to gun him down, he had to be stuck in an elevator with the most irritating woman on the planet. "That's supposed to be my line."

"What?" She was distracted as she studied the ceiling.

"The 'don't worry' line. The 'stay down' line."

She sent him a vague smile, then went back to inspecting their surroundings as if she knew what she was doing.

Clearly, she thought he was an idiot.

Kyle didn't need Jimmy to kill him. This nutcase in pink was going to do it by stress alone.

ANNIE STUDIED the ceiling carefully, while wracking her brain, conjuring up every action-adventure film she'd ever seen—of which there were many—for inspiration. "There's always a way out," she said. "I just have to come up with it."

The man behind her made a rude noise. "This whole thing could have been avoided if you'd only listened to me in the first place."

"Oh, you mean when you told me to *get out of here*?" Hmm, the ceiling had several panels. Assuming she could reach one, she might be able to crawl out. She was good at escaping. She'd mastered it at age two, when she'd escaped into her mother's royal closet to avoid eating her peas at dinner.

It had taken the entire army of Grunberg royal bodyguards to find her, as this had been before her mother's death, when the closet had been the size of a house and filled with enough clothing to clothe everyone in their entire country.

By the time Annie had become a teenager, she'd gained enough skill that no one could find her when she wanted to be hidden, not even Natalia—her sister and closest friend. No one could find her but Amelia, but since Annie was convinced Amelia really was a fairy godmother in disguise, she didn't count.

"If you'd stayed back," the man said, "I could have tackled him and wrestled away the gun. Arrested him."

She turned on him in surprise. Which was not an easy move wearing such a stupid dress. While the skirt might be too wide, the top sure wasn't. When she turned, she threatened to expose more of herself than she planned on exposing.

Secret exhibitionist fantasy or not, she didn't plan on showing off her wares to just anyone. Especially this man, with his intense eyes that gobbled her up and his tall, rangy body that could make a grown woman drool. Not that she was drooling.

No, not over him. He was too big, too…real.

Then what he'd just said sank in. "You're a cop?"

"What did you think?"

She had no idea. Hmm…a cop. He'd dedicated his life to serving and protecting others. How irresistible was that?

But he was about to get married. To someone else. If they lived.

Not that he'd have been interested in her anyway. Well, not past the tiara and prestige anyway. She'd learned, hadn't she? She should have had it down by now. No men. They wanted only one thing.

Well, make that two.

Sex and money.

Too bad she wasn't any good at the first and until she came into her trust fund in another year, had a lot less of the second than anyone would believe.

"Maybe," she said, "the other people in the store, the ones Jimmy sent outside, called the cops. Or maybe the shots alerted someone else in the building. Maybe there's help on the way."

"You're awfully full of maybes."

"Call me an eternal optimist."

"In that dress, you'd have to be."

She ground her teeth together. "This dress is hardly *my* fault—"

"Look, let's just get ourselves out of here before Jimmy figures out how to find us."

"Right." She figured they'd have to go out the ceiling, crawl along whatever sort of system there was and—

"We'll go out the ceiling."

She stared at him. "That was going to be my idea."

The look he shot her was nothing short of patronizing. "Right. I'll go first, and—"

"I should go first." She came up to him, startled anew by his sheer size. She refused to acknowledge how her head barely reached his wide shoulders, or the fact that his gaze dipped down to the barely there neckline of her dress, which she prayed had stayed in place. "I'll need a boost."

"Did you forget who's the cop here?"

"So you're one of those guys who have a problem with strong women—"

"I most definitely do not have a problem with women, strong or otherwise."

His voice had gone low and dangerously soft.

Sort of the way her father's got when he was really close to losing his temper.

She had a feeling seeing this man blow his lid would be quite a show, but they didn't have time for that right now.

A fact that was reiterated when another bullet hit the panel, again piercing the back wall above their heads and echoing throughout their small confines.

She put her hands over her ears at the same time he reached for her, covering her body with his.

"You have to stop doing that," she said against his chest.

Against his really hard chest. She wondered if he had a smattering of dark hair across it or if he was smooth—

"Shut up. *Please,*" he begged. "Just shut up and let me rescue you."

"I'll rescue myself."

"This is a nightmare. *You're* a nightmare."

She'd heard that before. "Just bend down and let me get on your shoulders. Do it quick before another bullet tears into us."

He stared at her, then shook his head. "This isn't some great adventure, you get that, right?"

"Of course—"

"Because I don't think you realize that if Jimmy

gets smart and gets upstairs before us, and your pretty little neck appears first, he's not going to drop his gun, give you a hand, and help you out.''

"Well—"

"Unless, of course, you do exactly that."

"What?"

"That." His eyes remained on her face, but his voice changed again. Silky soft now. *Very* silky soft.

And she was clueless. "Do…what?"

"Pop a nipple out of your dress."

# 3

BECAUSE HE COULDN'T handle looking at her for another second, Kyle turned his back. Counted to ten. Calculated complicated algebra problems in his head.

Didn't matter. He could still picture her nipple poking out from the top of her dress. Perfectly rose-colored and perky. Perfect size for a man's mouth.

He was a man. A typical red-blooded man. With sex now firmly on the brain despite the fact that they were on the run from a bad guy with a gun.

Damn it.

"Sorry."

This from behind him, in that voice that somehow screamed innocence and sex all at the same time.

"I haven't had my dress fitted yet," she said amongst the rustling of her dress. "And—"

"It's okay," he said to the wall. No way could he look at her and hold eye contact. Nope, his gaze had a mind of its own suddenly, run by the boss between his legs, and it wouldn't be able to hold back from taking another look to see if she'd managed to cover herself.

"I couldn't wear a bra with it because—"

"It's okay," he repeated, and pinched the bridge of his nose with his fingers, trying to think of something else, anything other than how absolutely delectable her nipple had been.

"Let's get out of here," he said in what he thought was a remarkably casual voice. "To do that, I need to concentrate. And to do *that,* I need you to be really, *really* quiet. Can you do that one little thing, do you think?" He risked a look at her.

Her eyes narrowed. Her mouth opened. Then closed.

"Good girl," he said.

"I'm not a girl. I'm a grown woman."

He knew his eyes went hot, knew his voice sounded low and husky, but he couldn't help it. "I realize that."

"Do you? Do you realize there's no need to be rude? Just because your manhood feels threatened by me suggesting you might need my help—"

His manhood didn't feel threatened so much as...horny. "I don't need your help—" He broke off when another bullet tore into the control panel, getting ensnared high in the corner this time. Not forgetting to save her ungrateful hide, Kyle drew her down into the corner yet again.

They stayed that way for a moment, until he realized how still she'd become. Damn. She'd probably, finally, gone into shock.

But then she shoved him off her, stood and hiked up her dress, revealing a pair of long, toned legs in thigh-high stockings rimmed with lace, held there by a simple white, devastatingly sexy garter belt.

His jaw dropped. "What—" His voice cracked like a teenager and he tried again. "What are you doing?"

"Did you see that? The direction of the bullet entry?"

Yes, damn it, he had. Jimmy was still below them.

"I'm safe going first." She put her lifted skirt between her teeth. Then she shoved not one, not two, but three hoops down her legs. Stepping out of them with a sigh, she took her skirt in her hands.

*Rip.*

Okay, she'd succumbed to the stress. He'd never actually seen it happen, but had heard of such things. She was going to tear off her dress and go running naked through the streets. Maybe even sexually attack him. He had to stop her, help her, but good God, he'd gotten a quick glimpse of barely there white-lace panties. Just a tiny little wisp of material between her legs, hardly covering—

With one last rip, she straightened and tossed aside miles of material, leaving her with the form-fitting bodice of the dress still in place, but the wild skirt was completely subdued and laying nicely against her body to midthigh.

"There," she said. "Better. Now... You need to lift me up to get us out of here." Without another word, she walked behind him and lifted her hands to his shoulders.

"Say pretty please with sugar on top," she breathed in his ear, "and I'll be sure to pause at the top to give you a hand."

He blinked. "What?"

"Boost me up."

"But..." What had just happened? Here he was, poised to fight off her sexual advances, but she hadn't jumped his bones at all.

"Come on," she said, pushing on his shoulders. "Up."

So that's how he found himself putting his hands over hers to steady her and going to his knees.

Helping her to his shoulders should have been a breeze, but by the time she'd plastered her chest to his upper back, then climbed up his body, rubbing her breasts against the back of his neck, panting in his ear, pausing for balance, he was sweating again.

"Okay," she said, balanced on his shoulders, still holding his hands. "I'm ready."

"Be careful."

"Just lift me up."

He had a moment to think again about how amazing she really was. How she was together and perfectly willing to pitch in to save their lives. That she was also annoying and bad tempered went without saying. Maybe it was her way of showing shock.

Her toes dug into his shoulders. They were bare of polish but she had a silver ring on the second toe of her left foot. Her hands in his remained cool and steady, and as he straightened, so did she, in perfect balance, reaching for the panel above them.

"Nice and easy," he said, sliding his hands from her ankles to her calves for extra support, then farther up the backs of her legs to hold her low on her thighs.

He knew, or his *brain* knew, that now wasn't really the time to enjoy the soft, smooth silkiness of her stocking-covered legs, but it wasn't his brain running the show at the moment.

"Nice and easy has its place," she said breathlessly. "But not here." Grunting, she manhandled the middle panel aside. Another grunt and she started to pull herself through the hatch above the elevator.

Kyle made the mistake of looking up.

Directly beneath her dress. With the help of his hands on her, she used her muscles to rise. He watched her legs strain, tremble. Watched her perfectly rounded butt clench.

And because he was watching where he shouldn't, he didn't see her foot kick out for purchase and find his face until stars exploded in his head.

By the time he could see again, she was gone. Completely gone.

"Hey," he whispered, panicked. Damn, he'd known better. He'd sent her, an innocent, no matter how irritating and sexy and brave, directly into the hands of Jimmy.

Then her face appeared in the hole above. "What's taking you so long?"

He was so weak he nearly stumbled back against the wall of the elevator. "You're okay."

"Of course I'm okay. Hey, cop man, hurry up, will you?"

He tore off his jacket, shoved up his sleeves and leaped up, but couldn't quite reach the top of the elevator.

"Hang on," she said, then vanished. She reappeared a moment later to toss down a large empty box. "I got this from the second-floor hallway. We're only a few feet short of that floor. Be quick, I think I hear him coming."

"Be quick," he muttered to himself, using the box as leverage, grabbing on to the opening to pull himself up.

"Took you long enough," she said in lieu of a greeting, waiting with barely contained impatience.

Kyle's fingers itched with an overwhelming desire to reach out and put his hands around her neck. "I'm here now."

"Good job," she whispered, absently patting his shoulder, as if he was an idiot. As if *she* was the one in charge. As if he was *her* burden. "Now stick with me."

"Wait a minute. *You're* sticking with *me* or I'll leave you here as bait. Got it? Good. Now I'll lead, so move over."

She blinked at him in surprise and he felt like a jerk.

Hell, he *was* a jerk. What had happened to his legendary patience? ''I'm sorry. *Please* move over.''

Not surprisingly, she thrust up that chin again. ''Saying *please* when you're still being a bully, does not make it okay.'' And with that, she took the lead and crawled through the space out into a dark hallway. Then she craned her neck to peek at him, her finger to her lips, because clearly he couldn't be trusted to know when to shut up.

''Wait.'' *He* was supposed to lead. *He* was saving *her*.

But she didn't wait, and it occurred to him, he'd never followed before. He didn't like that, or the fact that she was moving too fast, too recklessly. Surely she was going to fall and break her pretty little neck, or at the very least, alert Jimmy to their location. Reaching out, he grabbed her ankle and tugged.

And tugged.

''I said wait,'' he said into her ear when he'd pulled her to him. He had all that gold hair and sweet, sexy scent tangling his brain cells now. ''Get *behind* me.''

"Fine." Now *her* jaw was all bunchy. "But let's climb up to the third floor," she said.

He hated to admit that it was the logical thing to do. Going down was a bad idea, at least until reinforcements came. "Okay, back into the elevator shaft, to the third floor," he agreed. "Me first." He was fairly certain Jimmy wasn't smart enough to locate them, but if he did, Kyle wanted to be out front. "Did you hear me?"

"How can I help but hear you? You're yelling in my ear."

"Yeah, yeah..." He moved to crawl past her, his big body brushing against her much smaller one, and he was simultaneously bombarded with sensations. Temper and heat.

Temper and need.

But mostly just temper.

ANNIE DEALT with her own temper. "So who is this guy anyway?" she asked as they climbed. "Someone you've won over with all your considerable charm and wit?"

He stopped to send her a dry look. "He's the punk nephew of a mobster I just helped put away."

"Interesting life you lead." They'd gone about five feet up, when she stopped.

She sniffed and went still. "I smell smoke, cop man."

"Pull your shirt over your nose and keep climbing. We'll get out on the third floor, find the stairs and come back down," came the terse reply.

So much for comforting platitudes. She was climbing as fast as she could, which was pretty damn fast. Good thing she had an affinity for climbing. All her tree scaling and climbing walls or whatever she could get her hands on since she could walk, had come in handy today.

But the smoke burned her lungs, and she fought the urge to cough.

"I said cover your mouth," he said.

"I don't have a shirt."

"Then don't breathe," he said gruffly, and encouraged her to follow with a sharp tug on her wrist.

That was another thing about him, this soon-to-be-married cop. He kept touching her.

She wondered if his wife-to-be knew he had a thing with touching.

It wasn't often that she was touched, period. People in her country respected their royals, and kept a distance. She had her father, once a warm, loving man, but he'd lost much of his zest for life after her mother had died twelve years before. She had her sisters, when they weren't fighting.

Few others had been allowed to touch Annie, though there had been the occasional affair during her naive days, back when she believed there was a man for her out there somewhere. Once in a while she dreamed about that still, a man's hands on her. Solid and sure and arousing.

But the dreams had turned out to be better than reality.

The smoke was thicker now. She let out a cough, her lungs starting to feel squeezed.

"You okay?" He patted his hand between her shoulder blades, but she kept coughing, mostly because he didn't seem to know his own strength. "Damn, Pink, keep your lungs in your chest." Without a care for the loaned shirt on his back, he ripped it off, tearing the thing in half with his bare hands. He put one half over her face, before he covered his mouth with the other half.

Their eyes met, and she saw the frantic concern in his, so she nodded, then continued shimmying up the narrow hatch.

At the top, he held her back, making sure he was the first one out into what she feared would be an open hallway, making them easy targets.

But the third floor was some sort of warehouse, filled to the brim with huge storage containers the size of wardrobes, each probably filled with more torturous dresses. And while containers provided cover for them, they also provided that same cover to Jimmy.

Her cop—sooner or later she'd have to stop thinking of him as hers—reached down, grabbed her hand and pulled her up. For a moment, their bodies collided and he held her still, looking her over.

"I'm okay," she said.

"You're amazing, is what you are." He moved to a window and carefully peered out, leaving her with the most incredible view of his now bare, sleek back. "At least five black-and-whites down there. That's the good news."

"And the bad?"

He moved away from the window. "Until Jimmy is caught or gives himself up, we're on the third floor of a possibly burning building, the hostages of a wild idiot with a gun. Let's go."

"Where?"

"Out of ideas, are you?" He guided her to the west wall, where there was a door.

"Stairs?"

"Shh." He put his ear to it, then his hand.

She wrestled with the urge to put her ear and hand and everything else against his bare back.

*Taken,* she reminded herself. *He's taken.* "Let's go out the window," she suggested. "The cops can cover us."

"Unless you're Spider Woman, bad idea. There's no fire escape."

"No, but we can shimmy down the storm drain."

He stared at her. "Who the hell are you?"

"Cops aren't the only ones with nerves of steel," she said. "Try being a princess."

*"What?"*

"You want a formal introduction?" She curtsied, not an easy move in her cut-off dress. "Your Serene Highness Andrea Katrine Fran Brunner of Grunberg, at your service. But the at-your-service part is just a formality, you understand. I'm not really at your ser—"

"You hit your head in the elevator, right?"

"I came here for the wedding." She tried not to sound bitter about that, because really, just because he was big, strong and gorgeous didn't mean she wanted him for herself. Nope. He was too stubborn, too confident, too…everything. "You can just call me Annie, if that's easier."

"Annie." He was looking at her as if she was from Mars.

"I'm telling you the truth. Grunberg is a perfectly nice little country, right next to Switzerland."

"Uh-huh."

"Oh, forget it." She turned away, but he grabbed her arm.

"Don't you want to know who I am?" he asked, sounding a little surprised that she wasn't panting with the need to know his name.

"I already know who you are." She didn't want to hear him say he was going to get married. Not when he was the first man to stir her in a very long time.

No, wait, she wasn't stirred. She wasn't anything but sick and tired of this dress. "Let's get out of here," she said, suddenly very weary. "Before I start screaming and never stop."

He looked at her for a long moment, as if not quite certain she wouldn't do exactly that.

"I'm not going to fall apart," she said.

"You'd be entitled."

"A princess doesn't fall apart." At least not until she was safe, and he was far, far away.

# 4

THE WAREHOUSE was a bit of a mystery. For some-one of Annie's stature—that is short—it wasn't possible to see the entire room at once. Which, given the circumstances, was disturbing to say the least. "We need a better plan," she said, gaze searching, hoping Jimmy wasn't up here with them.

He was a cool one, her cop—no, he wasn't hers. She needed to remember that. But she had begun to think of him as such the moment he'd actually let her lead the way onto the elevator, because in her life how many men had let her lead?

Exactly none.

Not that she'd been neglected. The opposite, really. She'd been pampered and sheltered and pro-tected, even when it wasn't in her nature to hide behind someone. No, her nature was to come out fists swinging. "I think we should—"

"Stay here, stay down," he said, nudging her to

the floor. He placed his hand over hers and lifted it to her mouth. "Keep the shirt over your face."

So much for her leading. Fine. She could share the power, if she had to for now.

She just didn't want him to get used to it.

It wasn't until he vanished that she realized the smoke had followed them, and that suddenly she couldn't see more than a few feet. "Hello?" she whispered, squinting, but no one answered.

He'd left her.

She was alone.

*Keep trouble at bay.*

"Amelia?" Annie whipped her head to the right, then the left. Through the filtering smoke she would have sworn she'd just seen Amelia standing there, her silver hair neatly coiled on top of her head, her wire-rimmed glasses slipping down her nose, her satchel firmly at her side.

But that couldn't be, it just couldn't. Amelia was with Lili at a museum opening. And yet it had seemed so real, right down to Amelia's intense, all-seeing gaze.

Annie peered harder into the growing smoke. If Amelia was doing something magical, it wouldn't be the first time. Lili, Natalia and Annie had long ago come to terms with one thing. Amelia was... different. Very different. "Hello?"

Of course, there was no answer.

But thinking about Amelia made her just a tad homesick, not that she'd admit it to anyone. She longed for Nat, who would be absolutely no help.

She must be inhaling too much smoke. Must be near passing out. How infuriating. She never passed out. Fainting was for sissies, and no one had ever accused her of being a sissy.

If she passed out and ended up in a hospital in this dress, someone was going to have to die.

"Hey."

At the low, husky voice she blinked. "I don't want to die here."

"That makes two of us." His face was blurry through the smoke, but even so, he had such a way of looking at her. Like no one else ever had before. "Jimmy set a fire to smoke us out, I'm sure of it. He's a known pyromaniac."

"He's trying to kill us," she whispered, suddenly sad.

"He's trying to kill *me*." He hunkered before her, touched her face. "I won't let him hurt you."

Annie's heart did a stupid little leap at the brave, confident statement. *Taken, Annie. He's taken.* "If we get out of here, I'll never complain about this dress again," she said. "I'll wear it and smile through the entire wedding if I have to glue my lips into place."

"Uh…" His gaze ran over her body. "You do remember you ripped half of it off, right?"

Oh. Yeah. Mostly she just remembered him ripping off his own shirt. That had been nice. She felt a little funny thinking about it. A little light-headed. "Well, the dress does look better now."

"Yes, it does."

She felt his hand on her face. A big, warm, slightly calloused hand, and without thinking she turned her cheek into the palm and closed her eyes. Sighed. Wondered if she started coughing again would he rip off his pants this time. That would be nice. "Hey, cop man."

"Yes, Pink?"

She didn't open her eyes, just concentrated on the feel of his hand on her. "I thought I saw Amelia. From Grunberg. She's my fairy godmother. You know, like Cinderella had? Only she doesn't sing."

"Annie?"

"What would my old nanny be doing here?"

"Ah, hell," he muttered. Then he put his hands,

those wonderful hands of his, on her shoulders and gently shook. "Come on, baby, snap out of it. We've got to get out of here."

Baby. He'd called her baby. It made her smile dreamily. "I'll be your baby," she said. "If you call off the wedding."

"Come." He hoisted her up into his arms, which were deliciously corded with strength.

"Come?" She sighed against the delicious warmth of his bare chest. "I don't know about that." She sighed again and set her head on his very wide, very lovely shoulder. "I should tell you, I can't seem to have an orgasm with a man."

He made a rough sound, and for a moment went still.

She lifted her head and looked into his eyes, needing to know the truth from a man's perspective. "Do you think sex is overrated?"

He choked. His hands tightened on her, and since one was on her bare thigh, and the other on her ribs just beneath her breasts, it caused an interesting reaction within her own body.

*"What?"* he asked a bit unevenly.

"Sex." She put her nose to his shoulder because he smelled good. "I want to know if it's as overrated as I think it is."

"You think sex is…overrated?"

"Um…" Suddenly, with his hands causing such an interesting reaction, she couldn't be sure. "Put me down, I'm feeling better now. I can help—" She wriggled, trying to get loose, but he merely tightened his grip.

"Don't," he demanded, staring down at the bodice of her dress, reminding her that she wasn't exactly sewn in, and that any little unplanned movement could free a nipple without warning.

"Sorry," she said.

"It'd help if you didn't speak or move."

Yes. She could do that. Only because she felt dizzy and nauseous. In order not to stare at his bare chest—possibly the most distracting sight she'd ever seen—she tipped her head up. That's when she saw the corner loft. "There's one more floor."

Just as she said it, a sound came from the exact location they'd just been. The elevator shaft.

Their faces jerked toward each other. His eyes were the color of the darkest of dark chocolate. Her very favorite flavor. "I'm not going to die in this dress," she said.

He squeezed her gently. "Nor me in this tux."

"The loft?"

"The loft."

He set her down. She let him lead, because after all, it had been her idea. And if she had her heart in her throat, wondering if she'd feel the unspeakable pain of a bullet, she could try to distance herself by staring at his butt as they silently made their way to the loft.

Another woman owned that butt, she reminded herself.

They made it to the stairs, ducking and dodging through the rows of boxes. The problem became not the threat behind them, but the condition of the stairs and loft itself. Archaic was too kind a word. Given the heavy layer of dust and spider webs lining everything in sight, whatever was in the boxes up there on the small, rather thin-looking floor had been there a good long time.

Annie put her hand on the wooden banister that was more splinters than handrail. The stairs didn't look any better off, and she wondered if it would even hold their weight. "Good thing I skipped breakfast."

"It'll hold. It's holding all those boxes."

Good point. She wished she believed it. "So up we go then."

"That's right." He touched her arm. "You're

doing great. We'll get out of here yet, okay? Together.''

Together.

He was acknowledging her. Respecting her.

It was entirely possibly every single bone in her body melted right then and there, because never, in her rather adventurous life, had a man really respected her as an equal.

And he was getting married. Well, she'd go home and lick her wounds over the unexpected and startlingly real attraction she had for someone else's husband when the wedding was good and over.

First they had to survive. So up the stairs she went, carefully, wondering if he was watching her butt like she'd watched his. Just in case, she swung her hips, getting so into it that she was at the top of the stairs before she realized her cop hadn't followed her at all.

He was gone, vanished back into the smoke.

KYLE QUIETLY and quickly made his way through the warehouse back to the elevator shaft. Staying hidden by a stack of boxes, he peered out, and sure enough, there was Jimmy, peeking his head out the opening they'd climbed up. Waiting. Gun in hand.

Kyle pulled back. Where were the cops? Waiting for the smoke to flush them out? Did they even realize he and Annie were in here? He didn't know, and one thing Kyle hated was the unknown.

He could make his way to the wall of windows and wave around like a damn flag until they saw him, or he could go back and keep Annie safe until Jimmy was caught. If he'd been alone, he would have said the hell with waiting, and gone after Jimmy himself.

But there was the fire to worry about. And Annie. A princess of all things. He remembered now, in the distant corners of his crowded mind, being told that there would be some very special foreign royals attending the wedding. But he'd been told a million other details, all of which had made his eyes glaze over.

He definitely would have remembered if he'd been told a princess with golden hair and even more golden eyes was coming—a woman with major attitude, a smile guaranteed to drain all brain cells and a body designed to make a grown man beg.

He stole back to the loft. They had to move. But one look produced no Annie. His heart all but stopped. What if she hadn't stayed up there? What if she'd followed him back around, and was right this moment heading toward Jimmy-The-Scum, who took pleasure in hurting people, especially women?

No. She had to be up there. She was smart, she'd hidden herself. God, let her just be hiding. He took the stairs as fast as he dared, imagining her hurt, bleeding, or worse. Taking care, he made his way across the loft floor that was little more than floor joists and a few pieces of plywood tossed down. There were big, gaping holes between the wood that allowed him to see all the way through to the third floor beneath him, and he imagined the worst, imagined—

Anything other than the toes poking out from what appeared to be a stack of forgotten white wedding dresses. The toes weren't moving, and since Annie hadn't been still a single second from the moment he'd first seen her, his blood ran cold. He surged forward on the rickety planks and lifted the white dress.

"What took you so long?" she hissed, pulling his shirt away from her mouth, sitting up so fast he fell back on his butt, narrowly missing a huge gap in the plywood where he would have plunged to the floor below.

Did she worry about that? No, and as if his balance wasn't precarious enough, she smacked him in the chest, making him grab for purchase on a beam that drilled no less than three splinters into his palm.

*"You tricked me into waiting up here,"* she whispered furiously. "You—"

Everything she said was drowned out by the roar of adrenaline in his ears. Her pink dress had shifted again. The hem of the skirt had risen above the line of her silk stockings, and was so high on her thighs he thought maybe he caught another peek-a-boo glimpse of those heart-attack-inducing panties.

The blood roaring in his ears abruptly shifted south. Very south.

But above it all came the one thought that made his heart threaten to burst right out of his chest, the heart he hadn't realized worked.

She was unhurt. She was alive.

So he acted without thinking—which was why he wasn't a brain surgeon—and hauled her up on his knees to face him.

"What—"

He didn't give her time to finish the sentence. She was alive, her lips were parted and she had a very perky nipple once again poking out of her dress. There wasn't a man alive who could have resisted the urge, and Kyle didn't even try. He slid his hands into her hair, his thumbs skimming along the deliciously creamy skin of her jaw as he tilted her head and covered her mouth with his.

She tasted like heaven for one glorious second before a pain exploded in his belly.

Annie pulled back both her fist and her mouth and glared at him.

"Hey," he whispered, rubbing his gut. Being sucker punched wasn't the typical reaction he got when he kissed a woman. In fact, usually they melted like a charm and begged for more.

"You've bossed me around, you've tricked me, you've scared me to death and now you…you *kiss* me?"

"Well…" Logic defied him. "Yeah."

She yanked her dress back into place, which was probably a good thing because now he could concentrate on her face. Her eyes were filled with the fear she hadn't yet admitted to. That really got him, that flash of vulnerability.

"I don't care how good you kiss, you can't just go around—" She glared at him. "Are you listening?"

Yeah. He kissed good. That was what he'd

heard. He risked his life and touched her face. "I thought you were dead."

She didn't punch him, which he took as a good sign, but she did back away. "So that was...a happy-to-see-you kiss?"

"Something like that—" He broke off at the sound directly beneath them and he threw himself at Annie, using their momentum to take them to the far corner, just as a bullet ripped up through the plywood they'd been kneeling on.

Heart tattooing a frantic beat against his, Annie lifted her head to stare at him with horrified eyes.

"Stay here," he mouthed, praying she'd listen as he pulled back. He crawled across the treacherous floor to the stairs, then peered over the edge.

Below, off to the right and hidden behind a box, was Jimmy, his gun hand jerking all over the place.

Kyle glanced up and nearly had a coronary. Annie had scooted toward the ledge on the far side of the loft where he'd left her. Slowly, she stood. Slowly, she lifted one leg over the edge, then the other, holding on to the wood behind her as she prepared to... Good God. She was going to jump!

Down on top of Jimmy.

And Kyle was too far away to stop her, too far away to call out to her or he'd cause Jimmy to look up. He'd shoot her. Kyle had no doubt of that. Jimmy would shoot that bright, sassy, stubborn, amazing, beautiful woman without a qualm.

"Jimmy!" he bellowed, waving his arms. "Over here."

Dutifully distracted, Jimmy swung toward him, and with an evil grin lifted his gun.

Crying like a banshee, Annie let go of the wood and flew into the air. Pink satin whirred. Golden hair whipped her face as she jumped Jimmy.

It all seemed to happen in horrifying, terrifying slow motion.

Jimmy glanced upward. His jaw dropped. He slowly lifted his hand, the one that held the gun.

Kyle leaped over the banister, landing at a dead run and getting halfway there before Annie landed right on top of Jimmy.

The gun flew in the air.

Still in slow motion—or what felt like it—Kyle hauled Annie off of Jimmy, then reached down and flipped the thug over so he was kissing the ground. Kyle wrenched Jimmy's hands behind his back and held him still with a knee to his back.

"This isn't over," Jimmy spit out.

"For now it is." Kyle, breathless, lifted his head

and pinned a furious gaze on Annie, who sat where he'd dropped her. *"You."*

"Me," she agreed, coming to a stand, tossing back her hair, putting her hands on her hips, and overall looking so damn proud of herself he felt his anger dissolving on the spot. "No need to thank me."

His anger returned as he stared at her.

"I saved us," she said.

Jimmy laughed and Kyle dug his knee a little harder into his back. "You want to run that by me again, Princess?"

"Princess?" Jimmy repeated.

"Shut up," Kyle and Annie told him in unison, still staring at each other.

From the direction of the elevator came the sound of running feet. Through the smoke, several uniformed policemen appeared, all with guns drawn.

"Now they show up," Kyle said to no one in particular.

BY THE TIME the fire was put out and Jimmy was hauled off, Kyle had a killer headache.

Annie sat not too far away from him. Someone had tossed a blanket around her shoulders. Her hair had long ago rioted wildly around her face, and yet she looked every bit the princess—chin high, eyes flashing—as he approached.

"You coming over here to thank me?" she asked, and he had to pause. She was a most remarkable woman, he'd give her that. But he didn't want a tough-as-nails, know-it-all, irritating, sexy-as-hell woman in his life.

Annie rolled her eyes and stood. "Who asked you?"

He blinked. "What?"

"You just said you didn't want a tough-as-nails, know-it-all, irritating, sexy-as-hell woman in your life—thank you for the compliment by the way— but I'm wondering…who asked you?"

He'd spoken out loud. Perfect. He would attribute it to the usual adrenaline rush after a close brush with death, as he was most definitely feeling an adrenaline rush.

But he was deathly afraid he felt something else as well. A rush of lust for the hot princess with the cool head. "It's nothing personal," he said. "All I want right now is a nice long leave of absence and a one-way plane ticket."

"To where?"

"Anywhere." He needed to rejuvenate, needed

to figure out what he wanted to do with his life. And if a woman, or two, came along during that time and wanted to wear him out with wild sex, then great.

But he doubted a princess would fit the bill.

AND CERTAINLY no cop would fit the bill for Annie, though it had nothing to do with his profession.

In fact, his profession, and all the innate danger and excitement associated with it, was a turn-on for her.

No, it was his upcoming nuptials that stopped her. Even if just looking at him made her hormones quiver he belonged to someone else.

It was normal, she assured herself. He was a decorated, respected, intense, badass cop. She'd learned those details from his fellow officers, all of whom were as in awe of him as she was.

He was a magnificent specimen, standing there shirtless, his body tough and rugged. She could well imagine her sisters' reaction to him. Lili would blush. Natalia wouldn't. She rarely blushed over anything.

And suddenly Annie was grateful Nat wasn't here to bat her long lashes, and that she alone could look at this man.

He had a streak of dirt over one rock-hard pec and a bruise forming on his equally rock-hard jaw. She had a terrible urge to touch it.

"Well, I'm not interested, either," she said to him. A big, fat lie, but she had no qualms about speaking it, not when her own pride was at stake. "I don't covet other people's fiancés. Not one little bit."

Confusion flickered over his face. "What?"

Annie had plenty to say on the matter, but she didn't want to hear what a fool she was, so she whirled on her feet, taking herself and her destroyed bridesmaid's dress right out of his presence.

And this time, luckily, both nipples stayed where they belonged.

# 5

THE LAST THING Kyle wanted to do that night was play dress up again, but as the best man, he had little choice.

It was bachelor-party night. A time where grown men made utter fools of themselves, all in the name of wedded bliss.

Only a few more days, he told himself, and then he'd be finished with all wedding duties. Not that he didn't feel happy for Kevin, but who'd have thought having his brother get married would be so torturous—on *him*.

"Uh, Kyle? There's something you should know about tonight." Kevin pulled into the restaurant parking lot where the party was to take place, turned off the car and looked at him.

Uh-oh. Kyle leaned his head back against the headrest of Kevin's car and reminded himself that he loved his brother. "Why does the tone of your voice make me quiver in fear?"

"Hey, after facing Jimmy Tarintino, anything else should be a breeze."

Kyle studied Kevin's smile and decided it was a fake one. "What the hell have you done?"

"Oh. Well." Kevin looked straight ahead and shrugged. "It's no biggie, really."

"Then why are you sweating?"

Kevin let out a little laugh. "Have I mentioned I love you, man?"

"Spill it."

Kevin took a deep breath. "Lissa really wanted to be with me tonight."

"It's called a bachelor party, Kev, not date night. No fiancées allowed."

"Yeah." Kevin bit his lip. "She didn't want any strippers."

"Which is why we didn't get any."

"She wanted me to get a good night's rest before the wedding."

"Which is why we're doing the bachelor party tonight, two days before the wedding."

Kevin closed his eyes and dropped his head into his hands. "She really wanted to come."

"Yeah? So did Mom."

Kevin was silent.

And Kyle's stomach sank. Kevin had done

something stupid, he could feel it. "Tell me you didn't invite Mom."

"Worse."

"You told Lissa she could come." When his brother just groaned, Kyle sent his gaze skyward. "Terrific."

"She invited herself," Kevin said into his hands. "All the bridesmaids are coming, too. It's a bachelor-bachelorette party."

"Funny, Kev. You're a funny guy."

"I'm not kidding."

"Ah, hell." Kyle closed his eyes and pictured the scene perfectly. Lissa would be there.

Which meant so would Annie.

"Let's look at the bright side," Kevin said from behind his hands.

"There is no bright side."

Kevin dropped his hands and stared at him for a moment, then let his shoulders sag. "You're right. There is no bright side."

KYLE ENTERED the restaurant, expertly dodged the crowd that immediately swallowed Kevin, and headed straight to the bar.

The bartender was drying a glass as he eyed Kyle's maneuver. "You're good."

"Yeah. Something stiff. Straight up."

The bartender's brows lifted. "Buddy, maybe you'd better rethink this getting married thing if you're stressing already."

"I'm not the groom, I just look like him. If I was the groom I'd have hung myself by now."

The bartender slid him a drink.

Kevin came up and sat next to Kyle. "Hey, Kyle, I thought you stopped drinking after Uncle Joe tossed back one too many and wrapped himself and your beloved Jeep around a tree."

"I've gotten over both losses." Kyle slid his fingers around the cool glass and thought of the evening ahead.

Lots of required smiles.

Required politeness.

And worse, lots of Annie. He took a long swallow.

Kevin stared longingly. Lissa had asked him not to drink tonight, so they'd have clear memories to last them a life time. Kyle shook his head in disbelief.

Clear memories.

Why anyone would want clear memories of getting locked to another person was beyond Kyle.

Besides, he wanted some help forgetting the

events of the day. How he'd nearly bought it. How he'd nearly bought it for an innocent—irritating— woman with the biggest, most expressive gold eyes he'd ever seen.

Kyle went utterly still and ran that last thought again. Yep, he'd just been waxing poetic over a pair of eyes.

He tossed back the rest of the drink and waved for another, which came promptly. He lifted it to his lips but Kevin was just sitting there, looking a little regretful that he'd promised Lissa he wouldn't quench his thirst.

And with a regretful sigh, he passed the glass to Kevin. "Be quick about it, and don't tell her I gave it to you."

His brother put a grateful hand to Kyle's shoulder and took the drink in one swig. "Oh, yeah." He put a fist to his chest. "That's going to do the trick."

"Doubt it," Kyle muttered.

"Well, look who's here."

Kyle didn't turn because he knew that slightly nasal, slightly whiny voice. Lissa. The woman his brother had decided to marry. The woman bound and determined to set up Kyle to the same fate.

"Hey, baby," Kevin said with a smile. "You look real pretty tonight."

Lissa beamed. "It's my prewedding glow."

"No, it's you," Kevin said, and slipped his arms around her.

Kyle looked away and tried not to puke.

"Well, well, well," Lissa said to Kevin. "You're sitting next to the man who single-handedly destroyed one of my bridesmaid dresses."

He could feel her dark eyes boring into the back of his head and wished he had his drink back.

She put her face in front of his and he prepared to die.

"I wanted to thank you," she said, surprising him.

"Look, I'm sorry about the dress," he said a little defiantly. "And the tux." Okay, he wasn't sorry about the tux. "But I wasn't thinking about the clothing while trying to save—"

"I know," Lissa said, and her smile was genuine. "Kyle, I meant it." She leaned in, and kissed his cheek. "I really did want to thank you. And so does someone else." She pulled back and gestured to the woman standing next to her. "Kyle, I'd like

to formally introduce you to one of my bridesmaids.''

Kyle looked into the gold eyes he'd never forget.
She wasn't wearing any horrendous pink creation
now, but cream slacks and a thin sweater to match,
both of which seemed sedate, and almost boyish,
after what he'd seen her in earlier.

He liked it.

Everything about her, from the tip of her leather
shoes to the top of her head, screamed elegance and
sophistication. Her hair had been tended to, the
golden waves falling past her shoulders. She wore
little makeup, but she didn't need it. She looked
natural. Stunning.

And very much like a princess. A very...*angry*
princess.

''It's one of my mother's fondest wishes to have
her best friend's daughter in my wedding,'' Lissa
said. ''You don't know much about my family,
Kyle, but my mother called some very famous people her friends.''

Kyle could care less, but he couldn't take his
eyes off Annie. A woman he'd drilled Kevin about,
and now knew the basic facts. She really was royalty, one of the Three Jewels of Europe, so nick-
named by the European paparazzi. German was her

first language, though she'd been taught English at the age of two by a British nanny, which explained her almost-British accent.

Yet, she was so utterly…real. Tough. Amazing. And he couldn't take his eyes off of her.

Annie seemed similarly afflicted, although he had to admit, while he felt his eyes soften as they landed on her, her eyes most definitely did not soften. In fact, they sparked fire.

Lissa, oblivious to the tension, continued, "Kyle, this is Her Serene Highness Andrea Katrine Fran Brunner of Grunberg." Lissa turned to Annie. "And this is Kyle Moore, Annie. Kevin's brother."

When neither Annie nor Kyle moved, Lissa let out a little laugh. "You two do remember each other, right?"

Remember? He'd never forget. God, she was beautiful. So serene, so quiet and calm. Nothing like the kick-ass woman he'd traipsed with to hell and back today.

But then he looked into her eyes again, caught the flashing emotions, and saw his Annie.

*His* Annie? Oh, boy. Not good.

"Well, at least we won't have that sort of excitement tonight," Lissa said, smiling into the quiet tension. "No gunmen hanging around here, trying to ruin more wedding plans, not to mention wedding clothes.''

What would Annie say if she knew Kyle had grown rather fond of that ill-fitting pink satin dress? And that it had little to do with its inability to keep her perfect nipples hidden?

It gave him pleasure to remember how strong she'd been. He couldn't remember respecting a female more, and suddenly his forced smile felt warm and real. He stood, getting ready to make a little joke about how well she cleaned up.

But she stepped forward and stabbed a finger into his chest. "I remember you just fine."

*Really?* he wanted to say. *Do you remember that first heart-stopping sensation when I kissed you, just before you punched me?*

*Do you remember how we both melted, for that brief moment?*

*Or how about afterward, when we were both safe and there was that strange sense of loss because our time together was over.*

But Annie didn't look like she would enjoy a trip down memory lane. Clearly, she was furious.

Confused, Kyle looked at Kevin, who was gesturing to the bartender for another shot. No help coming from that department.

"Why did you let me think you were the groom?" Annie demanded.

He looked at her again. *"What?"*

"You heard me."

"Yes, but...I never told you I was the groom." Because the idea was so ridiculous, he laughed, and she poked him again, harder. "Stop that," he said, grabbing her finger.

"I made several mentions of the wedding," she spat out, pulling her finger free. "And you..."

"And I...what?"

"You wore that tux."

"Yes, but I sure as hell didn't say I was getting married."

"Yes, but..." She trailed off, staring at him, wide-eyed.

"Yeah," he said, nodding. "You're catching on, now, aren't you? I was wearing the tux because I'm in the wedding, too. Just like you."

She made a low sound that managed to perfectly convey that this was still all *his* fault.

Kevin, on his third shot of liquor now, snickered, but cut it off at a look from Lissa.

"Look," Kyle said, trying to appease, "I had no idea you had me pegged as the groom."

"Well you should have figured out what I was

thinking and corrected me," she said with another stab to his chest. "A woman would have."

He grabbed her finger, and this time held on. "I'm not a woman."

"I..." She swallowed hard. "I did notice that much."

# 6

KYLE STARED AT ANNIE.

Annie stared back.

Kevin lifted his arm for another drink.

Lissa shook her head at the bartender.

Kevin just grinned, already happily drunk. He turned that grin on Annie, who merely lifted a brow at him. For whatever reason, that made him laugh. "So…you really thought Kyle was me?"

"Well…" Annie divided a look between brothers.

Kevin just kept grinning. "Hey, tell me the truth. Now that you see us both together, you'd never make that mistake, right? Because clearly…" He stood and spread his arms. "I'm the best-looking one."

Lissa smacked Kevin on the back of his head.

"Hey," he complained, then let out another stupid grin. "She loves me."

"You should have told me," Annie said to Kyle.

Frankly, he was still blown away by what she'd assumed, and it took him a moment. "If I'm ever engaged—" *God forbid* "—I won't be lusting after a beautiful, scantily clad woman in pink satin while on the run for my life, believe me."

"You—" She looked confused. "You...lusted after me?"

"And I sure as hell wouldn't have kissed her," he finished.

"You *what?*" Lissa shrieked.

Kevin, who'd just sat down again, nearly fell off the stool. "Whoa."

"It was nothing," Annie said firmly, lifting that gold gaze to Kyle's. "Right?"

The earth had only moved, worlds had collided, hearts had bumped. "Right," he lied as their eyes connected. Held.

Shimmered.

"Nothing at all," Annie repeated, more slowly now, her gaze still locked in his. "And..."

Although they all were on the edge of their seats—especially Kyle—whatever else Annie had been about to say didn't come.

It was as if it was just the two of them. As it had been earlier. Scared and dirty and alone except for each other.

Unable to help himself, Kyle stepped a little closer, just a little.

Big mistake.

She smelled like some exotic flower, and his nose itched to press even closer.

"My God." Lissa stared at them, then let out a little laugh. "You two...together...who'd have thought that the sweet little princess and the hard-ass cop—"

"Hey, I'm not a hard-ass," Kyle said.

"Yes, you are," Kevin said.

"And call me sweet little princess at your own risk," Annie said. "But back to this."

"You mean you and Kyle," Lissa said.

"Yes. No! There is no me and Kyle."

"But about the kiss—" Lissa started.

"Yeah, about the kiss—" Kevin said.

"Forget the kiss," Annie said tightly. "It lasted only a second."

"So there *was* a connection," Lissa clarified.

"No," Annie said, glaring at Kyle. *Don't you dare tell them about what happened between us,* her eyes demanded.

Too bad Kyle didn't respond well to demands. Never had. "Now there's no reason to get anyone's panties tied in knots."

Annie shot him another silent dagger.

Oh, yeah, that anger in her eyes was a definite turn-on. "Kevin and Lissa just want to know what happened, right?"

Lissa's and Kevin's heads bobbed in collective agreement.

"But nothing happened!" Annie said through her teeth. *"Nothing."*

"Okay," Kyle said with a shrug. "Whatever. I was only there. What do I know?"

"Really," Annie said, weaker now in the face of Lissa's open curiosity.

Ooh, if looks could kill, Kyle thought as he absorbed Annie's staggering death look, he'd be dead as a doornail right here on the spot. "At least you remember who saved who, right? Because I definitely came to your rescue, Princess."

Annie fisted her hands in her hair and let out a strangled scream of frustration.

"And as the victim," Kyle went on, feeling pretty damn pleased with himself for some reason, "it's understandable you'd want to grab on to the person that saved you. It's a hero-worship thing, very common. Just try to restrain yourself."

"Oh, this is ridiculous! Leave it alone, all of you!" Annie let out a slow breath when Lissa blinked in hurt surprise. "I'm sorry. It's just that it was nothing. *He* is nothing."

"Hey," Kyle said.

But Lissa was standing in front of him, blocking his view as she hugged Annie tight. "Don't you worry about a thing, Annie. Not one thing. Forget about Kyle. Focus on the good news. I have five seamstresses working around the clock to replace your dress. Everything will be fine. Just fine."

Annie paled at the mention of the dress being remade, and Kyle thought maybe he enjoyed that even more than bickering with her. "Oh, Annie?" he called as she was led away by Lissa. He lifted Kevin's shot glass in a silent salute. "Can't wait to see that dress again."

She sent him a roll-over-and-die look before she allowed Lissa to pull her away.

*HERO WORSHIP, MY EYE!* Annie thought, so furious she could hardly see. She stormed out of the bar and through the restaurant, toward the wall of French doors at the far end. She figured fresh air would help cool her temper.

It didn't.

She figured the gorgeous view of tall mountains and mesas would help soothe her.

It didn't.

Unbelievable how riled up he could make her. He was just a cop. A tough, remarkably quick-witted and sharp cop, yes. Traits that under any other circumstances she might even admire.

*Might.* If he didn't drive her so crazy.

And he thought she worshiped him. Ha! "The only thing I feel for him is the insane need to wipe that smirk right off his face," she muttered, gripping the balcony railing with white knuckles.

"Careful," came a low, unbearably sexy, unbearably familiar voice. "You're talking about the guy who rescued you."

"You," she fairly spat out, refusing to look.

"Yeah." She didn't have to look to see his smug expression, she could hear it in his voice. "Me."

Her fingers gripped the railing even tighter as her mind and body warred. One wanted to look at him and the other wanted to—damn it—look at him.

She refused. "I came out here to be alone. As in just me."

He didn't take the hint, instead came forward and leaned on the balcony right next to her. So close his arm brushed hers. His face, when he turned it toward hers, was still smug, and so close she could see the setting sun dancing in his eyes.

Her breath backed up in her throat because he was so gorgeous. Too gorgeous. And incredibly sure of himself.

And damn, if that didn't make him all the more attractive.

"So...why are you so upset?" he wondered, reaching out with one finger, rubbing it over the crease she knew appeared in her forehead when she got herself worked up over something.

To say she was worked up now was the understatement of the year.

"Annie?"

"What?" she whispered.

"Why are you so upset?"

"Because..." *Because you do something to my insides and I don't like it. Because I'm melting over the way you're looking at me, and I don't like that, either.* "I'm not harboring some secret hero fantasy over you," she said defensively.

He lifted a shoulder. "Okay."

"I'm not attracted to you. Not in the least."

"You're sure protesting a lot."

"Did I mention I wanted to be alone?"

"Yep." He straightened and reached for her hand. "But what the princess wants, she doesn't always get. Not tonight, anyway. I was sent out here for you. There's something Lissa wants you to see.''

''Unless it's the Exit sign,'' she muttered, ''I'm not interested.''

His laugh was low and sexy. ''You should know I was ready to leave the moment I got here.''

That surprised her. He seemed the type of guy who could have fun at his own funeral. He'd certainly had enough fun at her expense. ''What made you stay?''

''Besides being afraid of Lissa if I left early?'' Suddenly there was no teasing in his gaze. ''You.''

She stared at him for one long beat, then tossed her head back and laughed. ''Right.''

''No, really. I—''

At that moment, Lissa and Kevin and a crowd of others, piled out onto the deck.

''You nearly missed it.'' Lissa grinned while two waiters put out a couple of chairs. ''Sit,'' she said to the groom and his best man. ''I've ordered you each a special present. Just because you allowed me to join you tonight doesn't mean you can't have a traditional bachelor party.''

Kevin and Kyle looked at each other. Annie tried to decipher the look on Lissa's face and gave up.

Two uniformed women officers pranced—and

there was no other word—onto the deck. Before Annie realized what they meant to do, they'd hand-cuffed each brother to their respective chairs.

This started an immediate party on the deck as the two cops began to dance.

The *woo-hoo*ing and catcalling got louder. The music was turned up.

And the two "cops," thrusting their ample breasts and booties in the men's faces, began to strip.

The crowd went wild.

Kevin blushed beet red.

Not Kyle. No, he just sat there, clearing enjoying the show. He certainly couldn't miss it, Annie thought darkly, as the exceptionally built, red-headed stripper kept putting her...parts right in his face.

It repelled her, disgusted her. It did.

But it also made her legs inexplicably rubbery. It made her thighs ache, and she couldn't tear her gaze away.

And when it was over, she was still standing there, mouth a little open, when Kyle came up to her, obviously still full of himself and mischief.

"Did you enjoy the show?" he asked.

"Of course not."

He lifted a brow. "You're not too uptight to admit that was fun, are you?"

Uptight? She wasn't uptight! There wasn't an uptight bone in her body!

"Are you a prude, Princess?"

She was still assimilating the uptight insult. When she managed to switch gears, she had to pause.

Uptight, no she definitely was not uptight.

But prude...? Damn it, maybe she was. Being a tomboy had given her a certain degree of freedom when it came to how she lived her life. But it had also limited her when it came to relations with the male of the species. "I just still think sex is overrated, that's all."

His good humor faded and his eyes darkened with a light of challenge she couldn't miss. "Then you haven't been with the right man."

"Oh, yes. Do tell." She crossed her arms to hide the fact that even her nipples reacted to his sexy voice. "I suppose *you're* the right man. Would that be correct?"

"Are you asking?"

*Was she asking.* Lord, no.

But his lids had dropped over his eyes a little

bit, giving him a sleepy, sexy look as he studied her mouth.

Her tummy fluttered.

"Princess?"

How was it possible that just his voice could render her a twisting, melting mass of hormones? No man had ever done that to her before, and she'd tried. Oh, baby, how she'd tried.

"Are you asking?" he repeated with infinite patience.

"No. I'm definitely not asking."

"Hmm." The sound assured her he saw right through her. "You be sure to let me know if you change your mind."

*Change your mind,* her body begged.

She ignored her body. Not an easy task since said body was fairly humming in a completely foreign way she suspected was helpless lust. "I won't." But because she sounded weak, she tightened her arms and repeated it. "Of course I won't."

But a little shameful part of her wanted to.

# 7

THE BACHELOR-BACHELORETTE party lasted a lifetime. Two lifetimes.

Annie couldn't wait until the last toast. Couldn't wait to get to her room, strip down, shower and go to sleep.

Once asleep she would dream of such comforting things as ice cream. Of her home in Grunberg where the sharp, magnificent mountain peaks and comforting, familiar alpine towns and people provided her with all she needed.

Or better yet, she wouldn't dream at all.

She certainly wouldn't think of pink satin.

Or the upcoming wedding.

Or of one sexy but cocky, stubborn, smart-aleck cop named Kyle Moore.

Nope. Not a single thought would be spared for the man she didn't care one iota for.

That decided, she smiled and toasted and actually salvaged a good time, from this nightmare party. And when it was over, she breathed a sigh of relief.

Once back at the inn, in her room, she switched her slacks and sweater for her favorite pj's, which consisted of a spaghetti-strap tank top and a pair of men's cotton boxer shorts.

"Perfect." She flopped on the bed, grabbed the remote, and prepared to be amused by late-night American television. *The Brady Bunch* maybe, or even her sister Natalia's favorite, an old Clint Eastwood movie.

*Nat, I wish you were here to argue over the remote with me. I'd even give it to you tonight.*

But then the phone rang. It was the front desk. A message had been left from Her Serene Highness Natalia Faye Wolf Brunner of Grunberg.

Natalia. Her best friend. One of the few people Annie trusted through thick and thin. Nat would never let her down, never. She must be coming in early, Annie thought with giddy relief. A familiar, loving face in the midst of this horrific wedding, thank you God!

Then what the desk clerk said sank in. "Could you repeat that, please?" she asked with remarkable calm, because clearly, she needed a hearing aid.

"Yes, ma'am, I can repeat. She has poison ivy and will not be attending the wedding."

"Poison ivy?"

"Poison ivy."

"But…" Annie shook her head. Natalia, the leather-wearing, multipierced sister who acted so tough, and yet was afraid of animals much less the outdoors, had poison ivy? Was that even possible? "How did she get it?"

"Well—"

"Where is she?"

"I'm sorry. That's the message in its entirety."

"It can't be."

"It is, ma'am."

Annie had no idea what the real story was, but it wasn't poison ivy. She set the phone down and felt far more sorry for herself than her sister, who certainly had found something better and more exciting to do than attend a wedding.

Annie would kill her when this was over. With pleasure.

Just then the door adjoining her room to another guest's opened, and in piled a group of women, with Lissa leading the pack.

Shocked, Annie sat straight up.

"Didn't I mention I had the next room over?"

Lissa beamed. "Cool, huh? Now we can have an official girl party."

She carried a tray filled with what suspiciously looked like makeup and accessories. Annie narrowed her eyes as the three women with her—Lissa's sisters, and all bridesmaids—plopped on the bed. "What is that stuff?"

"The ingredients for a girl party, of course." Lissa looked at Annie critically. "You've got good skin, but there's no telling what's just beneath the surface. A full facial," she said over her shoulder. "We'll all do full facials. Then we'll start in with the pedicures. Must have good toes. Did someone bring the pink nail polish?"

Facials. Pedicures. A fate worse than death. Annie hated makeup with the same passion she hated pink satin dresses and pink satin nail polish. She wore mascara because she looked like a zombie without it, and sometimes she even remembered blush. But gloss was the most she used on her lips, and she'd never, ever, had a facial. "I don't think—'

"You'll have to strip."

*"Excuse me?"*

"I brought this new breast cream for all of us. It'll give us great cleavage with our dresses."

"Lissa," she laughed, but no one else joined her. "This is a really bad idea."

Lissa, stirring the cream she actually thought Annie would put on her breasts, looked up. "What? Why?"

"Because…" Quick, Annie, think. "Because…"

"Oh, I'm sorry." Lissa's smile fell. "At home in Grunberg you probably have beauticians to take care of you. You'd never have to actually do this yourself. I…didn't think…other than I know our moms used to do this together, in boarding school. You know, give each other facials and do their hair and stuff. My mom talks about it all the time."

With the loss of her mother twelve years before, Annie's life had taken a drastic turn. There had been no more froufrou influence, no more pots of makeup and perfume lining her mother's room. Back then, Annie had already developed the tomboy side of herself, but without her mom, there'd been no stopping her. And she'd never looked back.

Lissa studied the cream in her hands. "I just thought for old times' sake…" She started to gather up the things she'd bought. "Never mind. I didn't mean to insult you. This all probably seems tacky to a princess, doesn't it?"

Annie sighed inwardly and managed a smile in Lissa's dejected direction. "You didn't insult me. Really. I just didn't expect—"

"I know. Forget it."

"No, this is *your* wedding," Annie said, feeling about an inch tall. "And whatever you want, goes." *God help me.* "If you want to slather sh— *stuff* all over your face—"

"And breasts," Lissa's youngest sister Sharise added helpfully.

"And breasts," Annie said bravely, suppressing a shudder. "Then okay. That's what we'll do."

"Oh, Annie. Really?"

Annie looked into Lissa's hopeful face and made herself keep smiling, even as she renewed her vow to kill her sister Natalia at the first opportunity. "Really."

"You first?" Lissa held up the cream.

"Uh…" Annie tried not to shrink back. She did manage, barely, to keep her hands at her sides rather than cover her breasts, which is what she wanted to do. "Well…"

"Do you want me to do it?"

"No!" Annie lowered her voice and let out a little laugh. "I can do it, thanks."

"You sure? My mom says your mom loved to be fussed over."

Her mother *had* loved being fussed over. A manicure or new hairdo had been her greatest joys, which she'd loved to share with her daughters.

They had all spent many an afternoon together, Annie's sisters and their mother, lounging in their castle home after school, waxing poetic over some new nail color they'd discovered, while Annie had chomped at the bit to get back outside and mess herself up all over again.

She lifted the cream with a hopeful expression. *Mom, I hope you're laughing in heaven.* "I've got it handled, thanks."

# 8

A GIRLIE PARTY was every bit as bad as Annie feared it would be. Which is how she found herself with curlers in her hair—so tight to her scalp she'd never need a face-lift—her entire face slathered in a mud-colored mask guaranteed to "pull out all those nasty wrinkles you haven't yet developed," and her nails painted the most atrocious color of pink that Lissa promised would match her new dress.

Goodie.

But all of it paled in comparison to the sensation of ice-cold cream applied to her breasts with the promise to "uplift and rejuvenate."

"Not that you need any rejuvenating," Lissa said cheerfully after the equally torturous removal of said cold cream. "You have great breasts."

"Um...thanks. I think."

"No, really."

Annie covered herself back up with the spaghetti-strap tank top and wondered if Kyle had thought so, too. Then she got mad at herself for wondering such a stupid thing and switched to wondering how long before she could kick everyone out of her room without insulting them.

Then someone knocked at the door.

"Grand Central Station," she muttered, and hopped off the bed, passing by a mirror and nearly leaping out of her skin at the sight of her curlers and mask. Please let someone have screwed up and sent room service up with ice cream.

With fudge to pour over the top.

Beneath her top, her breasts brushed against the soft material. They felt the promised revitalization, and were extremely sensitive. She wondered if Kyle would notice when she once again put on the dress from hell the day after tomorrow. Then she wondered why she cared what he thought.

She would have laughed at herself, but it'd crack the face mask, and if she cracked it, she was afraid Lissa would insist she start over.

If she had to start over with this beauty regime, she might go postal. And since weddings were supposed to be happy events, she took a deep breath and sucked it up.

Not that it was easy. For all her self-proclaimed

inner strength, she felt a little fragile. A little vulnerable. The events with Jimmy had taken their toll, no matter how she told herself it shouldn't. "Sucking it up," she reminded herself. With a sigh, she hauled open the door, prepared to kiss the feet of the room-service attendant bearing ice cream.

But the person standing on the other side of the door was not room service bearing ice cream.

Kyle stood there holding up the doorjamb with his broad shoulder, looking big and edgy and even yummier than she remembered.

"That's twice now," he said.

She was just stunned enough to repeat him. "Twice?"

"That I've made you speechless." He tapped her nose. "I have to say, I'm fairly speechless myself, Princess."

She gasped and brought her hands up to her face, remembering she looked like the Bride of Frankenstein. "Oh my God."

"Kyle?" Lissa came up behind Annie. "Honey, what are you doing here? This is girls only. Now scat. We've got facials and manicures and breast treatments going on."

Kyle stopped short. "Breast treatments?"

"Yes, they enhance and smooth," Lissa's sister cheerfully told him. "We've all been creamed." Her hands went to the buttons of her blouse. "Want to see—"

"No," Annie said quickly, stepping in front of her. "I'm sure Kyle here can use his imagination."

"Yeah. My imagination." Kyle was looking a little unfocused. A little dazed.

Until his eyes met hers. "How about you, Annie? Want to show me what you've creamed?"

"Very funny. Now get the hell out of here."

"You sound a little hostile there. If I didn't know better, I'd say you didn't want me to stick around— Hey!"

She'd put her hands on his chest and pushed. Big mistake. Not the push, but her hands on his chest. First of all, she didn't budge his solid mass. Second of all, her entire body quivered in delight at the feel of him beneath her hands.

Pathetic. She really was. "Just get out."

Lissa was grinning stupidly at them. "You two really do have a thing for one another."

"What?" Annie managed to laugh through her mask-stiffened face. "Don't be silly."

"It's adorable."

"It's crap," Annie said.

"I didn't know princesses could say crap," Kyle said.

"You like each other," Lissa insisted. "I can see it all over your faces."

"Lissa, my face has an inch of green stuff on it."

But Lissa wouldn't be deterred. "I've heard all about stuff like this, how under immense strain and pressure, especially under the threat of death, people who are polar opposites—and believe me, the two of you *are* polar opposites—come together."

"We did not come together," Annie said, flicking Kyle a dark look when he simply lifted a brow.

"Know what I think?" Lissa continued to bestow a proud, happy look at them. "I think there was more than a kiss. I think you did the wild thing."

"Okay, here's what *I* think." Annie didn't care if her hands were going to tingle forever, she put them back on Kyle and once again tried shoving him out the door. "I think we need to get rid of the single male ruining our female party."

"Oh, Annie, that's so sweet," Lissa said, putting her hands together. "I didn't know you were so into it."

"I'm...into...it," she puffed, trying to budge the unbudgeable Kyle. "Help, please."

"No, you know what?" Lissa let out a smile that didn't ease Annie one bit. "We're done here. I think we'll just leave the two of you alone. In case you have more...wild things to do."

"Funny," Annie said, but started to panic when the girls all packed up their stuff and headed for the door. "Wait! Don't go! My face—"

"Just wash off the mask in five more minutes," Lissa said.

"But my hair—"

"Take out the curlers in ten."

Annie plastered herself to the connecting door. "You can't go."

"Why?" Lissa asked.

"Yeah, why?" Kyle echoed.

Because then she'd be alone with Kyle, who stood there looking so damn sure of himself in jeans, a soft-looking shirt and hiking boots. Sort of like a walking advertisement for *Outsider Magazine*. She loved that magazine.

"Lissa, the breast cream," she said in a desperate, last-ditch attempt. "It didn't work. We need to do it again."

Lissa grinned and tossed the jar to Kyle, who caught it with ease.

"I love applying breast cream," Kyle said.

Annie felt a scream of frustration coming on, even as Lissa tugged her away from the door. "But—"

But nothing. The door shut in her face.

Leaving her alone with Kyle Moore. Cop. Best man, not groom. Tough and big and gorgeous. Holding breast cream.

*Please,* her body begged.

*No.* Flings weren't for princesses. She knew this for a fact, as she'd tried hard to make it work for her before. Flings weren't for women with secret dreams of happily-ever-after.

*And how are you supposed to get that happily-ever-after if you keep shoving everyone away,* a little voice asked.

She ignored the little voice. She stared at the wood door in front of her and willed herself to relax.

*You are not attracted to the man behind you.*

But she was.

*Well, then you will not admit to being attracted to the man behind you.*

No matter what he did or said.

"ANNIE?"

She didn't move, just stared at the door in front of her.

"Annie?"

"Go away, Kyle."

"But I just got here." He watched the back of her head covered in curlers, imagining he could see the wheels inside turning like crazy.

Poor baby. She was studying the wood grain of the door as if it held the utmost fascination for her.

*She* held the utmost fascination for him, though he felt vaguely uncomfortable with that realization. She wore only a skimpy little tank top and boxers, nothing else. Her bare feet curled into the rug. Her legs were toned and tanned and looked silky smooth. So did her arms. But it was the back of her neck, exposed by her tipped head and the fact that her hair was being tortured by the curlers, that really drew him.

He wanted to kiss her there. Then turn her around and dip his gaze to see for himself what that breast cream had done for an already perfect set of breasts and the most mouthwatering nipples he'd ever seen.

But she didn't move, and he sighed. She was going to be difficult.

"Problem?" he asked.

"No. No problem. What makes you think there's a problem?"

"Because you won't look at me."

"Maybe I don't like to look at you."

"Annie."

"Why are you here?" At her sides, her hands fisted. "Haven't you humiliated me enough today?"

"Humiliated? You're kidding, right?" He took a step toward her, so that the only thing that separated them was the ridiculous curlers in her hair. The tip of her head didn't quite come up to his chin, and the oddest feelings slammed into him.

Protectiveness.

Possessiveness.

Oh, man. Big mental step back here. *Biiiigggg* one. "I never humiliated you."

She let out a low laugh and continued staring at the door.

Ah, hell. Why *was* he here? He could no longer remember, but felt certain it had something to do with wanting to tease her about the strippers and her reaction to them. About offering to strip for her, just so she didn't feel left out.

He hadn't expected his tomboy to be wearing a

facial mask and breast cream, looking so...well, vulnerable.

"I'd like you to leave—" She gasped when he tossed the breast cream to the bed and whirled her around.

"That's better," he decided, keeping his hands on her shoulders to prevent her escape. "Talk to me, not the door."

"The door cares about my feelings more than you do."

That stunned him for a moment, during which time he realized he was still holding her. She felt good in his hands, damn good, and before he could help it, he'd shifted a little closer. "I care about your feelings."

"No, you care about the cream."

His gaze dipped down to the edges of the tank top, and the smooth curves plumping out of it.

"You're wondering."

He looked into her face. "Wondering?"

"If I still have the cream on."

No, he was wondering which bridesmaid put it on for her and if they'd let him watch next time.

"Kyle?"

He was lost in the fantasy. "Hmm?"

"I'm waiting with bated breath to hear why you're here."

Why he was here. "The strippers." He was pleased to remember. "You were bothered by them. And I…" Nothing to do here but speak the truth. "I was going to offer to make you feel a little easier about it. You know, the whole stripping thing."

"By…"

"Well…" He tried his most charming smile. It wasn't a tool he used often, but whenever he had put it to the test, it hadn't failed him yet.

Annie just stared at him.

Damn. It failed him. First time for everything, he supposed. "I was…uh, going to offer to strip for you."

She let out a laugh. "And that would have made me feel more comfortable, how?"

Her voice said, "not interested," but as he watched, her nipples puckered. *Gotcha,* he thought.

"You know this might be a huge shock to your ego," she said, crossing her arms and thereby removing his most excellent view. "But I'm not interested in you."

He took another step forward, watching with amusement as her chin came up. She refused to back up, though, his lovely, angry princess, which suited him just fine as it allowed her body to brush his. "Let's stick to the truth," he said.

"Which is?"

"Which is..." He reached out and ran a hand over her mud-slathered jaw. "You're attracted to me, every bit as much as I'm attracted to you. You're yearning and burning to find out if we'd be as combustible together as it seems. And..." he leaned in to speak directly in her ear, his lips just brushing her skin, causing a shiver that wracked his body as well as hers "...you want to know if making love with me would be...what did you say? Overrated."

She went utterly still.

"It wouldn't be, Annie. It'd be perfect."

He would have sworn she let out a little sound that conveyed her reluctant arousal at his words before she turned and jerked open the door.

"Good night." Her voice shook just a little.

"Annie—"

*"Good night."*

"Dream of me," he said, walking past her.

Because he sure as hell would dream of her, and misery loved company.

# 9

By THE NEXT NIGHT, Kyle had reaffirmed his decision to not get married. He'd truly had no idea how many functions one single wedding could create.

He'd been to breakfasts, lunches, dinners, meetings with caterers and florists and photographers, and quite frankly, was getting tired of holding his brother's hand.

"You're on your own," he finally told Kevin, the night after the bachelor-bachelorette party. They were standing in the open area downstairs, where Kevin was trying to talk Kyle into some partying on his last night of freedom.

Tuning out his brother, Kyle looked across the room and met a pair of golden eyes.

Annie had one hand on the stairs as if she'd intended to go up. She wore a pair of faded jeans and a simple T-shirt. Her hair flowed loose. Just a woman, a regular woman.

Who happened to be a princess.

Who happened to be more bossy than his own sergeant.

Who stirred his blood.

"Kyle?" Kevin waved a hand in front of his face. "Earth to Kyle."

"Yeah. I'm here." When he turned back to the stairs, Annie was gone. He ignored the quick stab of regret. "I'll tuck you in if you'd like, but then I'm going to crash."

"Never mind." Kevin's eyes lit with trouble. "I think I can find my way to a bed."

"Not Lissa's," Kyle warned. "It's the night before the wedding, remember? I think getting lucky is out of the question, unless you're getting lucky alone."

"Hey, I'm getting a marriage certificate tomorrow, which states I never have to get lucky alone again."

"You keep thinking that. And anyway, Lissa's at her wedding shower tonight, remember? Girls only." Kyle shuddered at the thought of having to attend a wedding shower. "She made me promise to keep you away."

"Don't worry, I'm not going to make you crash the shower." Kevin sounded disgusted. "I mean, heaven forbid you get lucky by accident. What's happened to you anyway? You used to be such a slut.''

Kyle didn't want to think about that, or why he suddenly—as in the past four days suddenly—wasn't interested in going on the prowl. He stared up the staircase, wondering if Annie was going to wear that skimpy little tank top and those sexy-as-hell boxers.

''Does this newfound sainthood have anything to do with one mouthwatering beautiful European royal?'' Kevin wondered, following Kyle's gaze.

''Of course not.''

''Of course not,'' Kevin repeated, then snorted his disbelief. ''Right.''

''Say good-night, Kev.''

Kevin sighed. ''Good night, Kev.''

''THIS ISN'T A *co-ed* shower, right?'' Annie wanted that clarified up front. ''Just us girls, right?''

Lissa laughed. ''Just us girls.''

A little suspicious after last night's fiasco, Annie walked into the lounge area of Lissa's honeymoon suite where she'd moved earlier that day. Annie was feeling on edge and overly alert.

The room was decorated for a bridal shower, no

doubt. Silver streamers cascaded from the ceiling. Silver and the all-too-familiar-pink balloons floated around the room, among flowers and presents and the biggest cake Annie had ever seen.

She hoped it was an ice-cream cake. She really needed ice cream.

With a broad smile, Sharise handed Annie a large silver-and-pink gift bag. "Here you go."

"What is it?"

"Your outfit."

Annie already had an outfit, thank you. She'd changed from her jeans and T-shirt into a very comfortable pair of slacks and a lightweight sleeveless sweater with a pair of flats she'd be comfortable in walking anywhere. "What do you mean?"

"Oh, didn't Lissa tell you? This is a theme shower."

Annie blinked. "A theme shower."

"Yes. Our theme tonight is lingerie. *Sexy* lingerie. A woman from an expensive boutique has put it all together for us. We were each supposed to log online and purchase an outfit for Lissa. Didn't you do that? We're going to model them for her."

"Um…"

"I can't wait to see how we all look."

Annie did not have a good feeling about this. "But as Lissa is the bride, shouldn't *she* try all the stuff on herself?" She hid her gift bag—with her own nicely wrapped present which was most definitely not sexy lingerie—behind her back.

Sharise laughed, then put her hand on Annie's shoulder. "You are so funny. Lissa and I had no idea how funny you were."

Being told she was funny when she was utterly serious gave Annie a very bad feeling. "Sharise, explain this bag you're handing me."

"The invitation explained it all, didn't you read it?"

Uh, no. She hadn't. Amelia had stockpiled all the invitations for her, warning her to go through the entire stack, which of course she hadn't.

*Told you,* came Amelia's stern British voice in her head, so crystal clear that Annie actually turned around and looked for the woman.

No one.

Annie shook her head. This wasn't the time to debate her sanity.

"Oh, you royals." Sharise laughed again. "I know how busy you are, and how many assistants you all have. I guess you never got around to reading about all the wicked fun we're going to have."

Wicked fun? Oh, boy.

"But *someone* picked out something for you to give Lissa." Sharise opened her own bag and lifted out a filmy white teddy that absolutely would not cover the essentials, and a matching "robe" that would only enhance the deficit. The matching slippers were white satin, four inches minimum, and fur topped. "This outfit is from me. Pretty, don't you think?"

Yeah, if one was a virgin sacrifice. "Well—"

"You should see the one Lissa has to wear tonight. It's this pink little number, and…"

"Looks like Little Bo Peep? Does it match the bridesmaid dresses?"

Sharise frowned. "Don't you like the bridesmaid dresses?"

Oh, dear Lord. "Sharise, you don't by any chance have any aspirin, do you?"

Sharise laughed. "Like I said, you're very funny. Show me what was picked out for you to model."

Annie looked into the bag and saw black. Black shiny vinyl. Black vinyl straps that couldn't possibly cover anything important.

"Oooh," Sharise breathed. "Very naughty. And check out those boots at the bottom of the bag."

Which were also vinyl with stiletto heels nearly five inches high.

"Can't wait to see that, a sweet little princess all decked out in dominatrix gear." Sharise tossed her head back and laughed.

"I'm not going to wear this." Whatever it was.

Sharise sobered. "Oh, but you have to. It's all part of the fun, you'll ruin it if you don't. Please?"

"Sharise—"

"I'd better come with you," Sharise decided, taking her arm, leading her to the bathroom. "I can't have you chickening out."

Chickening out? Is that what they'd think? Annie never chickened out, never. Two incredibly competitive sisters had made sure of that. Besides, she did have the kick-ass lingerie, shouldn't that make her feel a little better?

Sharise tried to go in the bathroom with her. "I've got it handled," Annie said, blocking the way.

"You might need some help getting it on." Obviously Sharise wasn't sure Annie would do it.

But Princess Andrea Katrine Fran Brunner of Grunberg didn't chicken out of anything. She peeked into the bag again and felt a little faint.

*Damn it, Natalia, this should have been you.* "I'll be fine."

"Okay," Sharise said doubtfully. "But call me if you need help."

"Call you. Got it." Annie shut the bag and tried not to picture how bad it could be. Whatever it was, she had the feeling she'd rather wear the Little Bo Peep bridesmaid dress for the rest of her life.

IT WAS A SURPRISE all right, the kind that provoked heart attacks. Stunned, Annie could only stare at herself in the mirror. Her frown made the entire getup that much scarier.

"Annie, hurry!" came Sharise's voice from the other side of the bathroom door. She'd been knocking every two minutes for twenty minutes now. "We're starting the games."

"Oh, yippee." Annie took once last shocked look at herself and opened the door to the virgin-sacrifice Sharise. "Don't want to miss the games."

Sharise's jaw dropped to the ground. "Holy smokes."

"What?" Was it worse than she thought?

"You look...wow."

"Yeah, yeah. Let's just do this." Annie started to walk past the white-lace teddy-covered Sharise, then reached back for the whip on the counter. With a grim smile, she stalked out of the bathroom.

Sharise just shook her head. "Honey, don't take this wrong, but you have the best ass I've ever seen."

Annie tripped over the stupid heels and nearly broke her ankle. "That's just because it's hanging out."

"That it certainly is."

At their arrival in the front room, the small group of lingerie-clad women all stopped talking and clapped. Lissa got up, dressed in what indeed looked like underwear Little Bo Peep would have chosen for herself.

Annie's eyes narrowed. "Wait a minute. How come yours covers all your parts?"

Lissa laughed. "Don't worry, my parts aren't nearly as fabulous as yours. I just hope I look half as good as you when I put that on for Kevin."

She was going to actually wear this for her soon-to-be husband. Annie looked down at herself. She wore a black vinyl thong—which brought new meaning to the word uncomfortable—and a black vinyl crop top that barely covered her nipples. The black garters and stockings—complete with seams down the backs of her legs—and the shiny, high boots, only added to the effect.

Then there was the impressive whip she held in her hand. "You're going to put this...this *outfit* on for Kevin?"

Lisa eyed the whip and waggled her eyebrows. "Of course."

Annie had had a hard enough time putting it on for the women to gawk at her. It was beyond her fathomable imagination to picture putting it on for a man. "In the daylight?"

Sharise laughed. "Annie, you are so funny."

Annie was beginning to dislike that statement. These people were insane. She hadn't come to New Mexico, she'd come to the twilight zone.

Feeling quite bare in the behind, as every little breath brushed air against her far-too-exposed butt, Annie was relieved to sit on the couch so the games could begin.

Her relief was short-lived.

"The first game is called Rate The Stud," Sharise called out happily.

Sure, why shouldn't she be happy, *she* had a robe to cover all her parts.

To play, they all had to stand up, face Lissa,

and tell her a studly thing about her soon-to-be husband.

Annie decided right then and there she needed a break. Actually, she needed air. Quickly, quietly, she escaped to the patio. No one followed her, and she felt like a death-row inmate granted immunity. Having been told the men were all out of the way for the night, she walked to the railing without fear of being discovered, leaned over and dragged in some air.

The wedding was tomorrow. Marriage. Commitment.

*Forever.*

Words she'd thought about in a vague sense, but had never really applied to any of her relationships so far. How could they when just by being herself—a rather opinionated, strong-willed woman, that is—she always scared men away?

If truth be told, she *wanted* a man to love her to distraction. She wanted a man who didn't care what she looked like in the most horrendous shade of pink that ever existed. She wanted a man who'd go out of his way to please her, even if it meant having a really stupid bachelor-bachelorette party.

She wanted a man to want her—not her title or her bank account—but her, Annie, the woman.

From inside came the sound of cheers, and Annie knew they must be doing the promised fashion show. She couldn't do it, she just couldn't.

Driven by these shaky emotions, that she couldn't have explained to save her life, Annie moved into the shadows and walked the length of the balcony. She'd just go back inside via the next room over and sneak up to her room.

Simple.

Only nothing in her life was simple. The next room, which looked like a den, was dark.

And locked.

The room after that, possibly a library, was also locked.

And so was the next.

And the next.

Something akin to panic drove her on, in her shiny, skimpy black lingerie that rode up where it shouldn't and threatened to uncover parts of her that should never see the light of day or, in this case, the dark of night.

Then she imagined having to go back to the fashion show, and pressed on.

Cool evening air caressed her skin. She tried not to picture how she looked—a solid mass of goose bumps on skin far too fair for a black vinyl thong.

A mosquito buzzed by her. She narrowed her eyes. "Bad mistake, bug, I've had all I can take tonight." She wielded the whip and hit pay dirt.

Then tripped on her heels.

Good thing the paparazzi hadn't followed her to Taos. She could only imagine the headlines.

Princess Annie Changes Her Image.

Tomboy Princess Annie Goes Hookerville.

News At Eleven.

Her father would kill her. Her sisters would never let her forget it. And Amelia...the woman who'd been like a mother to her, her mentor, her friend, would slowly shake her head and yet at the same time somehow make it all better.

Amelia always made it all better.

Annie wished she was home.

Especially when she found the next door locked, too.

*Keep your head,* came Amelia's voice, strong and real. Annie didn't bother looking around, she knew Amelia wasn't standing there. And then, good luck. The very next room, also dark, also very quiet, had an opened window, with curtains softly blowing from the light breeze.

*Keep your head.*

Just as always, from across the globe, Amelia came through.

Lifting a stocking-clad, thigh-high-booted leg, Annie swung it over the windowsill.

KYLE HAD HIT dreamland. He was waist-deep in a hot tub filled with big-breasted, naked women, all there to give him pleasure.

Maybe this wasn't dreamland, it was heaven.

*Water lapped at his chest. A blonde sank into the hot tub in front of him, with a knowing, promising, wicked smile on her face. Her mouth hovered right above where he wanted it...*

A sound startled his subconscious. *Don't wake up,* he told himself. *Don't even think about it.*

He sank back into the tub with the women, all of whom pressed closer to stroke their hands over his body while the blonde—

The window in his room slid all the way open.

Damn.

He came all the way awake, and was very unhappy about it. Dreams like that didn't come along every day, and he'd been just about to get lucky, very lucky, as he hadn't in some time.

Swiping a hand down his jaw, he blinked and stared at the figure straddling his window, one leg in and one leg out.

It was female.

He knew this because of the outline of the most luscious, curvy body he'd seen in a good long while. Slowly, a bit confused now, he sat up.

Was he still dreaming? The body silhouetted in front of him definitely could have been one of the bodies in the hot tub he'd just been dreaming about.

But, no. Not a dream. He was a cop all the way through to his soul. At the slightest noise he always came awake. He was definitely awake now. He threw the covers aside.

The woman, one leg in his room and one still out, went utterly still.

"Who's there?" he demanded.

Another long frozen second, and the woman shifted, started to pull back out of his window.

"Oh, no, you don't," he said, and surged out of bed to the window, grabbing one silky leg.

He knew that leg. He'd know it anywhere.

# 10

HE HAD HER by the calf, and there was no doubt in Annie's mind who he was.

His hand was gliding up, up, up, and then his fingers were gripping her thigh.

"Let go," Annie choked out, trying to pull back out of the window, panicked that someone would flip on a light any minute, and highlight the outfit she still couldn't quite believe she had on.

But for now, at least, they were in utter darkness. "Damn it," she snapped, her breath backing up in her throat. Of all the rooms in the entire place, she had to pick his. Just his fingers on her skin had her insides doing the happy dance. "Let go!"

"I don't think so."

"Well we can't just stand here."

"You're right. Don't move, I'll turn on the light—"

"No!" She lowered her voice with great effort. "Don't even think about it."

She heard his soft laugh. Soft, *sexy* laugh that the rugged, uncompromising man didn't let go of often enough. Her tummy fluttered. Her nipples tightened, which meant they scraped against the rough material barely covering them.

"You ever heard of the word *please?*" Kyle wondered aloud.

She drew a breath in and tried not to scream. "Don't turn on the light. *Please.*"

"Why?"

"Because…" Oh, hell. "Because I'm not exactly dressed for company, okay? Now let go of me and back off. I can't breathe around you."

"That's very interesting, and we'll get back to that in a second, but for now I'm interested in the not-dressed-for-company thing." His hand skimmed up her back, her *bare* back, and slid under her hair. His thumb caressed the sensitive skin there. His other hand moved up her thigh, then her stomach. Also bare.

He let out a low whistle, his hands still roaming.

"Kyle," she warned.

"I've *got* to still be dreaming." His voice was husky and a little thick now, as his hand settled high on her ribs. If he so much as twitched his thumb he was going to get breast.

"It's not a dream, it's my life and it's a nightmare," she told him grimly. "Now, I'm going to back out of this window. And you're going to go back to bed and pretend this never happened."

"Tell you what." His naughty fingers continued to play with her skin, causing shivers. "Let's do this all friendlylike, okay? You come all the way in here and tell me what's going on."

"Or...?"

"Or I flip on the light."

"How is that friendlylike?" she demanded, but as if he read her mind on jumping out the window, he tightened his hold on her.

"Come on now," he said, gently forcing her into the room. Before she could so much as knee him, he had her in the window and on his bed.

By the time she leaped back up, he had the window and curtains closed, and then she was blinking like an owl in the bright light he flipped on.

His jaw dropped. "Holy sh—"

"I told you." She crossed her arms over her chest, which didn't exactly help. When she did that, the whip she still held nearly hit her in the face. She stared at it, hissed in frustration and dropped that arm to her side. "I'm out of here," she decided, and stormed toward the door.

Giving him an unwitting view of the back.

Or lack of, in this case.

He swore again, reverently, then beat her to the door, holding it closed. "Princess." His voice was hoarse. "You're...missing a few items of clothing."

"Don't tell me, you were class valedictorian, right?"

He ignored that to let out a rough groan as his gaze devoured her. "You're...dressed like a dominatrix."

"Your powers of observation are startling." She pulled on the handle, but with his weight against the door, it didn't budge. "You might not have noticed this part of the costume." She lifted the whip. "But believe me, after tonight, I'm not afraid to use it."

He actually almost smiled. "Hey, I'm not afraid of a little role-playing."

He'd let her... Oh, good Lord.

"Let me guess." He fingered the whip. "The bridal shower?"

"You're laughing at me."

"I wouldn't dream of it."

"Great. Fine. Go ahead and get some amusement out of this. Just as long as you let me out of here.''

"You're just going to walk down the hall dressed like that?'' His eyes were dark, and very, very hot as they ran over her body, stopping at the plunging neckline of the bra that barely covered her nipples. "You're going to need that whip," he said. "As every single male you see is going to drop his tongue and follow you like a puppy.''

She snorted. "Oh, please.''

"Do you have any idea how you look? Or what the back of that thing shows off? My God, Annie. You're the most amazing—''

"Right.''

"—gorgeous, mouthwatering—''

"Are you going to be a gentleman about this or not?'' she interrupted, not pleased at how his compliments warmed her.

He considered carefully, then slowly, almost regretfully, shook his head. "No.''

"Kyle, damn it.'' All warmth vanished. "Give me a shirt at least.''

"You'd need more than a shirt, you'd need a potato sack.'' He craned his neck and took another good, long look at her butt. "Tell you what.'' He straightened, and this time his body seemed closer. "I'll rescue you. On one condition."

They were just barely touching now, and she realized she'd been so furious that she'd missed a very important fact.

He was wearing only a set of knit boxers. Very well-fitting knit boxers. "Um...you're not dressed."

"Yeah." He nuzzled at her neck. "You startled me out of a great dream, but this is even better."

"The condition, Kyle."

He just stroked a long finger down her jaw. "Hmm?"

"The condition," she fairly screamed. "You'll rescue me on one condition, though I'm almost afraid to ask."

His expression came slow and wicked and made every single bone in her body dissolve. "Oh, yeah. Be afraid. Be very afraid." He leaned close, whispering, "Because my condition is this." His finger slid down her throat now, and she shivered at the touch. At her involuntary movement, his eyes were positively slumberous. "You've said sex was overrated. I can't seem to get past that, Princess. Let me prove you wrong."

She slapped his hand away. "No way."

"What are you afraid of?"

Afraid? She wasn't afraid. Just the thought of letting him prove her wrong got her juices going. Hell, just his voice did that.

But she couldn't...it would be out of the question...*no*. She was terrifyingly close to caring for this rough and edgy man. She'd rather march down the hallway in this outfit than be here another moment. Than let him disprove the only theory she had that made her loneliness okay. Sex was nothing. Sex wasn't worth her time. Sex was overrated. Yes, she really had to stick with that theory. "Sorry." She reached for the handle again, hoping against hope she could make it to her room without anyone seeing her.

But what if she couldn't?

The thought of being discovered was enough to have her face burning. Her fingers were still on the handle though, and she'd lose face if he didn't try to stop her one more time. "I'm...going."

He nodded and stepped back. "Okay."

"No, really." She lifted her arms to remind him of how she was dressed. "I'm walking down the hall just like this."

"I heard you." He reached past her. "Here. Let me get the door for you."

Oh, God.

He opened the door, but before it got more than two inches, she slammed it shut, pressed her back to it and glared at him. "You're a jerk."

"I've been told." His lips quirked as he crossed his arms. "You have options, you know."

"The decent one would be for you to help me out."

"No one ever said I was decent." He shot her another naughty look.

"Kyle."

"Yes?"

She bit her lower lip, pride warring with common sense.

Finally, he laughed. *Laughed.* And if she wasn't so pissed, she would have loved the sound of it. "Oh, baby," he said. "If you could see your face. You want me to beg you to stay?"

"Please," she whispered.

"Don't you know, in that outfit, you could have whatever you wanted? Stay, Annie. Stay and let me prove you wrong. I'll make it worth your time, I promise. I'll let you do whatever you want, you call the shots." He fingered the whip and waggled his eyebrows. "Unless, of course..."

"Unless?"

"You're chicken."

"*Chicken?*" she repeated incredulously, forgetting her near nakedness and her nerves. "That's the second time today someone has said that. I'm not a chicken!"

But as she stood there, mind whirling, trying to figure a way out of this ridiculous mess, she knew the truth. She *was* a chicken. She was a big fat chicken who'd rather face public humiliation than what she felt for a man.

This man.

Because more than any other, he mattered. Stupid, stupid, stupid. Where was Nat when she needed her? No one on earth was more fond of telling Annie when she was being stupid than Nat was.

Okay, she just needed to play her usual routine she had perfected. Run hard and fast in the opposite direction. Which she would, as soon as she was fully clothed again. "Okay."

He lifted a brow. "Okay?"

Oh, wasn't he ever so confident, leaning back, arms crossed, lips slightly curved. She may be temporarily defeated but she wasn't ready to call uncle yet. "You said I could do what I want. Well, okay,

I'll do what I want. I'll…'' She looked at the whip in her hand. "I'll spank you."

His smug look vanished in a heartbeat. His arms dropped, and so did his jaw. In his gaze was such a shocked surprise she burst out laughing. "You should see the look on *your* face, it's priceless."

"So you were kidding."

"No." She shot him back his own smug smile. "Not at all." Lifting her chin, she flashed him eyes filled with daring. "I'm tougher than I look."

"Well you look pretty tough right now." His hand slid down her arm to her waist, which he gently squeezed. "Tough on the surface, anyway. But inside, where it counts, I'm thinking you're soft and sweet. Are you soft and sweet, Annie?"

"No." But she stumbled over the word, and not feeling so certain anymore, she drew in a shaky breath. "Are we still playing? Because if we are, I'm not sure I— You should know, I don't play well. Ask anyone who's ever dated me."

He lifted a hand and slid it beneath her hair to cup the back of her neck. "We've already established that they're all selfish jerks who don't know how to please a woman."

"They were diplomats and foreign royals and heads of state and—"

"Selfish jerks," he repeated softly, his breath warming the skin beneath her ear. "I know how to please a woman. I'd make it good for you. Now... let's get back to that not being able to breathe around me thing. Are you breathing now, Annie?"

She let out a shaky breath and stepped away from the door, which put her nearly up against him. "I don't know."

When she tipped up her face, he took it as an invitation. The first touch of lip to lip was electrifying. He kept it gentle, had to keep it gentle, or he'd lose it. Nibbling at the corner of her mouth, he drew in the scent and feel of her. When she let out a reluctant sound of arousal, he shifted to the other side of her mouth and figured he'd never get tired of her.

"Kyle..." Her hands came up to his chest, probably to push him away, but instead they held on. She breathed his name again, more of a sigh this time. A sweet surrender completely at odds with the outfit she wore. All the blood racing through his body drained to parts south.

"Kyle...is this part of it? Where you prove my theory wrong?"

He opened his eyes and looked into hers. She thought he was still playing. Still messing with her.

And to be fair, it had indeed amused him to tease her. It had amused him to watch her fumbling response.

It didn't amuse him to suddenly realize he *wasn't* playing.

Nor did he want to.

He'd gone and done the unthinkable. He'd let down his guard. And like the enemy that most emotions were, she'd sneaked in past his guard, wormed her way into the one place he thought she never could.

His heart.

"Kyle?"

He ran his hands down her slim back and felt the vinyl banded over the softest, most creamy skin he'd ever felt. "I have to be honest," he said, his voice hoarse as he danced his hands down to her hips. "I have no idea what this is."

She let out a sound that might have been a laugh or a sincere agreement, and pressed her face into the crook of his neck. "You smell good. Like a... *man.*"

Now he let out that same sound, only from his

lips it sounded desperate. Hungry. "Do we all smell the same, then?"

"No." Face still pressed against him, she shook her head. Her golden hair slid over his chest. "You smell different. Good different," she said quickly, lifting her head to smile. "I'm glad, because if this had been like any of my other experiences…"

Did she mean that they were going to… "Annie?"

"I want you to prove me wrong," she whispered, sinking her fingers into his hair and pressing that tantalizing body to his. "Please, Kyle. Show me what it's supposed to be like."

He had a vinyl-clad beauty writhing against him. This was what he'd wanted. His ultimate fantasy. Only, suddenly the implications were more important than the actual lovemaking. He knew that was because his heart had gotten involved, had thrown a whole hell of a lot of caring into the mix.

Her mouth was against his ear. "You still want me?"

"Only more than my next breath," he assured her, letting his hands slip as they'd been dying to, letting them roam over her perfect, round, and very nearly bare butt. At the feel of her, he groaned.

"Trust me, wanting isn't the problem. But the wedding is tomorrow and then you're out of here."

"All we need is now."

Yeah. That's all he'd ever lived for. The here and now. But...

"I'm not looking for promises, Kyle. Other than the one you gave me, that is." Her smile, a little shy, a little wicked, nearly killed him. "That sex isn't overrated. Can you still do that?"

"Oh, yeah."

"Here?" She put her mouth to his neck. "Now?"

"Here." He could barely stand, but he slid his hands up her sides so that his thumbs were just beneath her tightly bound breasts. *"Now."*

Their kiss was hot, long and messy, and made his head swim. He couldn't get enough, but eventually had to pull back or pass out from lack of oxygen.

She stood there, eyes closed, mouth wet, weaving slightly. He waited, and when she opened her eyes, they were glazed.

"Annie?"

"Oh, good." Her voice was husky, and she cleared her throat. "Annie. I'd forgotten my name."

He'd nearly forgotten his. He certainly had forgotten everything else. "I'm doing it right, then," he said with some relief.

She gripped his upper arms and slid her body against his. "Just keep doing it."

"Yes, ma'am." When his thumbs stroked over her nipples, her head thunked back against the wall. "Good?"

"Good. *More.*"

"More on its way." He leaned in to kiss her again but she slapped a hand to his chest.

"More *now.*"

He had just enough breath left to let out a low hum of agreement but he still didn't move faster. "If I rush, I might miss something. Annie, sweetheart, have you noticed you're overdressed?"

"Yes. Fix that."

"Absolutely, my little dominatrix."

# *11*

WHEN HER HANDS tightened in his hair, drawing him closer, warm skin brushed warm skin. But there was still that heart-stopping lingerie between them where he wanted nothing. His fingers met between her breasts, searching for the release hook.

Nothing.

He tried around back.

Still nothing. "Annie..."

"Hurry."

"Hurrying." Because he was feeling a bit desperate, he dipped down and cupped her bottom in his hands. Now that was good. He played with the little strap dividing her cheeks, following it down...

"*Kyle.*"

With one hand still cupping a cheek and the other splayed over the pure gold between her legs, he went still. "Are we stopping?" If so, it was entirely possible he would beg. Maybe cry.

"You said I was overdressed." Her voice sounded funny. Tight. Needy. "You said you'd fix that."

"Right." He pulled back just a little and frowned at the contraption still holding in her breasts. There was no apparent hook, zipper or release. "How did you get into this thing?"

She blinked, then pulled back, looking a little suspicious. "I thought you said you knew what you were doing."

"Yes, but—"

"How can you follow through on your promise if you can't get me out of my clothes?"

Good point. He tried harder, running his hands up and over her breasts, around the back, but—

Annie's breath was coming in little pants. Her eyes were closed, her mouth open a little, and he realized all his efforts to strip her was turning on someone else besides himself.

Which turned him on even more, if that was even possible. So he kissed her again, sliding his aching body to hers, lifting one of her thighs to his hip so that he could press even closer. Her hips arched up to meet the slow, desperate thrust of his. He bent, running hot, openmouthed kisses down her jaw, her neck, over the plump curves of her breasts plunging out her bra. When his tongue dipped beneath the vinyl to stroke a nipple, Annie's knees buckled.

Or maybe that was his. ''Bed.'' He was barely holding them both up.

Annie's hands streaked over his chest, his arms, his quivering belly.

''Bed,'' he said again, more weakly now.

''Yes.'' Then she dipped into his knit boxers and cupped him. By some miracle, he kept them both upright, but he had become blind, deaf and mute.

''You're really good for it,'' he heard her murmur in surprise through the roaring in his ears.

''What?'' he managed.

''Your promise. You're…really good for it.''

Good. That was good. He was good. Everything was good.

Her eyes were still glazed, her face flushed. ''I've never felt like this,'' she whispered in a hungry voice that brought him even closer to the edge, not to mention her busy fingers. ''I'm hot from the inside out, Kyle. I need your hands on my bare skin. Why aren't your hands on my bare skin?''

''I'm trying. How the hell do I get you out of this?''

Her mouth was racing over his face, leaving a trail of eager, hot kisses. ''I don't know. Rip it.''

"But—" He broke off because she took those long, warm fingers of hers and squeezed his erection. "Annie."

"Kyle."

Against his neck, he felt her smile. When had the power shifted, he wondered wildly? He felt like a damn virgin. All finesse had flown out the window. "I'm trying to concentrate on driving you crazy here."

"Just do it faster."

"Faster. Got it." He dipped his fingers into her cleavage. Magically found a hook and freed it.

Her breasts spilled into his hands. His mouth took over while his hands worked at losing the thong.

Then she stood there in all her naked glory.

She smiled. "You look…"

"What?" he asked, his gaze drinking her in. "Desperate?"

"Yes."

"Because I feel desperate."

"I think you really do," she said with marvel. "It's almost as if I have all the power."

"Baby," he said on a sincere groan. "You do. Right in your very hands."

She looked down at his most urgent erection and

let out her own wicked grin. "I'm doing it right, then?"

"Most definitely right," he croaked out as she slowly stroked him.

"Here. Now. Remember?"

Here. Yes. Here was good. Now was even better. But on the bed. Twisting from the door, he dropped her to the mattress. He slid his hands up the back of her silky clad thighs, making a spot for him. *Slow,* he reminded himself when she opened for him. *Make it good.*

He was still working on the slow part when she guided him to where she wanted him most, and he slipped inside.

Heaven. Hot, wet, glorious heaven. But—

"Kyle." Panting, Annie opened to him more fully. "I promise to never say sex is overrated again if you just..." Her inner muscles tightened around him. "If you would..." Her hands pulled at his hips. "Move!"

"Move. Moving." And ignoring the niggling in the dim recess of his mind, he moved them both to high heaven and back.

It wasn't until it was over, until they'd drifted off to sleep that he remembered what the niggling had been about.

A condom.

Or more correctly…the lack of one.

How had he so lost himself? Well, that was easy enough to answer. He'd started out the seducer and had ended up being the seduced.

Even more shocking…he'd fallen in love.

Wouldn't Kevin get a kick out of this. Hell, everyone he knew would get a kick out of this.

But what would Annie think?

He doubted she'd be doing the happy dance. Still, it all had to be faced, especially the condom part. He cracked open an eye, startled by the shift in shadows, realizing a good amount of time had passed.

And that he was alone.

KYLE DISCOVERED the hard way just how difficult it was to talk to a bridesmaid on the wedding day. Actually, it wasn't just difficult.

It was impossible.

By the time he'd managed to stumble out of bed before dawn to look for Annie, he realized two things. One, the entire place was asleep, and two, she'd helped herself to the pair of his sweats he'd stripped out of before he'd gone to bed.

He stepped on something and looked down at

the torn dominatrix outfit. The quick spurt of hot satisfaction sizzled out quickly as he realized he'd have to wait until the sun came up to talk to her because he couldn't go sneaking his way through the sleeping bridesmaids' rooms trying to find Annie, who obviously didn't want to be found—especially at 3:00 a.m.

But at morning's first light, he tucked the thong in his pocket, braved the stairs and entered what he and Kevin had dubbed "The Froufrou Zone."

It was empty.

A maid scurried by and he stopped her. "Where is everyone?"

She laughed in disbelief. "On the morning of the wedding? Are you kidding?"

Did he look like he was kidding? "No, really. Where are they?"

"At the salon getting their fingernails, toenails, face, hair and anything else that needs doing, done."

"But…" It boggled his mind. "That could take hours."

"Many," the maid agreed. "And if the groom is very, very lucky, they won't be too late to the church."

Great. Now he had to go the entire day without talking to her. Unless... "Which salon?"

"Don't even think about it, bro." Kevin came up the stairs and swung an arm around his shoulders. "Entering a woman's domain like that would be scary stuff. They might insist you need a facial or something." He studied Kyle curiously. "And I thought this wedding stuff gave you the hives anyway. What do you need a bunch of women for, when they're all running around like their heads are cut off?"

"Um..." What did he need her for? Let's see. First, he had the torn thong in his pocket. Second, they'd made love and had forgotten a condom.

Oh, and third—this was the biggie—he'd fallen in love.

But Annie had left him in the dark of the night, stealing out of his room without a word, so he figured he might want to keep that last thought to himself.

Kevin waved a hand in front of his face. "Yoo-hoo."

Kyle slapped his hand away. "Stop it."

"What do you need Annie for?"

"Who said I needed Annie?"

Kevin leaned back against the wall, looking awfully at ease for someone who was hitching his life to another person in a matter of hours. He also looked annoyingly full of patience. "Why don't you just admit that this love stuff is sorta addicting, Ky, huh? That maybe even you can fall and fall hard."

"I don't know what you're talking about."

Kevin had the nerve to laugh, the ass. "Look at you, tough big brother, all jittery. You're sweating, did you know that?"

Before Kyle could strangle his brother as he was itching to do Kevin straightened and headed for the stairs.

"I'm going to get our stuff," he said. "Meet me in the car, you're driving me to the church." He paused and looked back. "On the way there you can tell me about your night. I heard it involved black vinyl."

WITH THIRTY MINUTES left before Kevin put the ball and chain around his neck, Kyle stood in the church dressing room wearing only his shorts.

Where was Jimmy when he needed him? He could use a good hold up as a diversion right now. But, no, he'd had to go and get the guy thrown in prison. Which meant nothing could save him. He had to put on the tux hanging in front of him. He had to go out there and be the best man.

He didn't feel like the best man. He felt like a frustrated one.

Not talking to Annie was a good thing, he reminded himself. Not talking saved face and pride, because God knows, if he'd gotten a chance, he'd have only made a fool out of himself.

Yeah. That was the attitude he was going with.

With a sigh he reached for his pants but the door behind him opened and hit him in the butt. Righting himself, he caught a flash of pink satin.

"You're not going to believe this," Annie said, skidding to a halt in front of him and grabbing his arms. "Not in your wildest dreams."

"Uh…" He ran his gaze down her pink satin nightmare of a dress. "Your sheep ran away and you need me to herd them for you?"

She grimaced. "See? You think Little Bo Peep, too!"

"Baby, that's the last thing I think of when I look at you."

She went still, hands on his arms, eyes locked on his. "Kyle—"

"I've been waiting to talk to you," the stupid part of his brain admitted out loud.

Suddenly she seemed to realize he was more than half-naked. With a hard swallow, she covered her eyes.

"Hey, you've seen it all before."

"Just…take care of it."

"Well, okay." Purposely misunderstanding her, he put his hands on the elastic band of his shorts. "But you don't have to be so rough. I already proved how easy I am."

She dropped her hands and squealed when he went to pull his shorts down. "No!" She checked over her shoulder after her loud cry, then lowered her voice with apparent effort. "I'm not here for… for…"

"Overrated sex?"

"Look, torture me later, okay?"

"I'd like that."

"Kyle, Lissa is in the women's facilities."

"Is that princess speak for the bathroom?"

"Yes, the bathroom!"

"Oh my God," he said in mock horror. "Ring the press. The bride is in the bathroom."

"She's refusing to marry your brother, you idiot. I need your help."

"Well, damn, I thought you needed—"

"I know what you thought," she said quickly, covering her eyes again. "Just…get dressed. Fast."

"Yeah, yeah." He jammed his legs into the black pants, then slipped his arms into the shirt, fumbling with the cuff links on the shirt.

With a sound of exasperation, Annie pushed his hands aside and took care of it.

"You're good at that," he said, wondering if he should be jealous.

"I used to help my father," she said in an oddly soft voice. "Not…"

"Not…?"

"You know…other men."

That shouldn't have made his heart leap, really it shouldn't have.

"And…" She drew a deep breath, her hands brushing his chest as she buttoned his shirt for him. "Last night…well, you know."

"No, I don't."

"When we—"

"Ah. The black vinyl."

"It was more than black vinyl."

"Yes, it was. What we did was—"

"Yes," she said quickly. *"That."*

"For the record, are we talking about when we made love?"

"Sex. We...had sex. And it wasn't overrated, okay? It was...well, pretty much off the scale. Just so you know."

With that shocking, and arousing, statement, she grabbed his hand and pulled him out of the dressing room.

# 12

HE WATCHED her Little Bo Peep butt wiggle as she led the way. "Annie—"

"Shh," was all she said. "She's going to screw everything up unless you fix it."

Whoa. *He* was supposed to fix this? Hell, he couldn't fix his own life.

That's when she tried to tug him into the women's bathroom.

"Now just a second." The last time he'd been in a women's only bathroom had been in sixth grade. A group of ninth graders had forced him in, where inside had been the entire girls' basketball team, changing.

He'd been suspended for a week, and the horror of it still made him dig in his heels at the threshold. "I can't go in there."

"No?" Annie gripped his arms and went up on tiptoe to whisper in his face. "If you don't, she's going to break your brother's heart."

Damn. He tried to peer inside the bathroom. "If there's a naked basketball team in there, I'm going to be mighty upset with you."

She looked at him as if he'd lost his mind. "What?"

"Never mind." He walked in, his hands stuffed in his pockets, looking straight ahead. The place was decorated in gold angels, and had a couch. A *couch*. What did women need a couch in the can for? "Lissa? You in here?"

*"Go away."*

Ah, hell. The voice came from behind a locked stall, under which he could see a bunch of white satin. He crouched down and spoke into the space beneath the door. "Hey, maybe you didn't know, but they're playing your song. Here comes the bride."

He heard a loud sniffle.

Oh, God. *Tears.*

"I can't do it, Kyle," she sobbed. "I can't even remember why I wanted to."

"Uh…" He searched his brain and came up with the reason Kevin had given him. "Because you get to have sex every night— Oof." He rubbed his gut and glared at Annie. "What? It's true."

"That's a *guy's* reason," she whispered furiously.

From behind the door came more sobs, and Kyle could only sigh. "Lissa, I thought you wanted this."

The sobs increased in intensity.

Annie stared at him accusatorily, as if it was *his* fault his brother's fiancée had gotten cold feet.

He lifted his hands in surrender.

Annie pointed under the stall.

Oh, no. No. He wasn't going in.

She crossed her arms and gave him the you-are-pond-scum look that every woman seemed to have in her bag of killer expressions.

Ah, hell, he was going in. "Open up, Lissa."

"No."

Of course not. With another sigh, he went to his knees and prepared to climb under. "If I ruin another tux, I'm not taking the fall for it." He got stuck when his broad shoulders jammed under the door, and he bashed his shin, twice. Jerking back, he slammed his head into the stall divider. Stars clouded his vision. When he blinked them clear, he was blinded by white satin. Miles of it.

"Scoot," came a direct order from behind him. The next thing Kyle knew, there was also miles of pink satin as Annie slid under the stall with much more grace than he had, forcing him to put his arms on the walls to brace himself in the sea of satin.

Now all three of them were squished into place—Lissa sitting on the closed commode lid, he and Annie practically joined at the hip in the remaining few inches. Cozy.

"Well." He looked at both women, one of whom was sobbing into her hands, the other was glaring at him. Oh, yeah. Cozy as hell. "Let's go have a wedding, huh? We can straighten out all these details later."

Annie shook her head.

Lissa just cried harder.

"But…" He searched for a reason to end this. "Lissa, if you keep crying, you'll ruin all the makeup you spent too much on."

Annie rolled her eyes heavenward.

Lissa bawled.

"Lissa, please." He resorted to begging without hesitation. "I'm bad at this. Just talk to me."

"Talk to you?" She lifted her wet face and flung back her hair. "Can you tell me why I thought that love was so cool that I agreed to wear this stupid dress and march down an aisle in front of hundreds of people I'm not sure I even like to say, 'I do'?"

She swiped her nose with toilet paper. "And do you realize I can never wear granny underwear again?"

"Uh…" Kyle glanced at Annie, but there was no help coming from that department. "Look, I doubt Kevin cares what kind of underwear you put on."

"Men don't like granny underwear," Lissa wailed anew. "But that's what I always wear on laundry day." Standing, she gripped Kyle by the lapels. "So many things are going to change. What is love about, Kyle? Do you know? What's love? *Tell me!*"

Annie raised a brow and looked at him with less animosity than curiosity.

Oh boy. "Love is about…" *Blow this, and toss out any plans you had for great sex tonight.* "Well, it's not that difficult, really."

"It's not?" Annie frowned doubtfully. "Then tell us—er, Lissa. Tell Lissa."

He drew a deep breath, but no answers magically appeared. Then he looked into Annie's gold eyes and suddenly it became clear. "Love is about wanting that person safe," he said.

"Safe, smafe." Annie looked disgusted. "A person can keep themselves safe."

"Then...it's about making that person happy," he said, feeling brilliant. "Yeah, that's it."

"A person can make themselves happy," Annie said, with far less animosity now.

Two strikes. One more and he was out. "Then it's about how you feel in the other person's presence." He closed his eyes and dug deeper. "It's about how you become a better person because they've been in your life. How you want to be that better person for them."

Lissa sniffled and sank back to the commode. "Really?"

Well, yeah. Really. At least Annie didn't shake her head this time. Instead, her eyes filled with something other than anger, and he was pretty certain it was wariness now.

She thought he was messing with her again.

If only he was. She had no clue that she was the one woman who'd brought him to his knees. "Love is about always being there for that person," he added softly, staring right at her. "Even when you think they're being stubborn and ridiculous."

Another sniffle from Lissa, but Annie never took her eyes off Kyle. "Maybe you should keep talking," she said.

"Love transcends all barriers."

"Such as a distance of thousands of miles?" she asked.

It was as if it was just the two of them. If he didn't count the yards of silk and the bride sitting on the commode between them, glued to their every word. "Those miles mean nothing," he said, and meant it. "Nothing to a person not attached to any one place."

"But some people *are* attached to their one place."

"And some aren't." He wasn't. With his eyes he tried to tell her that, tried to decide if it even mattered to her. "With love, being together is all that is important. Everything else falls into place."

Lissa burst into tears again.

His heart sank. "Lissa—"

"Shut up." She stood so that the three of them had so little room they were breathing each other's air. "Just shut up. You had me with the stubborn, ridiculous part. Oh, Kyle…" She threw her arms around him. "That was so beautiful. Now get out of my way or I'm going to be late. I can't be late for my own wedding." She opened the door, but before she went out she grabbed both Annie and Kyle close to her in a bear hug that spread perfume and lipstick all over his neck. "I'm going to make this work because I love that big, old lug," she vowed. "But if he ever pisses me off, I'm going to kill him." She pulled back and smiled. "Just want you to know up front."

Then she was gone.

Silence reigned.

"That was quite a speech," Annie said.

"Yeah."

"Did you mean it?"

Before he could answer, Lissa was back, sticking her head in the stall. "Hey! If I have to go, so do you, remember?" She grabbed each of them and tugged them out of the stall, out of the bathroom and down the hall to the back of the church, where the music had already started.

"This is it," Lissa hissed, still holding on to them with a death grip. "Oh, God. Kyle, I hope you know what you're talking about because I'm about to get hitched. Now take Annie and escort her down the aisle. Be sure to turn around and smile at me when you get there to remind me this is a good thing, okay?"

Then she was shoving him, and Annie was on his arm, looking breathtaking in spite of the pink dress that didn't suit her, and they were walking down the aisle.

ANNIE WATCHED the wedding take place as if from a great distance. Through this nice, comfy, blessed distance she didn't feel much more than a stab of pain watching Kevin watch Lissa come down the aisle. There was so much love on his face it made the entire audience tear up.

From that same distance she watched Lissa repeat Kevin's promise of love and felt another stab. She watched them smile dreamily at each other and seal their vows with a kiss and felt yet another.

When it was over, her chest ached with the pressure. She was barely holding it together, and she didn't know why. Then she saw the one person in the audience that made her throat tighten all the more.

Amelia Grundy. She'd come. The sixtyish, rather tall and formidable woman was built as round and solid as a brick, but when their gazes met, Amelia's entire demeanor softened, and Annie felt weak with homesickness.

"Hello, lovely," Amelia mouthed, her sharp blue eyes warming. As always, her silver hair was on top of her head, and as always, she wore tweed.

At just the sight of her, Annie nearly burst into tears. On Amelia's lap sat the satchel she'd carried as long as Annie could remember. It was filled with all sorts of useful items like cookies and pliers and the requisite romance novel.

Wildly, Annie wondered if she had fairy dust in there, anything in which to sprinkle over Annie and make this all come out okay.

*Chin up, don't let him see you cry.*

Annie straightened, startled, staring at Amelia. She could have sworn Amelia had spoken that out loud, which of course she hadn't.

But how did Amelia know? Well, of course she knew, Amelia knew all. And the woman had always known Annie's mind better than even Annie knew it.

Suddenly she was driven by some need to turn her head. She found Kyle watching not the wedding, not the audience, but her.

He was tall, dark and heart-stoppingly gorgeous. He was rough and tough, intense, sharp and had a job.

Her favorite qualities.

But—there always seemed to be a but when it came to her happiness—they were worlds apart.

Literally.

Not to mention he had no idea she'd done the unthinkable, that she'd started to fall for him. It was asinine, really. They hadn't known each other long enough for her to even contemplate such a thing.

Which hadn't stopped her from tumbling into bed with him last night, had it? She'd done so with shameless abandon, and because it had been the best night of her life, she couldn't bring herself to regret it.

But it sure as hell was going to make it all that much more difficult to walk away. And she *would* walk away. Grunberg was her heart, her home, her life.

And she was going back tomorrow morning.

THE RECEPTION was loud, boisterous and joyful. But Annie had trouble putting a smile on her face. Around her people were cheering as the newly married couple walked around arm in arm greeting their guests.

Annie sighed and wished she was home. Or that Nat had made it. Wished she could find that distance again so she didn't feel the ache in her chest that she couldn't—or wouldn't—explain to herself.

*It's not like you to accept defeat, lovely.*

Annie whirled around, but Amelia wasn't behind her.

She was hearing things again. Telling herself the melancholy was normal—after all, she'd been through a lot in just a few days—she moved outside, desperate for air.

She'd be happy to go home, but...

No. No buts. She was a grown woman who'd chosen to scratch an itch, that's all. And the itch had definitely been scratched.

Only she still itched...

She heard someone walking toward her. Now she was going to have to smile. Make nice. The reception was in a fancy place made for such events, and Annie had moved as far away as she could, standing just outside a set of glass French doors. She leaned over the balcony and studied the glorious New Mexico landscape and willed whoever it was to keep walking.

But it wasn't just anyone. It was Kyle.

She didn't feel like smiling and making nice for him. She felt like slugging him because...she didn't even know. He'd been a temporary diversion. A very nice temporary diversion, and she'd never forget that he'd not only saved her life but taught her that sex wasn't overrated.

Not overrated at all.

In fact, just thinking about it, how his hard, hot body had fit to hers, how he'd—

"Whatever you're thinking," he murmured when he came close enough, "you're turning me on with just the look on your face."

"I'm thinking about the buffet table," she lied. "All that food."

"And that's arousing you?"

"How do you know I'm aroused?"

He looked down.

So did she, and then groaned. Having sensed the man who'd sent them into ecstasy the night before was close by, her nipples had thrust themselves against the restraints of the pink satin.

She crossed her arms. "I'm cold."

He tucked a loose strand of hair behind her ear. "Liar."

Just his touch made her want to lean into him and bite his chin. "I'm not a liar."

He gave her a half-closed, incredibly sexy look. "Uh-huh."

"I'm not," she said, much weaker now. Damn him. He did that to her, and he knew it. He liked it!

His body brushed hers, and if she'd thought she

couldn't breathe inside during the wedding, she was in big trouble now.

"You're turned on," he insisted, running a finger down her jaw and her throat, then down farther to play with the locket resting between her breasts, which tingled from the backs of his fingers.

Traitors. She tightened her arms over her chest.

He didn't look bothered. "And you're pissed. Incredibly sexy combination, Princess."

"You're sick."

"Yes," he agreed, then looked right into her eyes again. "I'm sick that this is it."

Panic welled, but she beat it back. He couldn't know. He wasn't a mind reader and she sure hadn't given him any indication of her feelings. Mostly because she herself didn't understand them. "Wh—what are you talking about?"

"You'll miss me," he said, holding her gaze with his. "Why don't you just tell me you'll miss me?"

The big, bossy jerk. "Why should I?"

"Because I'm going to miss you. Every ornery, stubborn inch."

# 13

"LET'S TRY THIS," Kyle suggested, and went to pull something out of his tux pocket.

"Wait!" Annie covered his hand with hers, looking frantically over her shoulder, but they were still alone. Or as alone as they could be at a huge wedding reception surrounded by hundreds. "Oh my God. *What are you doing?*"

"I'm trying to tell you. I'm—"

"You can't pull a gun here! It's a wedding reception."

He let out a sound of disbelief. "What makes you think I have a gun in my pocket?"

She was nose to nose with him. She had her hand on his at his hip. Her chest was mashed into his chest, and suddenly Annie realized that this might be the last time they touched. "You're a cop."

"Was."

"You...what?"

He looked off into the distance, at the mountain

peaks, at the sky, an inexplicable yearning on his face. "I wanted a leave of absence but I couldn't get one."

"You wanted a leave? But...why?"

"I told you that day we were held up by Jimmy. I need a break. A change of scenery."

"You're burned out?" she asked, softening, feeling her heart break a little for the man who'd given so much and needed something back in return.

He shrugged. "I suppose burned out is a good an explanation as any other."

"So you..."

"Quit."

Her heart started a heavy pounding. She didn't know why. "Which doesn't explain the gun in your pocket."

He turned his head from the view and pierced her with those amazing eyes. "I told you it wasn't a gun. But somehow, I think you'd be less terrified of a gun than what I do have."

"Then maybe you should keep it to yourself." Her pulse was definitely off the scale. And she didn't want to see what was burning a hole in his pocket. Not one little bit.

"You are going to be kind, aren't you?" he whispered.

"Kyle." She backed up a step. "You're scaring me."

"Yeah. Good. I'm scaring myself." He drew a deep breath. "Here goes. Annie…do you think you could rescue me one more time?"

"I haven't rescued you, *you've* rescued me. Several times now."

"No," he said quietly, stepping back to her side, solemn and breathtaking. "You've got it backward. From the moment you came into my life, wearing that horrendous dress—"

She put one hand over her chest and the pink satin she'd nearly forgotten she was wearing. "You told me it wasn't that bad."

"I lied. It's bad."

"Well, thanks a lot."

"I have something much more important to talk to you about than the dress, Annie."

"Oh." Her hand was still on his, and she prevented him from pulling it free of the pocket because…well, she wasn't sure exactly. All she knew was that she could scarcely draw in a breath and she was fairly certain it was all his fault, but then he shifted and tried to free his hand. "Kyle…what are you doing?"

"He's trying to propose, dearness." Amelia appeared at their side. "Only you won't be quiet long enough for the poor man to get his words out. Isn't that right, Mr. Kyle Moore?"

"Uh…" He stared down at the slightly plump, undoubtedly regal Amelia Grundy. "Do I know you?"

"No, but you will. You're the man who's going to make my Annie happy forever after or I'll beat you senseless with my umbrella." She hoisted it out of her satchel and waved it for effect.

Kyle lifted his eyebrows, then looked to Annie, who felt sorry for him even if he was a big stupid lug. "This is Amelia Grundy," she said. "My ex-nanny and current…"

"Keeper," Amelia provided helpfully.

"Hey! You mean pain in my—"

*"Annie!"*

Annie smiled and hugged Amelia tight. "I love you, Amelia. And I'm happier than I can say to see you, but I need a moment of privacy here."

"With this man?" Amelia eyeballed Kyle, who, though fearless in the face of the most ruthless of criminals, looked a little wary. A little unnerved.

A little…hers.

"Yes, with this man." Annie smiled at him even as she spoke to Amelia. "Amelia, it's quite possible I'm about to make a fool of myself."

"No, actually, the big guy here is going to do that." Amelia smiled up at a very confused Kyle with fondness and patted his back. "Make her answer your question, good man."

"Yes. The question." Kyle opened his mouth, then with an oath shut it again. "I've lost my place."

"You wanted to know if she'd rescue you one more time." Amelia smiled. "She hasn't yet answered you."

"That's because the question didn't make any sense," Annie pointed out. Oh, yes, definitely her heart was going to burst right out of her chest, because suddenly she knew. She couldn't just walk away. Couldn't just go back to her life without doing the one thing she'd never really done before.

Risk her heart. Oh, sure, she'd *told* herself she'd risked plenty of times, and that no man had ever really been interested.

A big fat lie.

She'd never risked at all. She'd always simply

sabotaged any kindling relationship before she could get hurt.

No longer. She *was* going to leave, she *was* going back to her life, but she wasn't running away, and she wasn't going to always wonder. She was going to tell Kyle the truth.

That she'd fallen in love with him.

That he was the best thing that had ever happened to her.

That she hoped he came and visited her sometime, not only so she could feel whole again, but so that she could have another heart-stopping, screaming orgasm like only he'd given her.

Well, she thought with a guilty glance at Amelia, maybe she'd keep that last part to herself.

Amelia lifted a brow.

Definitely, she'd keep that last part to herself. "Kyle." Oh, man, she was starting to sweat. Who would have thought opening her heart would be harder than putting on pink satin? "I—"

"No, I've got to go first," he said. "I—"

"Wait. Why do you get to go first?"

"Because I started first," he said, not so reasonably. "Annie, don't take this wrong, but I'm trying to do something here."

"Well, so am I."

"Children," Amelia broke in, stepping between the two of them as they came together nose to nose. "Let's not squabble. I'm sure we can settle this reasonably. After all, you're both after the same thing."

Annie's breath clogged in her throat. "Amelia, I know you're always right—"

"Oh, dearness, I do like a sentence that starts that way," Amelia said with a smile.

"But—"

"Now Annie, you know how I feel. Butts are better—"

"—covered than discussed," Annie said with her in unison. She had to laugh. "Yes, I know. But—"

"Stop." Kyle lifted a hand to his head as if afraid it was going to fall off. "Please, just stop." He took Annie's shoulders and lifted her clear off the ground so that they were indeed nose to nose. "Answer this. Do you care about me?"

His eyes were dark, deep and full of many, many things, but it was the uncertainty that reached her. So much so that she reached out and cupped his face. "After last night, I should be insulted you have to ask."

"I don't mean physically, damn it. I know you

care about me that way.'' Before she could take offense at his confidence, he was solemn again. ''I mean do you care about me...emotionally.''

She didn't hesitate. ''I care very much.'' *I love you, you ignorant fool.* ''In fact, that's sort of tied into what I wanted to say to you.''

''Shh, he's not done,'' Amelia admonished, still standing right beside them, unabashedly eavesdropping. ''Let the poor man finish.''

''Thank you,'' Kyle said, not taking his eyes or hands off Annie.

''No problem. She's terribly impertinent, always has been.''

''I can see how that must have been a huge problem,'' Kyle said.

''Must *have* been?'' Amelia laughed. ''Oh, my dear. She still is.''

''Hey! *She* is still standing right here and has ears,'' Annie said indignantly, waggling her toes, which were still a good six inches off the ground.

''Get used to it,'' Amelia advised Kyle as if Annie hadn't spoken. ''And, oh, she's getting her temper up now, isn't she? She might as well be a redhead, really, for all her ability to control it.''

''Amelia!'' Annie glared down at her friend, at the woman who'd been a mother to her since her own had perished. "I love you, but I'm afraid you're fired."

"This is the sixty-seventh time you've said that in our time together," Amelia said, unconcerned, studying her fingernails. "And for the sixty-seventh time, your father pays me, not you."

Annie tipped her head back and sighed loudly.

Kyle's eyes sparkled. "So, impertinent princess, can I finish now?"

"Oh, please. By all means, finish. Heaven forbid I try to have a say in my own life."

His hands tightened on her. His voice came sure and strong. It was only the flicker in his eyes that gave away his nerves, and caused hers. "Andrea Katrine Fran Brunner, will you m—"

"Excuse me," Amelia interrupted. "You have to say *Your Serene Highness* when addressing Annie formally."

Kyle nodded. "Sorry. You're right." He turned back to Annie. "Your Serene Highness, Andrea Katrine Fran Brunner, will you m—"

"No. I'm sorry." Amelia shook her head and tapped a finger to her lower lip. "You forgot the 'of Grunberg' part."

"Okay." Before Kyle turned back to Annie, he paused. "Is that all?" His voice was a little tense now.

"Yes. Please proceed."

"Amelia." Annie spoke in an oddly calm voice given that she could hardly get a word out past the lump in her throat, not to mention the hope bouncing like popcorn off the walls in her stomach. "I mean this in the nicest way. But shut up."

"Shutting up," Amelia said obediently.

As if she'd ever been obedient!

"Kyle," Annie said, still watching Amelia. "Put me down."

He actually did, but he didn't take his hands off her. "I have to tell you, Annie. I'm getting a little frustrated here."

"Join the club. Now." She drew a deep breath and looked into his beautiful eyes, because God help her, she had an inkling that this could be better than even her wildest dreams. "Go ahead. I promise to kill the next person who interrupts you."

"Not if I beat you to it." He ran his hands down her arms to their fingers, which he entangled. "Okay, here it is, Annie. I love you. I don't know how it happened. I sure never meant for it to, but from the moment we took on Jimmy together, things haven't been the same for me." He blew out a breath. "And now that I've said it out loud, I feel a little weak, so could you say you feel the same way before I pass out?"

He loved her. "I'm sorry," she finally managed, her voice thick. "I didn't hear anything past the *I love you* part. Do you think you could repeat it?"

He actually tried. His brow was furrowed with stress, his body tight with strain, but he tried. If she hadn't already loved him, she would have fallen in love right then and there. "I said, I never meant for this to happen," he repeated. "But—"

"I meant the 'I love you' part." She slipped her fingers into his hair because she had to touch him. She probably had to touch him for the rest of her life.

"I love you," he said hoarsely, dropping his forehead to hers. "I want to go with you to Grunberg. I want to be with you in *your* setting for a change, away from all this…this…"

"Pink satin?"

"Yes. God, yes."

"But Grunberg isn't America."

"You have cops there?"

"Well, yes."

"Then I can make a living. But first I want to just be, Annie. For a little while I just want to be.

With you. I want to marry you. Do you think that's something I can talk you into?'' He pulled a small box out of his pocket and opened it, revealing a beautiful solitaire diamond.

"Like I said." She managed a smile in with her tears. "All I heard was 'I love you.'"

"Is that a yes?"

"I love you back, Kyle."

"Is that a yes?" he pressed.

"So you really thought *I* rescued *you?*"

*"Annie."*

"Yes." She threw herself at him and kissed his face everywhere she could reach. "Yes, yes, yes."

Next to them, Amelia buttoned closed her satchel and nodded in triumph. "A job well done," she decided, even if she said so herself.

# *Epilogue*

GRUNBERG WAS GLORIOUS. Green and lush and perfect, it allowed for more adventure than a man could ever want.

Kyle lay prone on the hammock. He was surrounded by the tall, majestic mountain peaks of Austria and Switzerland. He had a soda balancing on his belly and thirty minutes to himself before a meeting.

"There's been a breach in security," came the hushed whisper from behind the tree off to his right. "The castle is no longer safe."

"Never fear, I'll rescue you, fair princess," came a second hushed whisper.

"No. I'll rescue myself."

"Don't be ridiculous. You're just a girl."

"That's right, and as *just* a girl, I've got the innate right and ability to kick some—"

"Hold it." With a laughing groan, Kyle sat up. "I've got the innate right to report the both of you to Her Serene Highness."

The two in question, lurking among the trees just before him froze, then hung their heads.

He studied them gravely, biting back his laugh, because God help him, his heart threatened to burst just looking at them. "Does Momma know you're running wild and free?"

"Oh, yes," reported his beautiful six-year-old daughter who looked exactly like her mother, all deep golden eyes, long gold hair and that sweet, irresistible smile. "She sent us to bother you. Said that it was time her Head Of Security trained his new recruits. But we don't need training, Dad. Or at least I don't." She glared at her eight-year-old brother.

He glared right back, and Kyle didn't need a mirror to know where he got that expression.

"I'm going to be Head of Security, just like Daddy," claimed his son. "You're just a princess."

She only let out a slow smile. "Maybe. But at least I'm not a *boy*." She dragged the word out as if it was five syllables long, then let out a squeak when her brother started after her.

Round and round they ran, until Kyle grabbed one kid under each arm, much to their squealing delight. "Hmm," he said, pretending to ponder as he walked toward the pond ten yards away. "I wonder if naughty little children melt."

"No, Daddy!" laughed his little princess. "I'm wearing my good clothes."

"Such a girl," her brother sneered, but screamed with laughter just like his sister as his father stopped at the very edge of the pond.

"My, my," came the calm voice of reason behind them.

Kyle turned. "I'm sorry, Your Serene Highness. I've discovered a serious breach of security. I've got it under control."

His beautiful wife of nine years smiled, love and warmth coming from her eyes. "My hero." She sighed. "Then I suppose there won't be any need for the cookies I just pulled from the oven."

More squeals and squirming, and suddenly his two children were but a blur on the horizon as they raced each other for the kitchen.

With a laugh, Annie moved into Kyle's open arms. "Ah, hear that? Silence. Isn't it grand?" She snuggled in closer. "No need to thank me, really. I'll just add this latest rescue on to your tab."

Kyle choked a laugh into her soft, silky hair and his arms tightened on her. "You can rescue me any time. Any time at all."

# The holidays have descended on

COOPER'S CORNER

## providing a touch of seasonal magic!

## Coming in November 2002...
## MY CHRISTMAS COWBOY
## by Kate Hoffmann

**Check-in:** Bah humbug! That's what single mom
Grace Penrose felt about Christmas this year. All her plans
for the Cooper's Corner Christmas Festival are going wrong—
and now she finds out she has an unexpected houseguest!

**Checkout:** But sexy cowboy Tucker McCabe is no ordinary
houseguest, and Grace feels her spirits start to lift. Suddenly
she has the craziest urge to stand under the mistletoe...forever!

**HARLEQUIN®**
*Makes any time special* ®

*Princes...Princesses...*
*London Castles...New York Mansions...*
*To live the life of a royal!*

**In 2002, Harlequin Books lets you escape to a
world of royalty with these royally themed titles:**

### Temptation:
January 2002—*A Prince of a Guy* (#861)
February 2002—*A Noble Pursuit* (#865)

### American Romance:
**The Carradignes: American Royalty (Editorially linked series)**
March 2002—*The Improperly Pregnant Princess* (#913)
April 2002—*The Unlawfully Wedded Princess* (#917)
May 2002—*The Simply Scandalous Princess* (#921)
November 2002—*The Inconveniently Engaged Prince* (#945)

### Intrigue:
**The Carradignes: A Royal Mystery (Editorially linked series)**
June 2002—*The Duke's Covert Mission* (#666)

### Chicago Confidential
September 2002—*Prince Under Cover* (#678)

### The Crown Affair
October 2002—*Royal Target* (#682)
November 2002—*Royal Ransom* (#686)
December 2002—*Royal Pursuit* (#690)

### Harlequin Romance:
June 2002—*His Majesty's Marriage* (#3703)
July 2002—*The Prince's Proposal* (#3709)

### Harlequin Presents:
August 2002—*Society Weddings* (#2268)
September 2002—*The Prince's Pleasure* (#2274)

### Duets:
September 2002—*Once Upon a Tiara/Henry Ever After* (#83)
October 2002—*Natalia's Story/Andrea's Story* (#85)

 **Celebrate a year of royalty with
Harlequin Books!**

*Available at your favorite retail outlet.*

**HARLEQUIN®**
*Makes any time special* ®

Visit us at www.eHarlequin.com

HSROY02

If you enjoyed what you just read,
then we've got an offer you can't resist!

# Take 2 bestselling
# love stories FREE!
# Plus get a FREE surprise gift!